New Roads
to
Old Places

a novel
by Phillip E. Norris

This book is a work of fiction. References to living and dead actual persons and past events are for historical context.

New Roads to Old Places
Published by Portals Press LLC
New Orleans, Louisiana
ISBN 979-8-9999461-2-6

New Roads
to
Old Places

This book is dedicated to the memory of E.D. Nixon and Clifford Durr.

TO THE READER

This novel depicts a pivotal time in U.S. history. I recommend that you read "Letter from a Birmingham Jail" by Martin Luther King Jr. (1963) to better understand the interactions between religion and politics in the 1960s South.

An Alabama Civil Rights Timeline and a web address for the letter are in the Appendixes.

CONTENTS

1. End of the Road

It was a beautiful morning on the first weekend of May in 1993 as I looked out over Lake Martin located just an hour northeast of Montgomery. I had owned this cabin for ten years, and I drove from Montgomery the first weekend of every month on Friday evening. The cabin was built on the tip of a small peninsula that provided a great view of the lake, and enough tree-covered land to assure privacy from the road. The cabin had three bed-rooms and a huge great room that was floor-to-ceiling glass windows and two sets of French doors opening onto a stone patio that stretched to the water's edge. A massive stone fireplace made winter my favorite season and the kitchen was unchanged since the house was completed in 1958, mid-century modern at its best. This cabin had played an important role in my past, and owning what was once owned and loved by another was part of my private reckoning with revenge. This was Dr. Frazier's dream house, built to impress his followers and create a sense of privacy and secrecy because Dr. Frazier had a plan.

The house was sold in 1965 when Dr. Frazier left Alabama to spend the next 17 years in jail. I know he thought about that enormous stone fireplace and his lake view on many a cold night as he sat in a New York federal prison, and I thought about him every day he was there.

I left Montgomery after graduating from Sidney Lanier High School in 1967 to attend The University of Alabama, and after graduating, I moved to Boston, Massachusetts, for six years until I received my Ph.D. in Psychology from Harvard University. I lived a solitary academic life in Massachusetts with few acquaintances and an occasional sexual encounter that never lasted for over a month. I was damaged goods, and it didn't take much time for others to realize there was a wall around my emotions, and I wasn't going to explain the reason for it to anyone. I did my schoolwork, I got terrific grades, I perfected my clinical skills, and I did what I needed to do to assure myself of a good income. I wanted to return to Montgomery and carry out my life plan. Living in Dr. Frazier's dream house was a big part of that plan.

I returned to Montgomery in the fall of 1977 and obtained my license to practice clinical psychology and rented an office before Christmas of that year. I taught part-time at the new Auburn University at Montgomery campus and volunteered at several non-profits to get known in the psychology community. My practice flourished and my income grew. I rented an inexpensive one-bedroom apartment and continued saving my money as I had been doing since high school so I could one day purchase Dr. Frazier's house. The same couple who bought the house in 1965 still owned it, but my surveillance of the house almost every weekend indicated it had very few visitors by 1980.

I called the couple that owned the cabin in the fall of 1981 and asked if I could meet with them to talk about buying their lake cabin. My timing was perfect; they had been talking about selling it for the last six months. I told them I had been interested in the cabin since I was in high school, and I would pay whatever they thought was a fair price. As it turned out, I had saved enough to pay cash for the cabin, and I closed on it two weeks later.

Step one in my plan for justice was now in place; I would enjoy his loss, and I would be close by on the first weekend of every month when his monthly Social Security check allowed him to get really drunk at Sergeant Tom's Roadhouse. This low-rent tavern was frequented by Auburn University students and local deadbeats and was located about two miles from my cabin, which had once been Dr. Frazier's dream house. Dr. Frazier now lived in a broken-down house trailer he had been given by an anonymous donor just prior to his release from prison. The house trailer was located about 300 yards from Sergeant Tom's bar, making it easy for Dr. Frazier to get loaded.

On every first Saturday of the month after 9 p.m., I would slip into a back booth and nurse a beer as Dr. Frazier got drunk and loud and fumed about what the niggers, the Yankees, the Jews and the Communists had done to him and how they ruined his life. It usually ended when he was ushered out of the bar, or he just ran out of vitriol and stumbled back to his trailer. On more than one occasion, I saw him drunk and crying on the rickety front steps of Sergeant Tom's Roadhouse. He was laughed at by the other patrons who referred to him as Dr. Drunk.

He hated me but never recognized the adult version of me. However, there I was, one night a month filled to the brim with schadenfreude. I loved his misery; I loved his pain. I hated my misery; I hated my pain. I hated what I had caused him to do with my youthful arrogance and ignorance. The price I would pay for stirring this evil man up was my cross to bear. I would go home and sleep in his bedroom, in his house, and look out at one of the most beautiful views on Lake Martin.

My ritual weekend started with my drive to the lake after seeing my last patient of the day. I arrived by 9 p.m. and was up the next morning watching the sun rise in the east. Then I headed for the Lake Martin Market to grab two freshly baked blueberry muffins, a cup of dark roast coffee, and a copy of the Saturday morning Montgomery Journal newspaper. I drove three miles home to have breakfast on the patio, read the newspaper, and wait for my trip to Sergeant Tom's Roadhouse at 9 p.m. After ten years of going to Sergeant Tom's the first Saturday night of the month, I didn't realize that I had made my last trip; I would never set foot in that raunchy saloon again.

When I got back to the cabin the coffee was still hot, the blueberry muffins were warm and smelled delightful, my butterfly chair was on the patio pointed at the widest part of the lake as the sun began its ascent over the lake. I placed my newspaper on the table beside my chair, took the lid of my coffee, and devoured the first of my two blue-berry muffins. I felt good. I sipped my coffee, put the other muffin on the table to enjoy after I read the headlines and the sports news. It was my father's birthday and on my agenda was to call him and wish him a happy birthday although I knew he would guilt me for not visiting him, but he also knew that nothing interfered with my first weekend at the lake house routine and we had had many tense discussions about my not allowing anyone to visit the lake house.

Everyone in my family except my mother had asked to visit me at the lake, but I told them that it was my private place, and they would have to accept that. My mother said she didn't completely understand about the lake house, but she knew it was in some way related to Evelyn's death and she would not pry into what I needed to do to find recovery from those terrible days when Evelyn was killed. She said she would pray for me to find peace.

The headlines that morning proved to be ironic: the South African government had agreed to hold biracial elections in South Africa, which would end apartheid rule and would quickly make Nelson Mandela the new President of South Africa. What great news that was, and I knew that Dr. Frazier would be in an extra furious mood at the roadhouse that evening. This was going to be a good night, a high misery night for Dr. Frazier.

It all changed when I opened the paper to page two. At the top of the page was an article about Dr. Frazier's body being discovered Friday morning in the front yard of his trailer home at Lake Martin. I was instantly dizzy and threw up my blueberry muffin while getting out of my butterfly chair. I fell sideways and hit my head on the patio stones; I was completely disoriented and lay there for half an hour crying and not understanding what was happening to me. I realized the shock of Dr. Frazier's death had sent me back to 1962 and the beginning of the story that had defined my life. Twenty-one months of my past flashed before my eyes in what seemed like, and may have been, the end of a long, torturous road.

2. Avoiding Consequences

My tortured past had begun to develop in the fall of 1962 when my parents forced me to leave my neighborhood junior high school so I could attend the New Roads School and College with my older brother and sister. The New Roads School and College was affiliated with my parents' and siblings' chosen religion, the New Roads Church. My sister's straight A average allowed her the opportunity to skip her senior year in high school and attend the New Roads College as a member of the freshman class. My brother, who would be entering the eleventh grade that fall, was overjoyed with the opportunity to leave the secular school system behind and live comfortably in the religious structure he found in our church. I, on the other hand, was quite comfortable in the secular world and looked forward to the heavy petting and the beer drinking that would come in the next few years when I got to high school.

At fourteen, I had very little say in where I would attend school, and I was in-formed of this often by my father. He explained that for the sake of convenience, be-cause of the three-student discount policy at the New Roads School and College, and the fact that I had been born with a proclivity to stir up trouble, that it was his opinion that the family would be best served by my joining my siblings in their morning carpool across town to the New Roads School and College.

I knew that my father had a valid point when he noted my inclination to cause trouble because, as he reminded me, I had recently been caught for subscribing to dozens of magazines using my science teacher's name and address and requesting that he be billed later for these subscriptions. Poor Mr. Clem and his wife were inundated with magazines and bill collection letters for months. I might have gotten away with that prank, but I had decided that Mr. Clem needed just a little more trouble in his life for the summer break, so in the late spring I liberated one of my sister's bras and stuck it under Mr. Clem's front car seat. My mistake was getting Betty Jones to write an anonymous letter to Mr. Clem's wife claiming to be in love with her science teacher, Mr. Clem, and she said she was three months pregnant from doing it in the back seat of his car every day after school. Mrs. Clem raised such a fuss with Mr. Clem after she received the letter and then found the planted bra under Mr. Clem's car seat that a thorough investigation ensued that matched Betty's handwriting to the accusing letter. Betty turned me in as soon as she was fingered, and I ended up as the one with summer trouble.

That spring was not my first brush with the school authorities or the first time I had set my sights on disrupting an authority figure. In sixth grade, my friends and I had kept our twenty-two-year-old newly graduated teacher in tears for most of the school year. We stole her answer book, changed the grades in her grade book, sent false notes to the parents of her star pupils denoting their almost certain academic failure, and submitted a letter to the Montgomery Journal editor urging the immediate integration of all public schools with her name signed to the letter. The poor woman spent half of the year sitting at her desk weeping but was rewarded for her pain the next school year with a first-grade class that did not suffer from the hormonal rushes of twelve-year-olds.

The bottom line was that I knew I had earned my father's sentence of isolation from my public-school peers, but I didn't like it and wasn't really sure that a change of location would also mean the change in my personality that my father was hoping for. I'm sure his dream was that I would adopt the New Roads lifestyle, which would nullify all my desires to stir things up. New Roaders were known for their passivity and obedience to authority, which I found quite ironic because their religious role model was a poor Middle Eastern Jewish rabble-rouser who did nothing but stir things up for the thirty-three years he lived. As my tenure at the New Roads School and College wore on, I found more and more to like and imitate in the words and actions of the New Road's savior. I am remembered to this day at the New Roads School for my own two years of shaking up the serenity of a once peaceful fundamentalist school, a dubious accomplishment given the price I have had to pay for my teen-age mischief.

As the beginning of the school year approached, I felt the apprehension of an unknown experience. The friends and classmates I had developed over the last eight years would disappear. I was going behind the New Roads School curtain to an uncertain future and would have none of my public-school friends to count on in these impending times of trouble. I did have an ace in the hole, however, and that was my grown-up next-door neighbor and personal teen counselor, Mrs. Evelyn Katz. Mrs. Katz could always be counted on for guidance and advice on surviving the great traumas of living; she had been my lifeline in the troubled beginnings of my puberty and adolescence.

Mrs. Evelyn Katz was an unusual woman by Montgomery standards: a Yale-educated, Jewish New Yorker whose beauty and wit overcame most of the inherent Southern dislike for both Jews and Yankees. She could disarm all but the most ardent bigots with her funny stories and her ability to get total strangers to tell her their most private secrets. She used her master's degree in psychology from Yale to push back some of the limits the racial, ethnic and religious norms of Montgomery wanted to restrict her with. This woman was my mentor and guide, she knew how to adapt and how to survive in an inhospitable environment; she was my idol whom I depended on for my advice on surviving adolescence.

I knew I needed some advice, so I went next door.

I jumped right in and moaned, "Mrs. Katz, you won't believe what my parents are making me do! They are ruining my whole life by sending me to that church school! How can I do this? What should I do? How can I get out of this mess?"

"Well Pip," she began, "don't you have a lot of trouble waiting on you at your old school for what you did to your science teacher and his wife? This plan of your parents may be the best way out of a potentially bad situation you are going to face at your old school.

"Pip, feelings of discomfort are common when we make big changes and I'm an expert, having moved from New York to Montgomery, on dealing with discomfort. I know you are clever and inventive and more than a bit mischievous. I know you have the skills to survive and do well and only trouble awaits you if you return to your old school. I think your Dad has found you a way out of the trouble that awaits you."

I answered, "Yes, ma'am, that's a fair statement, and I can see where this might be my best choice, 'cause I don't know what they will do to me for messing with a teacher."

Next, she said, "Well, this is how you handle it, then. Draw on your inner strength to make adjustments in your life. Do that crazy alpha wave thing you do and know that your creativity will get you through."

"Yes, ma'am," I answered again.

"Well, since you made it successfully through eighth grade without getting caught for your pranks until school was out, I think if you slip away to another school in the fall you should count yourself lucky to not spend most of next year in study hall."

I couldn't argue with someone who believed in my ability to adapt and change, because I knew she was right; I knew that I was a survivor. When I left her house that day, I knew she had worked her magic with me because she always made me feel better about myself after our discussions. She never judged me because I think she understood my natural dislike for authority.

3. Religious Hypocrisy

My family, with the exception of myself, were all members of the First New Roads Church of Montgomery. My brother's and sister's lives revolved around their friends from church and the many church-sponsored youth activities. I, on the other hand, eschewed anything to do with the New Roads Church except for the obligatory Sunday morning and evening services and the Wednesday evening prayer meetings that I couldn't weasel my way out of. The choice of the New Roads School and College was a natural for my siblings; their lives would become whole as they filled their days, nights, and weekends with their favorite people engaging in one hundred percent wholesome activities. My recessive genes were especially prominent in my mind as I looked at the differences between my family and myself, but I also remembered my aunt telling hush-hush stories about my father's wild youth and figured that I probably came by some of these genes honestly.

Church was a very important activity in the family in which I was raised. When the doors of the church were open, we were there, and in my family's choice of denomination, the New Roads faith, that was often. It seemed to me that every time I turned around, it was time to get dressed and go hear one more lecture on the evils of the secular world and the unbelievers that populated it, which were all those people who did not belong to the New Roads religion. This was not your everyday run-of-the-mill Christian denomination; they believed that they alone had been given God's rule book and the keys to St. Peter's gate. They were so theologically arrogant and self-assured that if you were not a member of their denomination, there would be no admission to Heaven.

There was one way to the Kingdom of Heaven and only one way, their way, by their salvation rules, and all others (especially Catholics) were on the slippery slope to Hell. I can remember pondering how strange and insignificant some of their rules of exclusion were. If you had any musical accompaniment with the church service, you were in violation of the rules of admission to Heaven because God didn't say a word about a pipe organ or any other form of musical aid in His book. Their emphasis on the theological minutia of Christian living perplexed me because they overlooked the most basic tenets of love and fairness when applied to someone of another race.

Where the rest of the family found this rigid black-and-white, right and wrong structure comfortable and comforting in their religious beliefs, I was born with a love for the shades of gray, a feeling that the truth was very elusive and even constantly changing. This was long before college philosophy and years of graduate training in psychology had put some meat on my primitive philosophical bones. I didn't know exactly what was wrong with my family's logic system, but I knew that their religious worldview just wasn't going to fit me like it fit them. This philosophical mismatch was how I ended up in the New Roads School; my parents and siblings were just trying to work out a way to make me fit better in the overall family structure.

The fourteen years of five hours a week of church on Sunday mornings, Sunday nights, and Wednesday nights, not to mention the two weeks of vacation Bible school in the summer, was not an adequate preparation for the total immersion that I undertook when I entered the land of the righteous on that fall day in 1962. Forty-five hours a week should have been enough to break my will, but the effect of this attempted conversion process was like pouring gasoline on a fire. The New Roads School experience started me on a perilous journey that almost consumed me and left me with permanent psychological scars, which I would have to bear for the rest of my life.

A significant part of my intense negative reaction to being forced to join the ninth-grade class at the New Roads School and thus make the New Roads environment virtually my whole existence, was the hypocrisy of these pseudo-righteous, self-congratulatory religious zealots. As they proclaimed their superior Christian status, the quest for basic human rights swirled around them daily because the heart of the American Civil Rights Movement was centered in Montgomery, Alabama. As a group, they acted no differently than the mass of white Southerners in Montgomery, but they had claimed the high road of morality as their own, and it seemed to me that they had special responsibilities that went with their very special Christian status.

When questioned about their lack of involvement in standing up for the principles of love and fairness mandated in the "do unto others as you would have them do unto you" rule, their reply was that the struggle for equality that filled the evening news was the doings of the secular world. I knew this was a philosophical dodge intended to keep the New Roads followers focused on the institution of the New Roads religion and away from the hard choices and certain disruption that would be the outcome of actualizing real Christian principles.

4. The Five Percenters

As the summer of 1962 dwindled down to the last few days, the dose of self-assurance I got from Mrs. Katz began to erode. I knew that all my old friends would be gone from my life when the fall semester began. I knew that absence did not make the heart grow fonder, that the reality was that I would be out of sight and out of the minds of the Floyd Junior High School students who had comprised the people in my social life. The world of afternoons at the YMCA, school dances, and the discovery of teenage sexuality was about to be placed in suspended animation. These things were not part of the New Roads School and the isolation that was about to be imposed on me would wipe out my past, an isolation that would change me by causing me to change myself. Survival was the initial feeling that overcame me on my first day at the New Roads School. I remember years later, my first day of classes at Harvard University in Cambridge, Massachusetts, having the same feeling as on that fall day in Montgomery, Alabama. I felt like I really didn't belong in either place, and in each place, I hoped I would survive the experience. In both cases, I did endure the initial shock. I found fear and confidence and adapted to the idea that this was where fate had placed me, and that I would find my way through the insecurity that is so often the natural byproduct of change.

The first few days at the New Roads School fused together from the combination of social disorientation and culture shock. I quickly came out of my fear trance and began to analyze what was going on around me and what the school was all about when the institutional structure was broken down. I knew that logic was my only ally, and it was imperative that I figure out how the New Roads School and College worked from a formal and informal point of view if I was going to stay in control of my life.

Many of the faces and people I knew and recognized at the New Roads School and College were people from my church life on Sundays and Wednesdays, the people who dressed up and sang without the benefit of musical accompaniment at the First New Roads Church of Montgomery. This had been my other social life, the one that had been crafted by my family. I had always been tolerated by the congregation but viewed with suspicion after being caught at a nearby convenience store during Sunday services with several other New Roads children when I was ten years old. I was blamed by the others for leading the exodus off the back row with the temptation of candy that awaited us down the street at the 7-Eleven convenience store. I knew from my First New Roads Church of Montgomery experience that most of these folks at the New Roads School and College were serious and intent on winning souls; there would be no tomfoolery for them, and those who didn't feel that way were sure to be fair game in this enclave of soul savers.

The larger group, comprising ninety-five percent of the students at the New Roads School and College, were easy to understand; they had a calmness and placidity about them that seemed to be a byproduct of their religious commitment. The sorting of this group, for purposes of self-defense, was by age and status in school. The range was from first grade to junior college and beyond to a bachelor's degree in religious studies if you were ready to take on the battle with the Devil as a lifetime occupation. The further up this educational hierarchy, the more intrusive these fellows (only men could be New Roads ministers) got in interjecting themselves into the lives of the school's nonbelievers. There was competition amongst the would-be preacher corps about which ministerial student would catch and convert a nonbeliever to the New Roads faith. These guys made my first month at the New Roads School a real learning experience. I learned to spot one of these preachers-in-training at a hundred feet, to duck, to dive, to melt away, and when caught and quizzed about my religious beliefs, to excuse myself quickly with a myriad of preconceived reasons. The only problem with living this way was that it burned up a lot of alpha energy, which could be replaced only by systematically interrupting one's sleep frequently throughout the night.

It was easy to see right away that I was going to have trouble trying to force-fit my personality to appease these religious soul savers; I saw hypocrisy in their beliefs, and I was not going to compromise my beliefs.

The school was comprised of faithful New Roads believers that was ninety-five per-cent of the students at the school and college and a five percent minority that was made up of thugs, Neanderthals, misfits, rednecks, and con men who had been banished from most of the public and private schools in Montgomery. The choice, no matter how poor, had to be made. I knew that I would never make it in my new school as a loner; making friends who knew the ropes of that place would be very important to my successful survival and happiness at the New Roads School.

The choice was a very simple one. When I looked at my qualifications, the group that most nearly fitted my perception of reality was the five percenters. I had a new and very different peer group than I had ever had before. The only cohesive element of the five-percent group was the fact that we were different from the majority that surrounded us.

The dominant group was knit very tightly together by their New Roads philosophy practiced in a nearly pure environment. The cracks in the veneer of both the majority and minority groups were coming in the fall of 1962 and all of us would be swallowed up in that crevasse of change that came with living in Montgomery, the Cradle of the Confederacy.

5. Archie and Pecker

The first friend I made, after getting over my first few cultur-al-shock-treatment days at the New Roads School, was Archie Thompson, a boy with a good heart and a relatively slow mind. In academics Archie was lost, but he was a genius when it came to common sense or anything practical. At fourteen, Archie could figure out anything mechanical. He knew when he was being bullshitted, and when and if someone could be trusted. We met because we shared the same interest of sitting in the back row of all our classes, which was easy because ninety-five percent of the class were vying for front-row seats. The first three days of class, I avoided conversation and tried to observe what was going on around me. On the morning of my fourth day before English class began, Archie took the desk next to mine and got right down to business.

He said, "Pip, I've been watching, and I think I need to give you the lowdown on how things work around the school before you wig out trying to figure it out for your-self. You see, there are two groups who populate the school, and now I'm hearing about you from some of the students who attend the First New Roads Church of Montgomery. The way I hear it, I figure you're a natural to belong to the untamed minority group here at school."

He pointed to the end of our back row at a medium-sized blond boy who was shooting spitballs out of a straw at everyone sitting on the front row.

Archie continued, "Now that's Pecker. He's the only other Hell-raiser in the ninth-grade class." Then he laughed and said, "Now that you're here, you've pushed the percentage of outlaws in the ninth grade beyond the norm for past ninth-grade classes, but," he added, "I'm not great at math, so I'm not exactly sure what size our ninth-grade minority is."

After English class, Archie introduced me to Pecker, a boy possessed of a quick wit and a very devious mind. Pecker had been asked to leave the public school system the year before in the middle of the semester at Baldwin Junior High School. Pecker was caught running a bookie operation where he got his fellow students to bet their lunch money on the outcome of the Thursday night Baldwin Junior High School football games. When lunch purchases fell off by a third on Fridays, the principal investigated and found out about Pecker's gambling operation. Pecker probably could have survived that faux pas with a suspension, but the principal also found out that half the winnings were being given to the quarterback of the Baldwin Junior High School football team to make sure that the point spread came out right.

I could feel the tension lift over the next two days as I found my friendship growing with Archie and Pecker. They pulled me into their routines and started my education on living as a minority at the New Roads School. I was introduced to most of the five percenters and given a briefing on who and what to watch out for in this very volatile segment of our school.

"Are there any special instructions for the majority?" I asked.

Archie said, "No, they're just passive and self-absorbed in their religious quest. But you'll have to keep an eye on the administration. They'll leave you alone as long as you abstain from cursing and fornication when they're around."

Then Pecker added, "Not really, all you have to watch out for is cursing in front of these guys who run the school, because the chance of having sex with a New Roads girl is nil."

Archie was an old hand in the underworld of the misfits and knew how to maneuver in the system that surrounded us, a knowledge that proved invaluable over the next two years. This was not a static system, however; as in any school, there was constant churning due to the infusion of new students, both the pious and the deviant.

The pious presented little challenge in the survival game except for the occasional hard-driving soul saver. The deviants, on the other hand, were varied and dangerous, removed from other schools for a variety of anti-social behaviors or forcibly enrolled to get the church manifesto engraved on their souls, or in my case, just yoked to their siblings for simplicity. Our sub-group was awash in pathology that could get you in trouble on a small scale or that could land you in a public boarding school that had a fence around it where the admission test was given by a guy wearing a black robe down at the county courthouse.

Archie had a wonderful asset: he was the biggest student in the school and had a menacing silence that projected "don't fuck with me" in a 360-degree radius. My first lesson in living in a strange and hostile environment was how important it was to pick your friends for their ability to preempt trouble before you get pulled into its vortex. When hanging out with a group genetically endowed with extremely short fuses, it's wonderful to have a best friend whose aura says, "there may be no limits to what I will do to you if you choose to invade my personal space." On more than one occasion when the tempers would flare without warning from one of the New Roads School thugs, Archie would turn his calming and demented eyes on any dissension that might threaten either of us and a deceleration of the violence curve would ensue.

Archie had to establish his bad-ass persona every fall when a new crop of toughs would challenge the existing pecking order at the New Roads School. Invariably, one of these public school retirees would want to take on the silent menace they had heard about. Eventually, Archie would give the most curious thug a beating and humiliation that would fend off attempts from others in that year's class of new bad boys. The first fall that I attended the New Roads School and College it was Peedrow Walker who decided to establish a new pecking order and was rewarded with an Archie thrashing and a dunking in a very nasty septic tank bog.

Everybody wants to take down the fastest gun in the West, but nobody wants to get shot to pieces doing it.

Archie was a classic, a big Southern country boy who had a killer look that scared the shit out of anybody who knows the danger of unpredictable personalities. The first thing anyone noticed about Archie was his rough exterior, but internally, he represented a philosophy that is the leavening agent in one of the most complex regions of America. Archie was a man (boy) of honor. If he said he would do something, you could count on it. Extremely honest about his commitments but more importantly about his feelings, Archie would call it the way he saw it and usually with very few words. I never heard him disparage another person or group including Negroes. His credo was live and let live, as long you didn't bother him, or those under his protection, everything was fine.

It was grown-ups that shared Archie's philosophy who kept the Deep

South from becoming a complete war zone in the 1960s. People who fixed their cold stares on the zealots and Klansmen and checked those adult thugs before they brought Armageddon down on everybody else that lived in the South. These were good-spirited people who would change their ways, if necessary, but they weren't going to lead any charges or participate in any marches on either side of an issue. These were people who had grown up in a segregated and racist South but weren't wedded to the notion that their well-being depended on having someone else further down the social and economic ladder. As long as you left them and their families alone, they would accept change. These were not progressives but rather isolationists, people who unknowingly reached beyond the myths of the Old South to the reality of the beginnings of the Southern experience, to a people who migrated South to be left alone to work out their lives as they saw fit. It all worked fine until they were pulled into the rich cotton planters' war to protect a decadent lifestyle that was not their own.

There was no shortage of evil and vicious segregationists in my school or my hometown, but these folks came in a variety of shades of hate. The undisputed leader of the hate movement, the real grand wizard of the segregationist faithful, was my former paper route customer, George Corley Wallace. Before the governor became the Governor, I was his paperboy and thus must take responsibility for not intervening when I had the chance by slipping an occasional pamphlet on tolerance into the sports section of the Wallaces' newspaper. This, of course, would have done no good because George had already made up his mind about the positive aspects of being a bigot. He had run as the candidate of tolerance in 1958 and vowed after his drubbing by an arch segregationist to "never be out-niggered again." Being the honest politician he was, he lived up to his word until Negroes began voting in large numbers and at that point discovered the error of his past beliefs.

The governor had, in his liberal days, been a friend of my father's when my father was a local labor leader. I remember my father being involved in the 1958 campaign and his enthusiasm for "the little fighting Judge from Barbour County." He would extol the virtues of this tough little man who, he said, would lead us down the path of moderation and toward the internment of Jim Crow, toward a new Alabama that would be the example for the other states in the South to follow. Well, my father got part of the story right, the part about leading the South; he just didn't know about my former customer's take-no-prisoners approach to power. Winning the 1962 election on the promise of segregation now and segregation forever thrust the governor to the forefront of the racist resistance movement all over America.

Alabama was the lead engine that would take us to that well-worn spot where the tilting at windmills had been occurring since the dawn of civilization.

6. Roy Harper, Jr., Preacher-in-Training

I had not been encamped in the New Roads School for long when word spread amongst the preacher corps ministerial degree students that I was not a member of their denomination. It was further noted that I had been seen hanging out with members of the campus five-percent minority of nonbelievers.

Knowing that I was from a "good family of believers" and the fact that I had a believing brother and sister in attendance at the school only persuaded the preachers-in-training that a soul-rescue action was needed posthaste. They moved on me with great force and concerted effort and were successful in running me, a scared fresh New Roads School teen, to cover several times a day. Brother Roy Harper Jr. was selected as the project manager and coordinator of my salvation case. The plan, as best I could understand it, was to badger me into submission, make me admit that only their group got the ride to Heaven on the big day of the apocalypse and that music in church services and dancing were unnatural and a sure damnation for the soul. I suppose it would have been easier to have "fessed up" to whatever they wanted me to "fess up" to and gone on about my business, but my life experience in the previous fourteen years convinced me to honor my individuality and internal guidance system or a fate worse than Brother Roy's badgering would get me.

After the ministerial assignment, Brother Roy was all over me. He explained the benefits of joining the majority group at the New Roads School and at the same time the ultimate elite that was assured a table at the big house in the sky on judgment day. Brother Roy, the would-be New Roads minister, was a scrawny country boy from Opp, Alabama, who I am sure is still selling cheap furniture in a warehouse outlet somewhere today. Roy was full of fervor and determination and very adaptive to my ducking and hiding ploys. He figured out that everybody has to pee, and if he stationed himself close to the bathroom, we could continue our one-sided conversation about the joys and righteousness of the New Roads faith. This ploy worked for three of the longest weeks of my life since toilet training; Brother Roy was joining me at the urinal every time I had to pee droning on about my eternal demise if I didn't join up with the New Roads church.

He was relentless in his vigilance of the bathroom, which forced me to give up my second milk at lunch so I could skip his afternoon urinal lecture. The human mind, however, is a wonderfully adaptive organ, it provides answers to vexing questions when called upon. Thirst and bladder discomfort spurred my gray matter to find a way out of this endless urinal tape recording; piss outside, it was a much bigger place and much less prone to marauding evangelicals.

I was an experienced player in the game of eluding the salesmen of salvation but was adapting to a new field of play. For two years before I entered the New Roads School and College, Brother Jonus Reed, the preacher at the First New Roads Church of Montgomery had had me, and all the rest of the blooming adolescents, on his list of those in need of conversion to the New Roads faith. His goal was to get us on the straight and narrow before we discovered the temptations of the secular world. He had harvested all but one of his prey over that two-year period, though many were back-sliding on the afternoon of their conversion. I had learned to avoid his ominous presence by staying in groups at church. It was very hard to have a deeply personal conversation with me when I was clumped in a group. Preacher Reed was a patient converter and watched for every opportunity to separate me from the other church teens. To his credit, I must confess, he never stalked me to the urinal. He did, however, pull off his greatest conversion maneuver of all our times together on the last day of our two-year New Roads conversion dance. By conspiring with my mother, he was able to arrange for me to accompany him on a trip to the Bible bookstore in downtown Montgomery. This was Preacher Jonus's last shot.

The next day, I would turn fifteen, which was way over the age of conversion. The gauntlet had been laid down with my parents; I had told my parents that autumn that I would only continue my passive resistance to the preacher's prying until my fifteenth birthday and at that point I would consider us at war for his interference in my personal and private life. My parents knew this wasn't a bluff because I had given fair warning that I would use any devious trick necessary to remove Preacher Reed from my personal life no matter what the punishment or consequences. It was time for Preacher Jonus Reed, minister of the First New Roads Church of Montgomery, to make the final pitch for the New Roads Church's pedagogy before I was lost forever to the impending sin that awaited me.

Preacher Reed warmed up slowly as we traversed the suburbs on our way to the outskirts of downtown Montgomery.

"So, Pip," he began, "how are your classes this year?" He continued, "Who's your favorite teacher? Don't you think it's cold for this time of year?"

At that point, we were just passing by the Governor's Mansion on Court Street, when out of nowhere, without pausing for answers to the previous questions, the reason behind the excursion exploded inside the car. "Is it that you don't believe in the New Roads beliefs, or do you just love the world?"

I was not surprised at all by the last question, and I tried to answer from my heart. "Preacher Reed, I sure have a hard time believing that God has chosen just one sect to bestow salvation on, and are you sure it's this one? I certainly have a vision of such a select group, but they're over in Africa helping out the sick and dying or trying to improve the lives of the poorest people in Montgomery, the Negroes who are in need of Christian love and support."

While I watched Preacher Reed's face turn beet red, I admitted, "I know I must have been influenced by actually reading the Bible, and what the poor Jewish woodworker from the Middle East said almost two thousand years ago, and I think he would be ashamed of what is happening in Montgomery and many white Christians not following his philosophies. As far as loving the world goes," I said, "now, I'm just patiently waiting for the opportunity to discover beer and heavy petting with real live, secular public school girls." At this point, I figured I had said enough.

The rest of the trip after my confession of disbelief in the New Roads roadmap to Heaven was spent in total silence. If I had known then what I have subsequently learned in years of graduate psychotherapy training, I would have recognized silence as an elicitor of compliance. Even without all that training, I knew that twenty minutes of silence might just remove one of the most ardent followers of my comings and goings that I had ever attracted. So, we parted ways with a handshake, the sporting analogy didn't escape me even at the age of fifteen years minus one day. Preacher Jonus Reed had thrown a Hail Mary pass to the end zone on a fourth down and long in the gospel championship game.

Unfortunately, his receiver wasn't interested in making the catch and had left the field.

Even with my previous two years of training in avoiding a full-fledged New Roads minister intent on conversion, the geek would-be minister from Opp, Alabama, Roy Harper Jr., was not going to be defeated by my old ploys, but at least I didn't have to carry on a war on two fronts since Preacher Jonus Reed had accepted defeat and moved on to easier prey.

My moves lead to countermoves by Roy Harper Jr. Since Roy couldn't catch me in the bathroom anymore, he figured out other biological necessities that he thought would lead to the capture of my soul for the New Roads team. Roy figured out that I had to eat and that this was a better place to have our little philosophical chats because it took a lot longer to eat than to pee. Roy was a man of cunning and social influence in the New Roads School, a ministerial student, and the son of one of the wealthiest members of the New Roads religion. Roy Harper Jr. was sure that he could overcome any obstacle that might block his path to his first hostile conversion.

When Roy checked into my lunch schedule, he found out that I was dining from noon until one p.m. in the New Roads' Bistro, the unofficial five-percenter name for our food-surplus cafeteria. My eating schedule presented quite a problem for Brother Roy because he had his class in evangelism from eleven thirty until twelve thirty, but Roy's family influence and his social standing kicked in to solve this minor problem of academic standards.

Roy explained his situation to his evangelism professor, Dr. Ronald T. Snodgrass, including the urgency of the intervention because I was being seen more and more in the grips of members of the five percenters.

Roy had a proposal. "Professor Snodgrass, I think I should be allowed to leave class at noon to do applied field work, and I'll base 50 percent of my grade in this evangelism class on the accomplishment of bringing Pip Cooper into the New Roads' fold before final exams."

The professor agreed, and poor Roy had doomed himself to the first F of his stellar academic career. Roy had also formalized his relationship with me by entering into this contract with the school administration. We were yoked together in a battle of the wills, and poor Roy had bet the farm on a pair of deuces.

Lunch had become one of the high points of my day, except for the occasional tongue-lashing for not praying over my canned food before consumption, because after lunch it was a time to gather with the rogues of the ninth-grade class. Archie, Pecker, and I would wolf down a quick plate of agricultural surplus food provided to nonprofit organizations by the U.S. Department of Agriculture. This was food for those who were not overly concerned about the human palate. After our bad meal, it was off to the cow bowl, the barn situated on the remnants of the working farm that was a mostly unused part our educational institution. The barn, where all the school's maintenance equipment was stored, was down a hill and removed from the rest of the campus and known to be a place where cigarettes and rabbit tobacco were consumed. For those five per-centers who did not know what rabbit tobacco was, their initiation took place in the barn.

My first experience with rabbit tobacco was one day when we had one cigarette amongst the three of us and Pecker said for us not to worry because he knew this plant that grew in the cow bowl and was just as good as real tobacco. The next thing I knew, Pecker was outside the barn rooting around in the dried fall weeds pulling off leaves. Pecker came back with three likely candidates, saying he couldn't exactly remember what it looked like. Being well-educated in the ways of the sophisticated smoker, we decided on a blend and proceeded to make three smokes by rolling our cow-bowl blend with the tobacco from our one real cigarette in a page from my math book. The math book didn't matter because we didn't show up for math that afternoon anyway. The Pecker brand of smokes caused great intestinal irritation, which led to the launching of our government-donated lunches. On that day I started to question any advice I got from Pecker.

Brother Roy knew where to find me after lunch before he cut his internship deal with Professor Snodgrass. The barn was considered unholy ground by the New Roads' majority, and a ministerial student would not want to be seen coming up the hill from the cow bowl unless accompanied by the school's maintenance man. Roy Harper Jr. knew that this was the way ugly rumors began, rumors like backsliding or coming under the influence of the power of the dark side, or being one of the five percenters who hung out below the hill in the cow bowl. With this stigma in mind, Brother Roy planned to do what he had to do by catching me early in my lunch break and sticking to me to keep me away from the cow bowl and especially my peer group of choice, Archie and Pecker. This proved to be one of the most difficult tasks Roy Harper Jr. had ever undertaken.

Roy was giddy the first day he was out of his evangelism class at noon. He caught me within thirty feet of the classroom building and proceeded, "Hi, lad, how are you this beautiful day?"

I knew that I was nailed for lunch and a five-minute prayer before I got to eat my lukewarm food that even the government didn't want. Roy had shifted to a new strategy for his New Roads' Bistro campaign to convert me. This approach was based on a theory of us becoming buddies because we were so much alike.

Brother Roy began with a few questions without waiting for answers, "So, Pip, what are some things that you like and what do you not like?"

This was where the rub came, I didn't much care for music-less church, softball, reading the Book of Revelation, or coin collecting, and he wasn't in the least interested in motorcycles, ditch walking, YMCA dances, or rock and roll music. I found his interests boring and he found mine evil. We were at an impasse, but Roy trudged on, he had no choice given his agreement with Professor Snodgrass. His challenge to bring me into the righteous fold was the talk of the New Roads' majority community and its outcome would determine if he passed or failed one of his most important subjects.

Within a few days, I had begun to perfect my response to these Hell-on-earth lunches with a litany of excuses about why I had to be on my way: had a test the next period and must go, needed to get to the library for the paper that's due tomorrow, and my least favorite, that I had to pee. When I used the bathroom excuse, Roy would suddenly realize that he had to pee, too. When he really did, I would fake a quick piss and be out of the building and into the woods and down to the cow bowl before Roy could zip up his fly and catch me.

This fleeing behavior wore thin real fast. I knew that I had to find a better way to cope with Roy soon or start studying the change in my pockets and bone up on the Book of Revelation. It was time to call on the five-percent irregulars, Archie and Pecker, if I was going to get my life back. I knew I needed the support of my own kind even though they had abandoned me to Roy the first day he had begun his lunchtime escort service.

After a narrow escape from the washroom to the cow bowl after two long weeks of having lunch with Roy, I told my friends about my problem with keeping my sanity and having my lunch spoiled every day. I said I needed my friends' help and support; and after a few minutes of reflection over a Marlboro, Archie said, "Pip, you should explain to Roy that he irritates the shit out of you and that he has a severe body odor problem to boot."

Then Pecker chimed in, "Pip, I think you should lure Roy into the woods by being a little slower on your bathroom takeoff, and then the three of us will beat the crap out of him." Neither of these solutions fit my personality; I just figured that Brother Roy was just trying to do his job as he knew it and fulfill his poorly conceived evangelism class contract obligations. I knew it was up to me to find a non-confrontational way to solve my problem with Brother Roy; I needed a plan without the side effects I perceived in my friends' ideas of how to send Roy back to his religious studies.

We left our powwow with the agreement that I would find a way to use their help and that I would let them know what to do the next morning. There was no TV for me that night, I was in my room dissecting my options. By morning, I had a plan that would give Brother Roy the same level of enjoyment that I had endured over our previous luncheon dates. I huddled before class with Pecker and Archie and gave them their scripts for our joint luncheon with Brother Roy.

I said, "Okay, guys, I need y'all to start joining Roy and me for lunch. Archie, your role is to steer the conversation to motorcycles. Pecker, it's your job to talk about rock and roll the whole time. And I'll be talking about how great it is to play in the drainage ditches after school."

Pecker said, "Well, why can't I just tell Roy to fuck himself?"

At this, we agreed to share the responsibility of talking about dances we had been to or would like to go to, but I knew I would have to carry the ball on this one, because Pecker and Archie had never been to a dance.

At noon that day, thirty feet past the classroom building, Brother Roy fell in next to me on the way to the New Roads' Bistro for our daily dose of canned vegetables and church dogma. Was Roy ever surprised when Archie and Pecker joined our little twosome! Brother Roy and I were already seated when the dynamic duo joined us and interrupted Roy's discourse on the sins of omission.

Archie jumped right on that line and changed the subject. "Roy, can you believe the amount of emissions that a Ducati 250 Scrambler gives off?" He carried on for ten minutes about the power baffles in the exhaust pipe and its additional power because of the shape of the cylinder heads.

Roy's eyes were glazing over when Pecker cut in, "You know, Roy, Jerry Lee Lewis rode a motorcycle." He carried on about Jerry Lee Lewis and other Godless rock and roll groups for a good fifteen minutes.

Brother Roy knew he had to take control of this conversation, so he said, "I don't know how you boys listen to that evil rock and roll stuff. That's not music! All three of you should be listening to Pat Boone and his music. I'm sure there will be plenty of Pat Boone music in Heaven and absolutely no Jerry Lee Lewis music."

Before my friends could take Roy to task, I cut in, "Roy, you've just got to experience the virtues of an afternoon ditch walk. It's about as good as Heaven! You get to see the wonders of how trashy your neighbors are when you look into their back yards."

Roy was starting to come apart; this was not what he had planned, trapped at a table with three teenagers from the five-percenter minority talking about worldly things. I saw Roy summon up his strength to give it one more try to take charge.

He cut me off in midsentence, "You are all dancing with the Devil, and y'all are absorbed with too many worldly things!"

That was all it took to start the three of us talking in unison about dances of the past and dances of the future. That was it for Roy. He became disoriented with all this talk of one of the New Roads' biggest sins. He went as pale as a sheet, his hands began to tremble, and sweat broke out on his brow. Roy stood, and in a faraway voice said, "I've got to go pee."

We waited, but Roy never came back that day.

7. The Bistro Conversion Room

Brother Roy was down but not out; he made several more runs at his new, but defeated, Bistro method of soul saving. The outcome was always the same, the three five percenters overwhelming his conversational moves about salvation and his having to endure subjects that he found abhorrent. After two weeks of trying politely to get us focused on the big sin sinkhole we were all headed for and getting in return, talk of dancing in ditches to rock and roll as motorcycles roared around us, Brother Roy's glue began to melt. We were having mystery meat and rehydrated mashed potatoes for lunch and enjoying driving Roy nuts when his fuse blew. Roy was on his fourth pitch at our luncheon to get right with God, accept the New Roads tenets, and turn away from the Devil and his agents on earth, the five-percenter minority.

At this point in our conversation, I made the fatal mistake of joining him in a theological discussion. I asked Roy if he didn't think himself and the rest of the New Roaders to be a tad bit arrogant in thinking that the kingdom of Heaven was reserved only for them. It was at this point that Pecker explained that he would rather spend eternity roasting in Hell than spend one more luncheon with a grease ball hick who must be using Limburger cheese for deodorant.

The man of God had had too much, he came up out of his chair with a bloodlust in his eyes and threw a wild punch at Pecker. At this point,

Archie put a bear hug on him to try to calm the situation. Archie was succeeding in getting Roy to calm down when Pecker dumped a full plate of mashed potatoes and mystery meat down Roy's pants. Roy began cussing Pecker and trying to get unstuck from Archie while I watched the gravy and mashed potatoes run down the inside of his pants and over his shoes.

The New Roads philosophy on cussing was one where heck or darn was a sin be-cause these were mere euphemisms for the real thing. Roy blew past any stand-in words in a hurry and was quickly into a discussion of Pecker's mother's canine past, questioning whether his parents were duly wed when his birth occurred, and if Pecker's head was composed of fecal matter.

Roy's display of foul language landed him in the New Roads School and College dean's office that afternoon. "Roy, what were you thinking, trying to ruin those boys' lunches? Why did you even think that was a good idea?" the dean asked.

Roy started to explain, "Sir, bringing in the sheaves is a lot harder than I was led to believe! I'm sure that Lucifer has returned to the earth in the form of a fifteen-year-old boy named Pecker."

"Son," the dean said, "let me tell you something. One more episode of foul language like that is going lead to your removal from the rolls of the New Roads' pastoral training program."

Roy realized that he had made a serious mistake in making his soul-winning deal with Professor Snodgrass, and then he asked the dean, "Sir, would it be possible to be let out of my bargain with the professor?

The dean said, "Roy, I don't see how I can let you out of it, because you've missed half of the evangelism class for several weeks. Besides, son, how hard can it be to bring a fifteen-year-old boy to his senses?"

Roy, who lived in the men's dorm on campus, took to his bed after his meeting with the dean. His display of a sailor's vocabulary before his Bistro buddies, the threat of expulsion from his chosen profession before it had even begun, and his failed approach to soul saving had overloaded his circuits. Revulsion turned to Christian charity on the part of his fellow would-be preachers after Roy spent three days in bed with the sheets pulled over his head. Meals were brought in, and sympathy was pouring out. After ten days, Roy returned to the world of the living and to class. I felt sorry for Roy; he defined the term boxed-in, and I knew that this could only mean trouble for me.

The five-percenter minority had spies everywhere; it was a prerequisite to survival at the New Roads School. You needed to know where the fire was if you didn't want to get cremated. The word on the sidewalk was that a Grand Council of the preachers-in-training had been formed, and their charge was to help in my soul rescue and to clamp down on the unholy activities of the five percenters. They were burning the mid-night oil in their dorm developing their plans. The positive part of this action for me was that I was left alone for weeks as the assault was planned. The first sign I got of the coming assault was from my brother, Ben, who grudgingly let me in on what he knew of the Grand Council's plan. Ben was from the Archie school of life philosophy and figured that his dog wasn't in this fight and so he didn't want to get involved, but he said he would keep me informed about what he heard of the Grand Council's plans.

About three weeks after the surplus-food-down-the-shorts incident, Ben told me that a group of ministerial students were trying to recruit him to participate in a plot to save me from myself and the gutter elements that the righteous had to share their school with. Ben was quick to tell them that he wished them luck, but he was having no part of it because he had to live in the same house as me and that he had spent enough years living around me to know that there would be a bill to pay for messing in what I perceived as my personal freedom. He advised them to proceed with caution lest they all find mashed potatoes and gravy in their shorts. He knew that my pursuit of principle could drive me to many a mischievous plan and so warned the members of the Grand Council.

My sister was next on their help list and much closer in age and academic rank than my brother to the Grand Council members. She was blunt and direct with the Grand Council. "As far as I know my younger brother is crazy, he isn't much for rules, he even found the Cub Scouts to be more structure than he could abide, and he sets his clock radio five times throughout the night so he can get more alpha waves in his life. I advise caution in dealing with him because you can never tell what a teenager hopped up on alpha waves might do if pushed too far."

In truth, I'm not sure my siblings wanted to change me because I certainly brought an element of entertainment into their wholesome lives. I figured that it was my job to cash in on the whole family's quota of sin and, besides, I think my brother and sister enjoyed the vicarious experience of my misdeeds. I could always be counted on for most of the bad press in our family's news and this, of course, kept the corrective attention on me and off them. With a brother like me, they looked great. All in all, it worked fine. I was who I was, and they were who they were, so we lived and let live in relative peace.

Having failed in their attempts to bring my family into the rescue, and thus having twenty-four-hour-a-day conversion coverage, the Grand

Council knew it had lost its best weapon in keeping the pressure on me. Roy had regained his strength and knew that the time of judgment before Professor Snodgrass's academic court was drawing nigh. Roy proposed a new plan to the Grand Council that involved the alteration of the interior of the New Roads Bistro. The renovation could be accomplished over the week-end if all the members of the Grand Council would agree to help. Roy said that they could all start working on his plan on Monday after the lunch period was over. They needed to do measurements, collect materials, devise a construction plan, and be prepared to do a renovation in one weekend. He knew he would have to involve Professor Snodgrass in his plan if they were going to succeed because they were only a group during the class day. Roy went to see the New Roads Professor of Religion that night at his home.

Professor Snodgrass was a bit wary when the cursing preacher-to-be called and asked if he could come to his home to discuss saving the school from the five percenters and the Devil, which he insisted were one and the same. When Roy arrived, he had worked himself into a righteous lather. Roy whipped through the door and into the living room before the professor got three words out of his mouth. Being aware of the Bistro incident and the days Roy spent in bed under the covers after it, the professor had second thoughts about being alone in the same house with Roy.

Roy got right down to business, "Professor Snodgrass, do you know that the New Roads School and College is being taken over by the Devil? Do you know that the cow bowl is a satanic recruiting station where innocent kids are enlisted in the work of the Devil?"

The professor answered, "As far as I know, the cow bowl is where the maintenance man keeps his equipment in the barn. The school seems basically the same to me, not like it's being taken over."

Roy's face turned bright red. He knew he was not getting through to Professor Snodgrass. In a fleeting thought, he wondered if Professor Snodgrass had also been taken over by the five percenters.

Roy decided to forego any more discussion of the big picture of the school's take-over and moved on to his plan for bringing me into the New Roads fold and thus dealing a knockout punch to the five percenters' corruption effort. Roy explained that he would need five of Professor Snodgrass's students in his eleven-thirty class for about a week. All the students had agreed to come to the professor's house every night if the professor would just repeat the morning's lectures then. Roy's voice was at a high pitch as he ended his presentation, and he seemed to be caught somewhere between exploding and imploding. The professor had lived too long to deny the request of a very desperate man and agreed to his plan to salvage his grade, even though it seemed destined to fail if Roy were at the controls.

Roy knew he was in the home stretch. Christmas vacation and finals were in three weeks. His world as he had known it was defined within a definite time span. The Grand Council went into action; they planned their renovation and got the cooperation of the maintenance supervisor, Estill Jarvis, and the construction work was set to begin. Over the next weekend, a private dining room was constructed in the Bistro's wall-less interior. Estill got the go-ahead from the administration to construct a private dining room for spiritual conversion if he could do the whole job over the weekend, if it didn't cost over $100, and if there would be no disruption of Monday's meal. Roy had sold Estill on his plan by assuring him that this action would break up the five percenters once the effectiveness of the conversion room was proven. He said that each member of the five percenters would be brought over to the New Roads faith and thus would never again be a problem in his barn. Brother Estill said he would work night and day if it would keep those wild kids out of his barn and restore dignity to his cow bowl.

Estill was more than a little concerned that his barn was known to be a gathering spot of evil spirits and was willing to follow any harebrained scheme that would stop the rumors about his primary workstation. Estill was a known backslider and from time to time would revert to his old sinful ways and this was incentive enough to help dis-associate his barn from evil in the eyes of his employers.

Construction began Friday after supper. All the Grand Council members and Estill showed up and worked hard for about two hours. At about eight o'clock, the workers started disappearing to the restroom, never to return. By eight thirty, all that was left of the original group was Estill, Roy, and the rest of the preachers-in-training conversion planning sub-committee and some of them were whining about going home. Roy's leadership talents and ability to lay down a heavy guilt trip on his fellow would-be preachers kept the group intact until Sunday night after church when the door was hung and the job completed.

Monday took me by complete surprise. There was a rumor from the five-percenters' information network that a Grand Council action was planned, but the same rumor had been around the whole week before. At lunch that day, as Archie, Pecker, and I headed for the Bistro, we noticed that there was a large gathering of the Grand Council membership standing by the front door. As we entered, I was shuttled off to the left into a previously nonexistent room. I had never seen this room in my life.

The door slammed behind me but before it closed, I noticed two Grand Council members standing guard outside. Surrounding me were

Brothers Roy, Peter, and Stride-X (a nickname for his devotion to the most popular anti-pimple cream of teens every-where), all members of the ministers-in-training program at the New Roads College. I gazed around the room and noticed trays of huge servings of the latest government giveaway food and a black velveteen portrait of The Last Supper staring down at me from the new wall. I told Roy that I felt like Rod Sterling should join us because I was in a room that didn't exist with artwork that you could buy off the side of the highway. Once again, I had said the wrong thing. Brother Stride-X let me know that his mother got that painting at an exclusive discount furniture store in Clio, Alabama.

Roy then formally invited me to a luncheon prepared especially for me, although I was sure that I was to be the main course of this luncheon. The style had shifted yet again. There was no more buddy-buddy talk; this was business and there were a lot of butts hanging out on the line. Roy began by assuring me that I was amongst friends and people who loved me. He said that the purpose of this luncheon, and every lunch I would eat until I saw the light, was to aid in my spiritual growth. Roy gave me the agenda for the rest of time: we would have lunch and discussions about wholesome topics and then we would discuss theology.

I wondered if their discussions of theology were open to any give-and-take, but I did not have to wonder very long. During the meal, they had a lively discussion about the Book of Revelation, coin collecting for fun and profit, and the latest scientific discoveries in the war on pimples. Then we got down to business. Peter started the ball rolling with the history of the New Roads Church, followed by a presentation by Brother Stride-X on the joys of not doing what any red-blooded American boy wanted to do: drink beer and fool around with secular girls. Last, but not least, on the speakers' roster was the captain of guilt, Brother Roy Harper Jr.

Brother Roy started out his attack on me, "Pip, you are the most selfish and destructive person I know! How can you let everyone around you be in agony by not joining the New Roads Church? Your parents and your wonderful brother and sister have to suffer from your inattention to your spiritual needs.

"This," he said, "cannot continue. Your brother and sister are now under suspicion for not helping wring the devil out of your soul. If you don't come around soon, they could find themselves facing fellowship isolation for your sins! Don't you even care?" "Well, Roy," I asked, "does this familial corruption extend beyond my immediate family? I have some cousins that I would like to drag into the swamp of sin with me." What little humor Brother Roy had begun the year with had all but disappeared.

He gave me a hard look and said, "This is nothing to laugh about. We're talking about eternal damnation and your soul flame-broiled forever and ever!"

I said, "Well, Roy, we should also not forget that we're talking about your grade from Professor Snodgrass's class as well."

Roy's face flushed bright red, and he began to stammer. I had cold-cocked him with a truth I wasn't supposed to know, but I was a member of the five percenters and had access to a superb spy network.

As Brother Roy was trying to regain the momentum and find a few intelligible words, I took the lead and began to quiz Brothers Peter and Stride-X.

I asked these preachers-in-training, "So, guys, will your association with this massive soul rescue attempt and subsequent failure have any kind of lasting impact on your grades? What about your careers? For y'all to jump right into such a dangerous under-taking before you all have even finished your training is foolhardy at best. You know, a recent study in the prestigious Journal of Ministry found that ministers who suffer an early defeat in their professional lives are marked for a life of ministerial failure. Can you believe that fully ninety-five percent of these eager-beaver failures go on to become drinkers, fornicators, and furniture salesmen?"

Peter was thinking about what I said, and Brother Stride-X was seeing his life rolling before his eyes, selling Barcaloungers and velveteen furniture in the Clio Furniture Barn, going home to his common-law wife to drink himself silly until the next day.

Brother Stride-X turned to Roy, who was stunned by my divide-and-conquer strategy, and explained, "Look here, Roy, I don't want to sell furniture for a living, and I'm headed back to evangelism class right now, before you or anybody else ruins my life!"

Brother Stride-X knocked both guards down on his escape from Roy with Peter following close behind.

The remaining members of the Grand Council sub-committee came rushing into the room wanting to know what had happened to Brothers Peter and Stride-X, but Roy was back on overload after being deserted by his most loyal followers.

Roy blurted out, "This little son of a bitch devil from Hell has wrecked my plan!

Not only that, but he's also trying to wreck my life!"

The remaining Grand Council members stood with mouths agape, in shock to hear the cursing preacher from Opp using his foul language again. It was at this point that I jumped in again.

"Remember what I said a while ago about the rapid demise of preachers who fail early in their careers? Why would y'all want to follow this foul-mouthed, would-be geek preacher anyway?" I asked.

That's all it took; the rest of the Grand Council sub-committee was headed back to class. Roy got up to close the door but not before Archie and Pecker had slipped in. Pecker said that he was glad that Roy had had the foresight to build a cussing room so he could stay out of trouble with the dean. Archie said he liked the painting, but Roy should try to get the other two that comprised the set: the dogs playing poker and Elvis on black velvet. This opening gave Pecker the ammo he needed to start a monologue on why Elvis was the king of rock and roll. Roy was smoking with anger and began to dog cuss the three of us. Pecker asked, "Roy, is this cussing like a sailor a new form of preaching being taught in the New Roads' religion program?" At which point Roy started to throw government-reject food in our direction. We were hugging the floor as the Salisbury steaks flew over our heads. Archie reached the door before the next course, dessert, was fired and the three of us were across the dining room by the time the chocolate pudding came flying out the door.

Roy was back in the dean's office that afternoon to explain why he had thrown perfectly good ex-government food all over the dining hall and was heard cussing a blue streak. Disoriented once again, Roy tried to explain in broken sentences that he was chasing the devil with a Salisbury steak. The dean knew that this was no time for another expulsion warning, that this boy needed pastoral counseling. The dean sent Roy to see the resident expert in pastoral counseling, Professor Ronald T. Snodgrass. Professor Snodgrass was lounging in his office above the chapel building when

Roy arrived with an envelope from the dean. The dean had given instructions to the professor to fix this mentally ill, tuition-paying preacher-to-be. Roy at this point was going catatonic after thinking about what he had done and said, and the professor was once again wondering if he should be left alone in the same room with Roy. When the professor asked Roy what seemed to be the problem, he thought he had hit Roy's instant-replay button. Roy started babbling about the five percenters, the devil named Pecker that lived in the cow bowl, the takeover of his school and the newly constructed "convert the evil" private dining room. The professor had helped many a student through a life crisis, but he had never tried to aid someone with Pecker's disease. The best thing he could think of was sending Roy to his bed, which was exactly what Roy was thinking.

After just two days under the covers in his room, Roy emerged with a very strange look in his eye. Roy took to wearing the same clothes every day and forsaking the bath. With Roy's over-active scent glands, this created quite a problem for his fellow students and for Professor Snodgrass who had to see Roy every day for counseling. The sessions tended to be short because Roy smelled awful and would only say that he had a secret plan to save the school and free the world from sin. Professor Snodgrass figured that the semester would be over in only two weeks and then Roy could go back to Opp and be committed to the mental hospital from there.

Life for me had returned to as normal as life could be at the New Roads School: boring teachers, boring food, and a midday reprieve at noon in the cow bowl. We would talk and look for something in the barn to get into. We always kept a sharp eye and ear out for Estill, but only an emergency at lunch would dislodge Estill from his full hour of packing in all the free government food that he could lay his hands on. There were four exits from the barn and dozens of places to hide and besides Estill was slow and nearsighted.

One day, the week before the holidays, we were taking our break down at the cow bowl barn when Pecker discovered a case of bottles in the back of an old storage shed in the barn. They were full of multicolored liquids and had been stored in the barn for years. Upon further inspection I found this substance to be Army surplus food coloring. Upon closer inspection I found out that fifty percent of the ingredients were listed as alcohol, the great demon of the New Roads Church and School. What were we to do? Here we were in the dark soul of the universe, the cow bowl barn, of course we had to drink it.

Being more worldly than my two friends, I took the first slug of the blue food coloring, it was awful but so were my first 600 beers years later. I guess food coloring, like beer, is an acquired taste, but that noon we acquired about half pint of blue, green, and red taste adaptation. What we failed to notice while enjoying our chemical cocktail was Brother Roy sneaking in by the old quail pen at the back of the barn. About the time that food coloring kicked in, Brother Roy was on us, wild-eyed and full of revenge. He said, "Now I have caught you demons up to no good, y'all are breaking God's and the school's rules about drinking and doing something mighty wrong and ungodly." I explained through a food-coloring high that we were sent down here by Mrs. Jamison, the Bistro cook, to fetch a case of food coloring and we were merely tasting it to make sure we had the right stuff.

Roy started to crumble before our eyes as it sunk in that we were on a mission for the school, and we almost got away with it. I told Roy, "Get out of our way so we can do our duty," just when Pecker fell on the floor and began the laugh that only the demon alcohol brings on. Roy was revived in seconds, grabbed the food coloring bottle and read the ingredients. He then realized what we were up to and proceeded to tell us what was going to happen when the school's administration and our parents found out that we were drunk on food coloring.

Roy should have saved the lecture and gone about his tattling. When Roy turned to run, he ran right into the waiting bear hug of Archie. Archie said to get the old pen open quickly, and that's where Archie deposited the flailing Brother Roy. The pen was about five-feet-tall and four-feet-wide, enclosed on three sides with wood, and on the front with a very strong chain-link gate with a padlock. Roy was hollering and screaming, cussing and yelling. He was pissed that he had been locked up by a bunch of degenerates zoned out on food coloring.

Pecker decided that this was the perfect opportunity to see if Roy might like to join the five percenters. He proposed this idea to Roy and pointed out that it would be a record-breaking occurrence because there had never been a five percenter from the New Roads School of Religion. Roy went manic with this suggestion; he accused Pecker of being the Devil. Then, Pecker stuck out his red-food-coloring-dyed tongue, and Roy began banging his head against the cage like a wild animal, screaming, and singing "Rock of Ages" intermittently.

"What should we do about him?" Archie asked.

"I think we should leave Roy caged until Estill brings the tractor back, and then Estill can let him out," I suggested.

Pecker added, "I think we should sing a medley of rock and roll songs for Roy." Unfortunately, Roy's renewed dog cussing nixed that idea.

Archie wondered, "Do you think we'll get in any trouble for treating Brother Roy like a quail?"

Roy chimed in, "Y'all, the shit is going to be so deep for us, it's going to take weeks for us to get to the surface."

At that point, I mentioned, "Roy, you should mind your language around young people. You have a reputation around campus for being psychotic. Any attempt to frame us will not be credible. Besides, there are a dozen five percenters who will testify that we were on the ball field at lunch, and there's nothing you can do about them."

That's when Roy quieted and moved to the back of the quail pen; defeat was written all over his face.

After putting the food coloring back where we found it, we needed to figure out what to do in our altered state with math class starting in five minutes. This was not as hard a problem as it seemed because our math teacher was Dean Leatherbury's great aunt who had already retired from two different school systems. Sister Nelson had lucid days but not any that week, so escaping once class started was easy. We just had to walk straight, take our seats at the back of the class by the window that opened onto the front porch, wait for the senile math teacher to turn to the chalk board, and then slip out one by one. This was a flawless plan that had us back in the cow bowl in ten minutes.

We checked on Brother Roy who had bent the gate in our absence but was still secured in his quail cage. Roy, that man of many faces, was now in a reasoning mood. "Hey, why don't y'all free me and forget the whole thing?"

Archie wasn't buying it and said, "Not a chance, Roy! You know you'll be in the principal's office in five minutes."

I asked, "So, what do you say, Roy? Is that true?"

Roy then promised and said, "Archie is dead wrong! I'm not going to the principal. If I do, y'all might lock me up like this again!"

Archie, who hated to see a grown man treated like a quail asked him to promise. "Roy, will you swear to God that you won't turn us in?"

Roy gave Archie a long hard look and then began beating his head against the gate again, screaming and swearing. Archie figured that meant no, but Pecker had another solution.

Pecker had to shout over Roy's commotion, "Would you just quit thrashing around in your pen? If you'll take a swig of this food dye, we promise we'll let you out."

Roy said, "I've never had a drink of alcohol in my mouth, and I'm not about to start now just to make you boys happy. I'll live like a quail until judgment day before I'll do that."

I worked out a compromise I thought we all could live with and suggested, "Roy, how about this? If you'll just rinse your mouth out with the food coloring, we'll let you out."

Roy wasn't sure of the theological implications of putting alcohol just in his mouth without swallowing. I assured him that the New Roads prohibition was against swallowing booze, not rinsing with it.

Roy agreed, and I brought him our best vintage of blue. Roy did as he was told and took a big swig and moved it around his mouth for no more than two seconds before he spit it out.

Pecker told Roy to try it again for at least a minute or he would be forced to get Nurse Archie to administer the correct dosage. Roy thought about being force-fed and followed Pecker's instructions.

We unlocked the pen and told Roy he was free to go, at which point he started right where he left off before he had become a human quail.

Roy started screaming again, "I'm headed for the principal's office! You boys should stay here in the barn until I come back with the school authorities. Your evil ways are at an end, and justice is about to be carried out!"

I said, "That's fine, Roy, but you need to think about this. When the authorities come down here, I'll point out that you brought us down to the barn and made us drink food coloring. All they'll have to do is look at your bright blue tongue to know you were taking part, too, and you're not just an informant."

Roy thought about this for a moment and began the psychological slump he was getting known for, and I suggested that a day under his sheets might do wonders for his disposition.

Roy spent that afternoon and night under his covers but was ready for action the next day and went on a hunt around the dorm for someone to help him catch the red-tongued devil that had appeared in their midst. Roy found no takers for his mission because everybody thought he was nuts and besides, they noted, finals began the next day. Roy's last hope was to get Brother Stride-X to help him because he knew what Pecker Power had done to Roy. Brother Stride-X had had all he could take from Roy. He said he was going to study for his exams, and he suggested that Roy do the same. Roy said that studying for exams was the last thing on his list, saving the school from the Pecker Devil came first.

Roy couldn't find anyone who would stand up to the forces of evil from the cow bowl and was about to give it up in favor of studying when he spotted Estill traversing the campus. Estill was an experienced demon rooter-outer. Here was a man who was a lifelong member of the New Roads Church, a man who had done battle with the Devil in his many years of backsliding. Roy knew that this was the man he needed, a man who had experience in taking the Devil to task. Estill had told Roy of his years of drinking, womanizing, cursing, dancing, and even playing music at the church gatherings of other denominations. Estill had done it all and had come back to the church after beating the tar out of the Devil. The two of them, with Roy's preacher training and Estill's knowledge of worldly things, could pull the fat out of the fire, they could overcome the takeover of the school by the five percenters. Estill and Roy began their partnership that day although it was with great trepidation on Estill's part.

8. The Best Laid Plans

Exams had begun and there was no sign or any information from the five-percenter spy network to cause me to think any further actions were planned. The opposite was what we heard: that Roy was off the deep end and no one wanted to go swimming anymore in his psychotic swimming hole. The only bit of information I got that disturbed me was that Roy was not studying for exams because he was never around the dorm except to sleep. I knew there was meaning in this information, but I couldn't figure out what it was. I had seen and smelled Roy around the classroom building, so I knew he was going to class, but he made no attempt at contact with me, he even averted his eyes when we passed in the hall. The days and exams passed quickly that week, but I could feel a tension around me that told me all was not well. I began setting my alarm clock for every hour on the hour after I went to bed; I knew that I would need extra alpha waves to get past Roy and on to the semester break.

When I raised my general feeling of discomfort about Roy with Archie and Pecker, they thought Roy's paranoia was rubbing off on me. Pecker was sure that Roy's stint as a quail with a blue tongue had dissuaded him of further attempts against such devious foes. Archie figured he would be in the bozo ward of the Opp Memorial Hospital by the weekend when his Momma and Daddy got a look at him. I, on the other hand, realized that we still had two and a half days until we were released from New Roads' grip for the holiday break. We needed a plan to watch our backsides until Friday afternoon, and I knew that I was going to have to develop it.

Archie and Pecker agreed to go along with me until my Roy Paranoia Syndrome wore off. It was decided that we would move as a group from early morning until we went home in the afternoon. We would eat, pee, and go to class and chapel together. The bladder timing was the only part that proved awkward; we spent three times as much time in the bathroom as we did before our defensive action began. The other part of our security arrangements involved checking the barn carefully before we entered and doing rounds in the barn several times during our lunch break. I only had half-hearted support in my barn security from Archie and Pecker; my friends' humoring behavior was erratic at best.

Things went well the next day; there was nothing out of the ordinary that happened except I noticed that Estill was not in his usual corner consuming his hour's worth of government surplus food. This caused us to be on full alert as we descended the woods and approached the cow bowl barn. We had three smokes that I convinced the guys to park in a tree until we could see if the coast was clear. We entered the barn from the side and went to dead stop for a full five minutes; there were no sounds, we heard nothing. We searched the barn from top to bottom including the loft but there was no threat. Pecker retrieved the smokes but they were wet from being parked in the tree so our lunch break was completed without them. The gnawing feeling that all Hell was going to break loose wouldn't leave me.

Our exams were over the next day at noon so we had the afternoon to kill until my brother and sister would be ready to leave at three o'clock. After one of Mrs. Jami-son's famous rehydrated meals, we were off to the barn. I had made it through a full semester at the New Roads School, and we had all finished our exams. Vacation had begun and we would not have to worry with Roy for two weeks and maybe forever if they bypassed Opp Memorial and sent him on to the state mental hospital in Tuscaloosa. What we had failed to pay proper attention to was the fact that Estill had once again missed his noon-time feedbag at the Bistro. We approached the barn with some caution, but not much. We gave the silent listening trick about twenty seconds, found our usual spot in the middle of the barn floor where some benches were gathered, and sat to enjoy our smokes. As we got comfortable, I noticed a picnic table had been set up at the south end of the barn.

The door was closed at that end, so the light wasn't very good. I could make out a stack of magazines and what looked like a whiskey bottle and three glasses. We decided to investigate this strange oasis, but as we got close to the table, we were startled by the two side barn doors being slammed shut. We were flying full tilt for the one remaining door when it slammed shut as well. We could hear the bolt being slid across this outside door, and we knew that we were trapped like rats in a sinking ship.

Estill and Roy were whooping it up outside, congratulating each other on their cunning and skill. Roy was screaming for God to be praised because the Pecker Devil was caught and would be exiled to the secular world outside the New Roads School.

As usual, I took on the task of being the spokesman for our group. "So, Roy," I hollered, "what are your terms for our release?"

"Oh no, Pip, there's only one thing that will change my mind," Roy said, "and that's if you'll swear allegiance to the New Roads faith and promise to abide by our tenets, that's the only way I'll let you go free."

"What about Archie and Pecker?" I asked.

Roy said, "Pecker and Archie can't go free. It's high time that the Pecker Devil and his sidekick, Archie, be expelled, and that's what will happen as soon as Estill gets back with the principal. Dr. Allen will boot Archie, Pecker, and you out of our school this very afternoon unless you repent and join our church this next Sunday. You better decide now, Pip."

"We won't get expelled for being in the barn, Roy," I said.

Then Roy said, "No, you'll be expelled for being in the barn with a half empty bottle of Early Times bourbon, three packs of cigarettes, and half a dozen nudist magazines."

I had to appreciate Roy's trap; he had set us up and then expected me to turn on my friends to save myself.

Roy had devised a plan to save his evangelism grade and get some revenge for his semester of torment. If I had done what he wanted, I would truly have sold my soul to the Devil.

Dr. Allen was a nice guy who was big on administration and small on running a New Roads faith–converting business. He let the five percenters slide as long as we stayed out of too much mischief; he even expected us to cause a little trouble.

Whiskey, pictures of nude women, and smokes would push the good doctor over his limit, and the shit would hit the fan in three Montgomery homes that night. I knew I could not let this happen; it was time for a very good plan to get us out of this predicament.

Then Roy asked, "Pip, are you ready to come out?"

"Maybe, Roy. How did you figure all this out anyway?" I asked.

I knew I had to distract Roy while I figured a way out of this mess. Roy was very forthcoming about how he and Estill had made the plan.

"Well, here's the thing, Pip. We drove to Birmingham yesterday and obtained all the incriminating evidence. Then, we each hid behind a side door when you all entered, and all we had to do was slam and bolt the doors when y'all went to the south end of the barn. Then, we ran to the other end and closed you in before you could get there. Now, you need to make up your mind quickly before Dr. Allen gets here. What do you say?"

I pulled my friends in close and said, "Follow me, and don't say a word!"

I grabbed one of the glasses on the picnic table and one of the nudist magazines and announced loud enough for Roy to hear that we should hide in the loft. My friends were right behind me as we ascended the stairs to the loft. I barked out hiding instructions as I waved my friends to the far end of the loft away from the end of the barn where Roy stood guard. At the end of the loft where we headed, there was a hay loading door that had not been used since the school was an active farm. On the other side of that door was a set of boards nailed to the wall forming a ladder. As I got ready to open the old hay door, I had Archie dump a stack of tin roofing down to the barn floor, the noise covered the sound perfectly.

Roy's voice echoed through the barn, "What are y'all doing?"

"You'll never take us alive, Roy!" I roared. This scared him, and he began the slow process of opening the heavy door by himself as we went out the hay door, down the ladder, and into the woods.

Roy was yelling and screaming for us to come down from the loft as we topped the hill in the woods behind the barn and saw the principal and Estill entering the front of the barn.

Roy explained, "Dr. Allen, me and Estill caught Pip, Archie, and Pecker drinking whiskey, looking at filthy magazines, and smoking cigarettes!"

The principal asked, "Well, where are they?"

Roy announced, "They're up in the loft. I can go up there right now and get them." When he got up to the loft, Roy saw the open hay door and knew what had happened. At this point, he let out a sting of profanities and then went to howling like a dog, which was the last thing we heard as we walked back to campus above the barn.

Archie and Pecker were ready to make a run for it when I persuaded them to wait for me on the steps of the library and act as if nothing had happened. I proceeded cautiously to the back entrance of the men's dorm, then down the quiet hall and into Roy's room. I set his matching whiskey glass by the bed and opened his American Nudist magazine to a full-page spread of a group of young naked females playing volleyball and left it on his pillow. I was back at the steps of the library in sixty seconds and reassured my friends we were fine because if anyone asked, we would say that we had been sitting here for thirty minutes. They got the drift of our denial strategy.

About the time that we got comfortable on the steps, we saw Roy, Estill, and Dr. Allen heading for us. Dr. Allen was short and to the point; when he got to our resting place, he said, "Have you boys been drinking whiskey, looking at nude pictures of women, and smoking in the cow bowl barn?"

We all gave him our most surprised looks, and I asked, "Where did you ever get an idea like that, sir?"

"Boys, don't lie to me. I saw a half-full bottle of whiskey, packs of cigarettes, and nudist magazines in the barn. Brother Roy and Brother Estill said they saw you all down there doing what I just described."

"How long ago were we supposed to have been there?" I asked. Dr. Allen said, "Less than three minutes before right now."

"Sir, that's not possible since we've been sitting on these steps for the past half hour," I said.

This is when Roy blurted out, "Goddamned lying little bastards!"

The principal was taken by surprise since he had not spent as much time as we had with the swearing preacher-to-be from Opp, Alabama. Dr. Allen snapped around, "Roy, you need to shut your filthy mouth, and you'll speak only when spoken to."

I jumped right back in as counsel for the defense.

"Dr. Allen, why don't you smell our breaths and see if you smell whiskey or cigarettes or anything we might have tried to cover it up with?" I asked.

He complied with my request, smelled our breath, and pronounced us innocent of the whiskey drinking and smoking charges. The principal turned around then and said, "Estill, are you sure you saw them in the barn?"

It was then that Estill realized what Roy had gotten him into.

Estill said, "I didn't see anybody because I was behind the door where Brother Roy asked me to stand and push on the barn's door. Roy is the only one who did the seeing. I might have heard some voices, but I'm hard of hearing and couldn't really tell."

Brother Roy was in the middle of a psychological meltdown.

Then the principal asked, "Roy, would care to explain the situation?"

Roy exclaimed, "I just need to go to bed. I need to get under the covers, and I don't want to discuss the Pecker Devil anymore."

Dr. Allen decided to go with Roy to his room in case he tried to do something to harm himself before Professor Snodgrass could be summoned to give emergency pastoral counseling.

About two minutes later, we heard what sounded like a dog that had been hit by a car, but the sound was coming from the men's dorm. I said it was time to go see if we could provide assistance to our brother in need, Roy Harper Jr. When we got to Roy's room, there were six Grand Council members and Dr. Allen looking very disturbed and confused. They were confronted with their first exposure to pictures of naked women and a possible werewolf preacher-to-be. Roy was curled up on the floor emitting a low howl and muttering about Pecker Devils. Dr. Allen turned to Brother Stride-X and told him to go find Professor Snodgrass and bring him right away to Roy's room and for the rest of the group to help him get Roy in his bed. Since we were in the room, we counted ourselves as part of the group and started grabbing Roy's arms and legs along with the others.

About the time we had Roy almost to his bed, he noticed Pecker holding one of his legs, which sent Roy into a wild panic. Dr. Allen was the first to fall from a convulsive kick to the head from a writhing Roy Harper Jr., who was being held aloft by his fellow New Roaders. The leader of the rescue team was down for the count and out cold as Roy broke free and went after Pecker. Pecker jumped up on the dresser while Archie and I formed a protective perimeter and the rest of the would-be preachers dragged their fallen leader, Dr. Allen, out into the hall. Roy had saliva pouring down both sides of his mouth like a dog with rabies, and he made two runs at the cornered Pecker, cursing and spitting as he charged. We landed Roy on his ass both times, which only seemed to increase his determination. As we braced for the third attack, the frail academic pastoral counselor appeared in the doorway and was set to flee when Brother Stride-X gave Professor Snodgrass a push into the room and closed the door behind him, with a comment to Roy that everything would be fine now that professional help had arrived. The professor seemed to be in shock, a normal response for someone that was dragged out of his office, who had to step over the comatose body of a fallen colleague and had been locked in a room with what appeared to be a mad dog intent on dismembering one of the school's younger students. The professor cried out for God's help in getting out of there alive as Roy made his third lunge at Pecker, which ended with Roy being dropped to the floor by Archie's oversized shoulder.

Professor Snodgrass snapped out of his lapse of professional conduct and asked a very dazed Roy what seemed to be the problem. Roy seemed to calm somewhat at this question and was trying to formulate an answer.

Then Pecker responded, "Isn't the answer to your question self-evident? This room smells like a grammar school restroom that hasn't been cleaned in a year because Roy gave up personal hygiene some weeks ago, and what now stands before you, Professor, is a drooling half animal that curses and howls and tries to hurt innocent children.

"The answer," Pecker continued, "as to what is wrong with Roy should be evident to any first-year ministerial student, Roy is obviously possessed by the Devil."

At this comment, Roy went back into a rage and started screaming that he was just trying to protect the school from this Goddamned Pecker Devil who was hiding out in a child's body.

Pecker said, "We need to send out for a Catholic priest to exorcise this Devil and get Roy back on his regular bathing schedule."

The suggestion that a Catholic, the archenemy of the New Roads faith, be brought into the case sent Professor Snodgrass into a snit.

Professor Snodgrass yelled, "No Papist, even the President of the United States, should ever set foot on New Roads soil! Those people believe in drinking, annulment, musical accompaniment, and the preeminence of their church over all others!"

I said, "It seems to me that the Catholics' main sin is that they were better competitors in the marketplace of religious ideas. Isn't that what really gets the goat of you New Roaders?"

Professor Snodgrass screamed at me, "Boy, you better shut your mouth before you commit a sin that cannot be forgiven, a sin that will doom you to the fires of Hell forever."

I said, "I'm only trying to shed some light on religious market competition in a free private enterprise economic system."

My comment was overlooked, though, because by now, the professor's attention had returned to the problem of what to do with Roy.

All this emotion on the part of the pastoral counselor seemed to have calmed Roy because the next thing we knew he was in his bed with the rather rank sheets pulled up over his head, singing "Rock of Ages" in a low voice. Professor Snodgrass was pale from his theological discussion with Pecker and me and quietly asked if I would escort him to his office.

When we opened the door, Dr. Allen was just regaining consciousness as I escorted the shaking professor back to his office. Dr. Allen asked what had happened in there and Pecker explained that Professor Snodgrass had performed an emergency exorcism on Roy, who was now resting quietly. Archie noted that this was the first New Roads exorcism ever performed so the effects might not be long-lasting, and someone should call Roy's parents and also notify Opp Memorial Hospital that they should expect a new patient for their bozo ward by nightfall.

Dr. Allen posted two student guards and followed Pecker's advice by calling Roy's mother and telling her that she and the judge should come right away because it appeared that Roy had suffered an emotional breakdown and might need to be hospitalized. The principal wasn't big on the possession theories of theology and didn't mention the first ever New Roads exorcism to Roy's mother. The next order of business for the principal was to check on Professor Snodgrass and find out why he was performing exorcisms since the New Roads Church didn't believe in Demonic Possession.

Dr. Allen found the professor in his office lying on his couch with a cold rag that I had procured for him stretched over his face. I had told the professor that in the movies they always got a glass of whiskey for people in his condition and that I would be glad to run down to the cow bowl barn and get him one from Roy's supply if he wanted me to. The professor regained enough strength to start yelling at me to get out of his office and his life, at which point the principal, who had arrived moments earlier, pointed at the doorway and asked me to wait for him outside. I was down the stairs in a heartbeat. When Dr. Allen came down, he was still angry after his conversation with the professor. He approached me. "Pip, what did you see happen in Roy's room while I was knocked out?"

I said, "Sir, it was very confusing in there and I don't remember exactly what happened, but I do remember a lot of screaming and yelling and maybe even some chanting."

Dr. Allen asked, "Was Professor Snodgrass the person doing the chanting?"

I said, "I can't be sure if it was the professor, or Roy, or even if it was chanting, but it seemed that it might be."

Dr. Allen then explained, "Exorcisms and chanting are Catholic rituals, and these practices have no right to be performed on New Roads property."

Dr. Allen reentered the professor's office and confronted him about his use of a Catholic ritual. Professor Snodgrass denied performing an exorcism; he even became violent and began throwing textbooks. He demanded that Dr. Allen leave him alone. So, Dr. Allen said, "If this purported exorcism had indeed occurred, I'll have to report it at once to our president."

After leaving Professor Snodgrass, Dr. Allen asked me again about what I saw and heard, so I told the principal, "I can't be sure of what I saw or heard, but I think the prudent thing to do is to report it to the president and let justice take its due course."

Archie and Pecker were waiting for me on the steps of the library, and I decided that we should lay low for a while and see what would happen. I went to the classroom building and found my brother, Ben, and told him that he and my sister should go home that afternoon without me because I was going to spend the night with Archie. I called my mom and got approval for my plan to spend the night at Archie's house, which was only a block from the New Roads School. We were then off to the cow bowl barn to debrief from our afternoon adventure. We decided that we had no desire to get Professor Snodgrass in more hot water than he was already in, so we would testify that after com-paring notes on what all three of us had seen and heard, we would say that we thought it was Roy giving himself a self-exorcism. We thought that we might recommend further study into this self-exorcism technique because it seemed to do Roy a world of good at the time.

After getting our story straight on Roy's self-exorcism, we went down to the barn and noticed that the bourbon, cigarettes, and nude magazines were right where Roy had planted them. What's a five percenter to do when confronted with temptations of the flesh like these: light up, pour a drink, and flip through some American Nudist magazines. It all went well until we got to the part of actually drinking the Early Times, we each took a small sip, and it tasted awful to each one of us. Pecker suggested that we mix it with the only other beverage in the barn, food coloring. I had had a blue tongue for a week after our last go at blue dye number two and knew that a Pecker cocktail would cost me my lunch. Archie said in the Western movies they just poured a couple of ounces, threw their heads back and let it fly, so that's just what we did. Within five minutes of each of us gagging down a mouthful, we were all in the cow bowl disgorging our lunches. We decided that Early Times was not very important to being a five percenter.

We agreed to save Roy and Estill from the evidence of their duplicity by running down to the creek at the back of the cow bowl and dumping the booze and filling the bottle half full of creek water. When we were back at the barn, we pulled out the brown food coloring and blended just enough to make the creek water look like Early Times. Next, we burned all the American Nudist magazines, including the planted one in Roy's room that I had grabbed as I escorted the professor out. I sent Archie home to grab a stack of Boys' Life magazines, and Pecker up to the 7-Eleven to get three packs of candy cigarettes. When they returned, we set the picnic table just as we had found it. We then went to the loft to wait on the school officials to come to confiscate the evidence.

About thirty minutes later we heard the president and the principal coming down the hill toward the barn. As they entered the barn, I heard the president talking.

In a bewildered voice, he asked, "What went on this afternoon? I don't understand why Brother Roy Harper Jr. would set a trap to try to lure three perfectly innocent children into sin as the boys claim. And, if that's true, how did he get Brother Estill to go along with such a hare-brained scheme?" Then, he said, "And now, a New Roads Professor of Religion has been accused of performing a Catholic ritual on New Roads soil, but the worst is having whiskey, nudist magazines, and cigarettes brought onto the New Roads campus."

At that point, the principal pointed out the evidence on the picnic table in front of them. The first thing the president did was to uncork the Early Times and give it a smell.

The next thing he did was stick the bottle under Dr. Allen's nose and ask the principal, "Does that smell like any liquor you've ever smelled?" The president then flipped over a copy of the Boys' Life magazine and told the principal, "Now, I'm sure there's nothing indecent in that magazine."

After he opened one of the packs of cigarettes and ate a couple of candy cigarettes, the principal was looking very confused. He said, "I'm sure it was real booze, cigarettes, and dirty magazines when I was here before."

The president suggested, "Well, the light is poor in here, and you've just completed a long exam week. Maybe it would help if you had someone to talk to about the stress of the job. I think you should start seeing Professor Snodgrass on a daily basis until you feel more like yourself."

9. Judge Roy Harper, Sr.

Archie had cleared the way with his mom for Pecker and me to have supper at his house when he had gone to fetch the Boys' Life magazines. While we all ate that night, we got the usual parental questions.

Archie's mom asked, "How are exams going for you boys? Did anything interesting happen at school today?"

Pecker piped in, "Well, we did aid in the rescue of one of the ministerial students, Roy Harper Jr., who went psychotic this afternoon, but I was able to talk him down be-cause I convinced him he needed daily personal hygiene."

"Archie, did you and Pip help with Roy?" Archie's mother inquired.

"Archie and I provided moral support, but Pecker seemed to have had Roy's full attention," I told her.

She said, "You kids are such Good Samaritans with your helpfulness! You all should keep an eye on Roy in the future; any one of you might be able to help again with his issues."

We assured her that we would help Roy whenever we could and that we would go over to his room right after supper to see how he was doing.

We crept up to the men's dorm by cover of darkness and saw the president, the dean, the principal, and a mighty pale-looking Professor

Snodgrass standing on the porch of the men's dorm.

While we waited for the arrival of Roy's parents, Judge and Mrs. Roy Harper Sr., we maneuvered into hearing range.

The president was pensive. "Exactly what should I tell the largest contributor to the annual fund about why his only son is filthy and insane after three years as a stellar student and the president of his senior class? When Roy left Opp in September to return here, he was happy, well-adjusted, and enthusiastic about his future."

The dean was at a loss for words and ideas, and asked Dr. Allen to respond. "I've got it!" the principal exclaimed. "We'll have Professor Snodgrass explain the situation to the Harpers. He's the resident pastoral counselor, and he's the only one with the academic and theological experience to explain Roy Jr.'s breakdown. Maybe an update from Snodgrass will keep the judge from destroying the college after he sees the condition of his son."

All four of the men knew about the judge's bad temper, and the dean had personally crossed swords with the judge and had no desire for a rematch. Professor Snodgrass, who had already had a bad day, knew there would be no getting out of it, he would have to explain why the judge's son was such a mess.

The president said, "I agree. Snodgrass will handle talking with the judge. If every-thing goes okay with that conversation, we'll just forget all about the Catholic ritual you performed this afternoon."

The professor perked up from his morose mood and started a shrill denunciation of liars and false witnesses when a big, new white Chrysler Imperial came up the drive to a stop in front of the men's dorm. Judge Harper was an imposing man who stood well over six and a half feet in height and weighed over two hundred fifty pounds. He had a shock of gray hair and the demeanor of a man who always got what he wanted. Helen Harper was the typical wife of a powerful, rich, rural Alabama land baron of the 1960s. She was quiet, demurred to his every wish, and was very close to her son. The judge had walked on the wild side as a young man and was brought to the New Roads way of life by Helen. As part of his late 20s settling-down phase of life, the judge had moved back home to Opp after a decade of sowing wild oats at The University of Alabama, the Tulane Law School in New Orleans, two years in the Army, and two years with a large law firm in Birmingham.

The judge was no stranger to the top ten sins of the New Roads Church because of his past experience with sin prior to joining the New Roads Church and his back-sliding to worldly temptations since then. After all, the judge would explain to anyone who asked, he was the richest and most powerful man in Covington County and their Probate Judge, and these things caused temptation to move in his direction. The judge figured that he did about as well as the next New Roader in resisting sin if you looked at it from a percentage point of view. His burden to bear, he would explain, was that he had to deal with temptation much more often than most other New Roads members. Interestingly, the other members of the Opp New Roads Church had adopted this philosophy for judging the judge as well, because the judge had been chairman of the building fund for ten years, ten years in which the Opp New Roads Church had become the biggest church in town with the newest building.

Helen had grown up in Opp, the daughter and only child of the town's undertaker and funeral home director. She graduated from Opp High School and married the judge two years later. When Dr. Bailey spoke at the Opp New Roads Church in 1950 about his new Christian college in Montgomery, she knew this was the perfect place for Roy Jr. Having been raised in the New Roads faith, she was excited about the whole-some environment in which he would be able to go to college and get his degree in ministry and spend his life preaching the gospel. Her father had arranged for her to meet with his old friend Professor Snodgrass and his wife when Roy Jr. was a boy. She had returned to Opp assured that Roy Jr. would be guided through his college experience and theology training by Dr. Snodgrass.

The judge let Helen know on their first date that he was anxious to find a pretty, wholesome girl like her to marry and get on with his family life and career and he would leave the child-rearing decisions to her. Helen decided that she would raise Roy Jr. to be an ally. After several years of marriage, she figured that she could tame any wild ways the judge might have left in him with the help of her growing son because she hadn't been very successful by herself.

After the judge and Helen were engaged, he agreed he would give up his Episcopal church membership and join the New Roads Church. The judge's only comment was to ask if that was the church that wouldn't allow a piano or organ to be played at church services.

The judge agreed to her religious dogma, thinking that he could live without musical accompaniment and was comforted by the fact that the New Roads Church of Opp was a growing church that might help him with his political ambitions. After three years of marriage, the judge had been elected as the county's Probate Judge, he had a fine young son, Roy Jr., and he was a stalwart in the Opp New Roads Church. As the judge's power and money grew, so did the temptations of the flesh, and there were rumors around the New Roads Church about the way he conducted his life. The judge was confronted about the rumors only once by an overzealous assistant minister who then got the judge's view of righteousness being defined by the percentage of sin a man resists, sort of like a batting average of sin. He said he would put his "sins avoided" average up against any man in the church. He then asked the junior minister if he had thought about what part of the state he would like to move to, because the judge said, as chairman of the building fund and finance committee, he was sure that the current cash shortfall, due to a cutback from one of the big givers in the church, was going to force the church to lay off the assistant minister until the financial picture improved. Brother Bob Leatherbury, soon to be the ex-assistant minister at the Opp New Roads Church, knew that he had walked into something a lot bigger than he had anticipated. He also knew when he was beaten. Brother Bob noted that he had been thinking about going to the New Roads Graduate Seminary in Atlanta. Having made his point, the judge offered to call his friend who was the president of the seminary and see if a full scholarship couldn't be worked out if the assistant minister would resign and leave peaceably with no further discussion with anybody about the judge or his temptations. The batting average calculation of the judge's sin was considered as a legitimate sin-scoring method for the judge from then on at the Opp New Roads Church.

The only disappointment in the judge's life was his son, Roy Jr. He had been fine as a kid, and the judge braced himself for his rebellious teenage years. As Roy went through his teenage years, though, the opposite happened. He adopted the New Roads life, hook, line and sinker. The judge had expected and even desired a son who would do what he had done, get out there and kick his heels up a little bit, or maybe even a lot.

Roy's devotion to the New Roads' way of life drove a wedge between him and his father. As a child, Roy loved to go up to his father's hunting camp for the weekend with his dad and a bunch of his father's friends. At fourteen, Roy Jr. informed the judge that he no longer wished to be in the same cabin with men drinking alcohol and using foul language and thus did not wish to join him anymore. Roy Jr. also pointed out that they always missed the Sunday morning service when they went to the hunting camp for the weekend and that was reason enough for neither of them ever to go to the hunting camp again.

The judge gave Roy Jr. a hard stare for a full minute and told him that he didn't ever want him to give him advice on how he lived his life again because it was none of his business.

As Roy Jr. got older and started college in Montgomery, he didn't live up to his father's command and reminded his father of his transgressions against the New Roads' way of life on a more and more frequent basis. This is when the judge knew that he had to put a stop to his offspring's meddling because they both had to live under the same roof, even if it was just occasional weekends and summers. He called his son into the study one Sunday afternoon and closed the door. The judge sat Roy down in a chair directly across from his, with their knees touching and his face about six inches from Roy Jr.'s.

The judge began in a low, soft voice explaining to Roy Jr. that he, Roy Jr., had his view of religion and right and wrong, and that he, Roy Sr., had his. In a little louder voice, the judge said that the way he wanted this disagreement in the interpretation of sin to be resolved from this moment on would be for Roy Jr. to keep his opinions about right and wrong to himself, and he, the judge, would do the same about his son's choice of a religious profession. In just two octaves above a speaking voice, the judge told his son that this was the way it had to be, or his only child might find himself on the other side of the state, at the Marion Military Academy, for his next semester in college. He ended by telling Roy Jr. to keep this little father-and-son chat to himself, to say not a word to his mother because he would hate to see him in one of those stiff, itchy military uniforms.

Roy stuck to his orders and stayed out of the judge's personal interpretation of the scriptures from then on, but this confrontation did convince Roy Jr. that he should draw his strength from his mother, who walked the straight and narrow, and try to forgive the judge for his weaknesses of the flesh. Roy's mother told him often about the relationship she had developed over the years with Professor Snodgrass when she visited Montgomery and the New Roads College and the wonderful feeling of being amongst a campus full of believers. She had groomed Roy to believe that this was to be his school and that she felt he had been called to the ministry. In Roy's senior year at Opp High School, he knew he had to let the judge in on his future but feared his reaction. The judge had thought for years that this New Roads' lifestyle was just a passing fancy and that his son would loosen up and be ready for fraternity life at The University of Alabama when it was time to go to college.

When the spring of Roy's senior year rolled around, and the judge asked Roy if he had gotten his application into The University of Alabama, Roy had to confess that he had only applied to the New Roads College in Montgomery. The judge should have seen this coming when he asked his son that spring who he was taking to the senior prom and was curtly told that dancing was a sin and that he would be with his Bible study group on the Friday night of that heathen dance.

The judge was beside himself; his only child was going to miss the best years of his life, a time of football games, fraternity parties, and spring breaks with lovely women at the beach. The judge couldn't believe what he was hearing and told Roy Jr. that he would send him to a Catholic Seminary in Boston before he would let him destroy his life by going to a dinky church school that didn't even have a football team.

Helen interceded and worked out a compromise. Roy would attend the New Roads College for his first two years and then he would transfer to The University of Alabama unless he felt he was called by God to the pulpit. If so, he would be allowed to go into the New Roads ministerial program. The judge didn't like it, but he knew a best last offer when he heard one.

With Roy Jr. now enrolled in his senior year in the New Roads ministerial program, Helen called the judge at the courthouse from their home in Opp and said, "Roy's in trouble. The college administrators think he may have had a psychological breakdown at school."

The judge asked, "What do you mean, Helen? What else is going on?"

Helen replied, "That's all I know. When I got the call from the school leaders, they said we should get to Montgomery right away."

Before the judge left his office, he called the president of the New Roads College, Dr. Slim Bailey, to get some answers but was told by his secretary that the president was out with the principal of the school, investigating an incident where a ministerial student was caught trying to injure one of the younger school kids who, the ministerial student thought, was possessed.

The judge wanted to know if his son was involved in this mess and what in the world this younger student was possessed with. She said she didn't know but Professor Snodgrass was involved because he was the resident pastoral counselor, and she could transfer his call to Professor Snodgrass if he wished.

When the judge was put through, the professor had just completed his tantrum with Dr. Allen and was still holding a textbook above his head, ready to fire. The once kindly professor picked up the phone and yelled into the receiver that he was having a nervous breakdown and didn't wish to be disturbed.

The judge inquired if he was speaking to Professor Snodgrass and identified himself as Judge Roy Harper Sr. At this point, the professor went into a tirade, "Your son has gone psychotic. Roy Jr. is convinced that a ninth-grade New Roads student is the Devil, and your son is also trafficking in booze, nudist magazines, and cigarettes here on the most holy ground in Montgomery."

The judge presided over all the forced legal commitments to the state hospital from his county, and he knew a nut on the phone when he heard one. He told Professor Snodgrass to tell the Goddamned president to have his damned ass at the dorm when he arrived in two hours. The professor responded, "I will tell the president what you said, and I now know where Roy Jr. gets his profanity problem from."

As the driver's door on the Chrysler Imperial opened, the group visibly tightened up. Professor Snodgrass was the exception; he was melting into the sidewalk as this huge man approached the group with his mousy wife in tow. Dr. Slim Bailey, president of the New Roads School and College, was down the steps and trying to shake the judge's hand as the other school officials descended the stairs.

The judge went right to the issue of his son and spouted out, "What kind of a zoo are you people here running? What in the damned Hell have y'all done to my boy?"

President Slim Bailey was unused to hearing profanity like this and in a tone of caution, urged, "Judge, please. Think about your language in front of ministers and your lovely Christian wife."

The judge was not one to be told what to do, as the dean could have told President Slim Bailey if he had asked.

The judge looked at the president and remarked, "Listen here, I will kick your sorry ass all over this parking lot if you don't answer my questions or if you say one more word about my choice of language." The group then decided that there were two insane Roy Harpers they would have to deal with that night.

President Slim Bailey knew when it was time to delegate, and he began explaining, "Judge, Roy Jr. is in the pastoral training program, which comes under the authority of Dean Bob Leatherbury. Since I, as president, spend so much time on the road doing fundraising for the school, I feel that Dean Leatherbury can best explain the situation with Roy Jr."

The president had clutched and wasn't following the plan to hand this hot potato off to Professor Snodgrass, and as the dean looked for the professor, he noticed that he had slipped out of the group and was sitting on the steps with his head in his hands weeping softly.

Helen went to her old friend and asked, "Professor, what's the matter?"

The professor looked up from his hands and said, "I just think that someone is going to get the stuffing kicked out of them when you and your husband see the condition Roy Jr. is in. I'm low man on the totem pole in this group, and if anybody is going to be thrown to the lions, it's probably going to be me."

"No, Professor, the judge wouldn't dare hit you, but you should defi-nitely prepare yourself to hear some strong language," she said.

The judge stared at the dean for a full minute without saying a word, studying his face and trying to remember where he had seen this man before when it came back to him that this was the nosy little shit of an assistant preacher from fifteen years before.

The judge then realized that the dean couldn't get his Roy Harpers straight, the old one, that he had irritated fifteen years before, was to be left alone, and the younger Roy Harper was to be watched. He noted that there couldn't have been much watching if young Roy Jr. was now a slack-jawed psychotic.

The judge told the assembled group, "Now, listen here, gentlemen. I'm quite experienced in the field of mental illness because I've com-mitted a hundred people a year from my county to the state hospitals in Tuscaloosa and Mt. Vernon. My theory of mental illness relies on the traditional "nature versus nurture" argument. In my opinion, there are two causes of mental illness: genetic and environmental, and my boy can't possibly suffer from the former because he comes from one of the strongest gene pools in the state of Alabama. This, of course, leaves only one possible explanation, environmental," the judge said.

Then he continued, "When Roy Jr. left my home in Opp in early September, he was happy and mostly well-adjusted except for an overac-tive religious gland. So, as you all can see, the problem must be with the New Roads College. It's turned my happy twenty-year-old into a raving lunatic."

Dean Leatherbury had experienced enough with the judge to know that his logic was not to be messed with. He remembered his theory of batting averages for sin and decided to let the New Roads Professor of Religion and resident pastoral counselor handle this environmental theory of madness that the judge had proposed.

The dean then jumped back into the conversation, "I am not an expert in mental illness like you are, Judge, but Professor Snodgrass is a highly trained professional pastoral counselor, and he can surely explain what happened to Brother Roy Jr. It's definitely not the school's fault, and whatever did happen was an external influence not associated with the New Roads School and College."

Professor Snodgrass had dried his tears but was shaking like a leaf in a windstorm when the judge turned a cold eye on him and said, "Professor, you better explain Roy Jr.'s madness to my satisfaction, or you just might find yourself behind bars for working on my boy without the proper degree and license." In 1962, a degree in pastoral counseling in Alabama was not an accepted authorization to work in the mental health field. "Unfortunately for you, I am good friends with all the judges in Montgomery County, and I can see to it that you are tried and convicted and on a road gang by the end of the week!" the judge said.

At this, sheer terror swept over the professor like a tidal wave; he could see himself in prison whites in the back of a big orange prison truck, headed to some lonely stretch of highway to pick up trash all day. His days and nights would be spent with the vilest of sinners listening to their stories of lust and corruption.

The professor didn't know how he got in this jam, but he knew he had better come up with a very good story about Roy Jr.'s breakdown or his next meal would be a corn dog in the county jail. The professor decided to go with the story that had popped up that afternoon, a story that might even get him out of the bind of providing psychological services without a license. The professor then said, "Judge, I believe Roy Jr. could be suffering from Demonic Possession, but I'm not absolutely sure."

"Where the Hell did you get an idea like that? I've never heard of such a thing in my twenty years as a member of the New Roads Church! I've seen several Catholics before my bench that thought this had happened to them but never anyone from the New Roads Church," the judge said.

"Well," the professor explained, "this is new territory in the theology of the New Roads Church, but if anyone else here can give another explanation, I'd like for some-one to step in and tell the judge what it might be."

The president could think of nothing else and said, "This certainly seems plausible to me, but the dean is in a better theological position to judge the merits of the Demonic Possession hypothesis."

The dean knew he was caught between a rock and a hard place, and he said, "Roy Jr. has been a model student until just a few weeks ago. This theory of Demonic Possession absolutely fits the circumstances, and that makes it a third factor to consider that's neither genetic nor environmental but an external force. The Devil is trying to get control of our best ministerial student."

"This is very plausible," the president said, "because Roy Jr. comes from such intelligent stock, the Devil would try to snatch him before any other student."

Dr. Leatherbury, the dean, spoke up, "I was in the room when Roy Jr. was howling like a dog. He went into a fit and injured Dr. Allen. Then, Professor Snodgrass was called, and he proceeded to perform the first ever New Roads exorcism. I must say that the effect was remarkable given the fact that the professor had never attempted a one-on-one fight with the Devil before!"

The judge had to think about this reasoning, but he figured that the Devil was out there because he sure gave him his share of temptations. He reasoned that it would make sense for the Devil to go after Roy Jr. because, as far as his father knew, the boy had a slate clean of sin.

The judge asked, "Dean Leatherbury, how exactly was this exorcism carried out, and what was the outcome?"

"Well, Judge," the dean said, "I don't know all the specifics, but I do know it involved having some pure and innocent children in the room and some chanting of special words. I'm sure Professor Snodgrass can give you all the details."

The professor was beginning to resemble one of the slack-jawed mental patients who came before the judge's court as his mind tried to process what he had just heard.

From our dark hiding spaces, we knew that our story of keeping the professor out of any more hot water had just changed from a Roy Jr. self-exorcism to one where we helped the professor drive Lucifer from Roy Jr.'s body.

"Professor, what did you do, and how has it affected Roy Jr.?" the judge asked. "Judge, the details are still a bit hazy, but during the situation, I remembered the importance of having sin-free youth around when charging the Devil. I also remember asking God to help while chanting 'Rock of Ages.' Then, the next thing I knew was Roy Jr. was back in his bed and sleeping peacefully," the professor explained.

The judge said, "It's possible, gentlemen, that I may have judged you all too harshly." That's when we saw from our hiding place a collective sigh of relief from the New Roads administrative group who were gathered in front of the men's dorm that Friday night.

"Also, gentlemen, if you don't mind," the judge said, "before I leave Montgomery, I'd like to see these brave children who participated in the first New Roads exorcism. I'd like to thank them personally for what they did for Roy Jr."

"Two of the boys live right here in the neighborhood, and I can go get the third boy for you, Judge," the principal said.

The judge agreed, "That's fine. While we're waiting, Helen and I would like to see Roy Jr."

Professor Snodgrass then warned. "Judge, I hope you're not expecting too much because Roy Jr. has been through quite an ordeal, and he might not be himself yet. After all, this was my first New Roads attempt at removing a demon, and Roy Jr. might need a booster exorcism."

While this discussion was going on, I sent Pecker around the back of the dorm to sit on the steps of the classroom building to intercept Dr. Allen and let him know the three of us were to meet in twenty minutes to shoot some hoops in the gym. This idea worked as I thought it would, and the principal instructed Pecker to bring Archie and me to the men's dorm as soon as we arrived. Archie and I went to the rear of the men's dorm and took our position below Roy Jr.'s bedroom window. The two student guards posted by the principal to watch Roy Jr. were just outside the door because the smell of the room and Roy Jr. was more than they could take even with the windows open. We were peering in from the bottom of the window when the entourage arrived. The judge was shocked by the pungent smell of the room and the sight of his son hidden under the covers.

His anger was rising when he turned to Professor Snodgrass and asked, "How can you all let your students live like this?"

"Judge, this is simply the olfactory after-effects of the demon being driven from Roy Jr.'s body," the professor answered.

The judge seemed to accept this and went over and pulled the sheets off his bewildered son.

The judge said, "Son, your mom and I are here. How are you doing?"

After a few seconds, Roy Jr. said, "I'm feeling some better, Dad, but I'm being chased by the Pecker Devil."

The judge figured that this was a sexual reference and remembered the trouble he had had all his life with his pecker trying, and sometimes succeeding, in getting him into a whole lot of misfortune.

Then he told Roy Jr., "Son, I understand." That's when he thought to himself that his son's problem might be a testosterone backup from having never been laid. He filed that information away and thought of an attractive open-minded woman he knew as a possible treatment option that he could easily arrange for Roy Jr. once they got back to Opp.

"Right now, though, I want you to get up and go take a shower, shave, and change into some clean clothes."

Roy Jr. jumped right up and gathered some fresh clothes and headed down the hall to the showers. He seemed almost relieved to have a voice of authority giving him instructions and structure.

At about the same moment, Pecker returned to our hiding place below Roy Jr.'s window, and we knew that it was time to make our debut with the judge. I led the three of us into the dorm.

The principal introduced us to the judge and his wife but instead of calling Pecker by his nickname, he introduced him as Ralph, his real name.

The judge said, "Boys, we can't tell you all how thankful we are for what you've done for Roy Jr. It was such a brave thing for y'all to face this challenge as mere children."

"Sir," I told the judge, "it was the least I could do for the man who taught me the joys of coin collecting."

Pecker then said, "Judge, I tried to help Roy Jr. before the professor's exorcism by giving him some thoughtful advice, but I guess my advice on the healthful practice of daily personal hygiene was not enough to break the hold the Devil had on Roy Jr."

The judge was overcome by the caring that this little boy had shown for his son and reached out and grabbed Pecker in a bear hug. He said, "Son, the world would be a much better place if there were more kids like you." At that same moment, Roy Jr. walked into the room.

Roy Jr. felt like he had been hit on the head with a hammer! Before his eyes was his own father embracing the Pecker Devil and saying there needed to be more of them in the world. Brother Roy Jr. charged his father and knocked him and Pecker to the floor.

Roy Jr. let out a howl and screamed, "The Pecker Devil has the judge!"

The judge thought his son misrepresented what he saw and thought he, the judge, was making a sexual advance toward this child in his arms. He told Roy Jr., "Boy, my pecker devil only sends me after full-grown women. But my pecker devil has left me alone since I married your mother."

Roy Jr. couldn't phantom what the judge was talking about, but he knew he had to get his hands on the Pecker Devil. He made another lunge at Pecker, but Pecker moved to the right causing Roy Jr. to slam his head into a plaster wall. Roy Jr. was dazed. Professor Snodgrass then had an idea and took charge. He instructed, "Alright, everybody out! I'll stay in here with the children; it's time to give Roy Jr. an exorcism booster."

Pecker took his place up high on the dresser while Archie and I moved Roy Jr. forcibly to his bed. The professor took a glass of water off the bedside table and poured it over Roy Jr.'s head, which had the desired effect of clearing the insane would-be preacher's mind. A low wail started to come from Roy Jr.'s mouth when the mild-mannered professor told him, "Shut the fuck up."

Roy Jr. was so shocked at hearing the New Roads Professor of Religion utter a profanity that he stopped in mid-moan.

The professor explained, "Boy, we all have the Devil in us, just like we all have God in us. If you don't cut that Pecker Devil stuff out, you're going to end up on the back ward of the state mental hospital in Tuscaloosa. You are not to ever speak of the Pecker Devil again. You're going to go with your parents and act normal, or I'll call down the curse of Job on you and your whole family!"

Roy Jr. finally saw the big picture and realized that he had better go along with this plan. He decided to go home, build his strength, and take on the Pecker Devil the next semester when he was feeling better.

The professor instructed us all, including Roy Jr. "Now, I want all of you to chant 'Rock of Ages.'" And so, we did.

Roy Jr. was packed away with his mother in the Chrysler Imperial.

The judge thanked the three of us and the professor for our help. Archie, Pecker, and I were each given a twenty-dollar bill and the professor was told he could expect to receive a grant to continue his work in New Roads exorcism research.

The judge then turned to his old assistant New Roads preacher, now the dean, and asked, "Have you received Roy Jr.'s grades from his teachers yet?"

The dean had a sheepish look on his face as he told the judge, "Well, Roy Jr. skipped, and failed, all his final exams. Under the circumstances, I'm sure I can get him a C in every subject except evangelism. This is because he missed most of the lectures in evangelism class and he'll have to take that class over."

We knew Roy Jr. wasn't through with us yet, that he would go back to Opp for the holidays and think of ways to avenge himself for the misery we had caused him. We knew that we had better get our battle plans down over the holidays because it was going to be a very, very long spring with a recuperated Roy Harper Jr. plotting and at-tempting to carry out his retribution.

10. Multiple Religious Personality Disorder

Twenty dollars in 1962 was one hell of a lot of money and the subject at hand that night was how to spend it in a way that would piss our parents off if they knew. We calculated that we would get fifty dollars from our assortment of aunts, uncles, family friends, and others who would rather give us cash for Christmas than think about what teenagers were desirous of.

We each had about twenty-five dollars in cash saved, not counting the twenty the Judge had given us for driving Roy Jr. to the brink of madness. We calculated a grand total of fifty dollars in Christmas money among the three of us, plus another ten for ex-changing goofy practical gifts that we were given, added to the seventy-five in our cash savings and sixty from the judge for a grand total of one hundred and ninety-five dollars. We figured that this was plenty of money to get in trouble with if we could just find something exciting to spend the money on.

We had all turned fifteen in late November and early December and this was the magic age at which an Alabama boy becomes eligible to apply for a motorcycle license. There could be but one plan for the three of us: we were about to become ghost riders from Hell. The plan was simple: collect and pool our various funds, find someone who got a new motorcycle for Christmas, and make the purchase of their used motorcycle from that someone who now had one motorcycle too many.

As the saying goes, the best laid plans often end up with a big hole in the middle. The biggest obstacle, other than finding a cheap, dependable motorcycle, was where to keep the motorcycle once we bought it.

If we were successful and our parents found out what we had done, we would all be on restriction until we were on Social Security. The next problem was that we were not old enough to register a motorcycle and get a tag so the cops would leave us alone. We knew that we had to buy the motorcycle from an adult who was willing to work with us on the illegal side of the law, because no one under nineteen could register a motorcycle in Alabama.

Pecker wouldn't let us get down and dejected as we thought of all the problems, so he said, "Look guys, we have the most important element for our plan to succeed, MONEY, and as we all know money talks and bullshit walks."

We had a mission: we were in search of a person nineteen or older who would like to have cash money, no bullshit, and owned an unneeded motorcycle. This man was none other than a fellow New Roads School student Jim Bob Brewer, a nineteen-year-old high school senior at the New Roads School and member of the school's five percenter group.

Jim Bob had been ejected from every school in the city and even the Marion Military Academy but was bound and determined to get his diploma and go to a state teachers college where he could find lots of secular girls and fulfill his ambition of be-coming a high school coach, so he could be on the other side of the whipping board for a change.

Jim Bob was the proud owner of a 1958 Triumph Tiger Daytona 500 motorcycle that he had owned for four years. Jim Bob knew how to start and ride his Triumph, but any mechanical problems sent him into a tailspin because Jim Bob didn't know a piston ring from a crankshaft, which was good news for us because Archie could take that motorcycle apart and put it back together in half a day. We ran into Jim Bob that night as he was packing to leave for the holidays. Jim Bob said, "Guess what, boys? I just got a deal on a 1955 Buick that's going to be much more conducive to my new life once I get to one of the state teachers colleges next year."

"Well, Jim Bob, are you looking to get rid of your motorcycle? How much do you want for it?" I asked.

"I'll take three hundred fifty dollars," Jim Bob told us.

This statement threw Archie into a fit, and he said, "Jim Bob, you know that bike's not worth over two hundred fifty, tops."

Jim Bob responded, "Well, I know that none of your parents would let you buy a motorcycle, and I would have to get the extra hundred bucks just for taking the chance of selling it to y'all. I'll tell you what, y'all let me know your decision to buy my motorcycle by the middle of January because my uncle is bringing me the Buick during the holidays, and I need to give him some down payment money as soon as possible." I left the meeting with Jim Bob knowing that I would never know the freedom of personal transportation till November when I would be old enough for a car driver's license and I would be able to get in line to borrow the family Ford when my senior siblings weren't using it.

Pecker looked at me and Archie and said, "Don't worry, fellas, because I've got a plan that will have us mobile on our own Triumph by the middle of January. It's still got a few bugs in it, but I'll let y'all know all the details of the plan shortly after Christmas."

What could I do but trust the devious Pecker mind to find a solution?

The holidays flew past. My attempts at reestablishing past relationships with my public school friends proved hollow without the day-to-
day contact at Floyd Junior High School. We seemed to have drifted beyond the point where we could find enough common ground for comfort.

I found that the world at fifteen was defined by your shared experiences with friends and these experiences revolved around where you
spent your school day. You could maintain these relationships, but only
with a great deal of expended energy because there were so many things
that happened at school and new people who had to be explained; the effort was just too great. I was a five percenter whether I wanted to be one
or not. I was destined to be a minority and felt a very small tinge of what
it must feel like to be a Negro in Montgomery, Alabama.

This was my first experience of being outside the norm, at least outside my definition of what was normal. At the same time surrounding
me were thousands of people in Montgomery who were redefining the
concept of normal in Southern culture. In a strange way, I drew strength
from these brave people with whom I lived in an apartheid culture, in a
time when the news you got was censored by the local newspapers, local
television stations, local radio stations.

George Wallace was going to become governor in a matter of weeks,
and his rhetoric was going to lead to violence. I was realizing that I lived
in a place and a time when I might actually see, with my own eyes, a
historic shift that was centuries in the making. There was a rejuvenation
of resistance to integration and a virulent racism that was fed by Wallace's victory.

The bus boycott victory was one of my earliest political memories.
I was about six years old riding into downtown when I saw over fifty black people walking in a pouring rain. My mother thought the bus

regulations were absurd and would say so. She would drive our house-keeper, Lulu Harris, home when she got home from her job, but this was two hours after Lulu normally went home. Lulu chose to walk with her friends except on really stormy days. I asked her about the boycott, and she told me, "Pip, you don't have to worry about it because God is going to make things better for the Negroes in America and I will walk the three miles home every day if it will bring that day of liberation sooner."

My methods for surviving my time at the New Roads School were different, but the lesson from the larger community struggle went with me to my school environment and was reinforced every night on the televised national news.

I had developed an awareness of the political struggle that surrounded me from listening to my father and his friend, Mr. Clifford Durr, discuss the changes that were coming to the South. I knew that courage to be who you are is hard-won when you face a gentle, and for the most part, loving adversary, but what kind of resolve does it take to put your life on the line for the right to be what you could be if the system would give you the opportunity to try?

My bonding with the idea of minority oppression began that holiday season. I was given the opportunity to taste the bitterness of living within but being on the out-side.

As the war for racial and economic freedom raged around me, I saw for the first time what an awful system of oppression we, as white Southerners, had built and nurtured and brought back under guises other than slavery: convict leasing, Jim Crow, poll taxes, and literacy tests all proclaimed as a state's right to discriminate. Undoing this mess was going to be hard because a violent minority had been empowered by the new governor.

For four months, I had been hearing about the work of the Devil from the cussing insane preacher-to-be from Opp and most of the rest of the students, staff, and faculty at the New Roads School, but no one connected the Devil's activities to the White Citizens' Council or the Ku Klux Klan or Governor Wallace.

It was beginning to seem obvious to me that the Devil had taken Montgomery as his workshop. I thought I would test my new insight about the Devil being holed up in Montgomery in Sunday School class, which was run by Brother Calvin Walker. Brother Walker was the music-less song leader as well as the teenage group's Sunday School teacher. I'm sure that down deep in his heart he sometimes wished there was a powerful pipe organ to drown out some of the most horrible screeching voices that were part of the New Roads Church service.

On the next weekend in Sunday School Brother, Calvin Walker was warning us that the Devil was lying in wait for every teenager to stumble and fall into his grasp.

"Now, as I was saying, kids," Brother Walker said, "alcohol, premarital sex and petting, profanity, and roving Catholic missionaries are the Devil's tools of seduction, and you've got to be aware at all times! In my work as a city police officer," Brother Walker explained, "I'm on the front lines to see the Devil's handiwork, and it's not a pretty sight."

At this point I raised a question, "Brother Walker, do you think the Devil might be up to other, more corrupt evil than what you've told us so far?"

He said, "Boy, the things I've seen in my work, the Devil's business, is too horrible to discuss with such an innocent group like this."

At this point, I stepped right into Brother Walker's shit and asked,

"Sir, how about the beating and threatening of fellow Christians, who happen to be a different race? Could that be a very clear example of the Devil and his agents at work?"

The answer to my question was quick and edged with anger and irritation. Brother Calvin Walker nearly shouted, "Son, the Bible said to give unto Caesar what was Caesar's and unto God what was God's, so Caesar's law, the law of the State of Alabama, and the law of the City of Montgomery must be followed!"

"Doesn't the Bible," I asked him, "indicate that God's law must be followed if there's a conflict with man's law?" With that one question, I had just punched a hole in his very weak theological position.

Then he asked, "Pip, have you been talking to any of those Yankee carpetbagger false preachers that are down here stirring up trouble with the Negroes? You know, those outside agitators?"

"No, sir, Brother Walker," I explained. "I came to this realization all on my own, by reading the Bible for my religion class at school."

Brother Calvin Walker was turning red in the face as he pondered a way out of this theological dilemma.

The other Sunday School class members were beginning to discuss the merits of Christians beating other Christians, and the teacher knew that if this discussion went on for much longer, he was going to be caught in a religious temporal rift, which might blow him out of his teaching and singing duties. To get the class back under control, he reached back to the Old Testament and pulled Job out.

"The Negroes in Montgomery," Brother Walker explained, "have to suffer because it is God's will, just as Job had to suffer because that was God's will."

I asked, "Sir, do you think true believers who have a hand in the support and implementation of this purported God-ordained suffering are at risk of violating the laws that Jesus set up in the New Testament?"

Brother Calvin Walker's mind was racing, and he was wondering if this was a trick question that this boy had been put up to by one of those Yankee preachers that were in town to stir up the Negroes.

Before he could answer, I said, "I can understand using the Old Testament for answers if you're Jewish, but my next-door neighbor, Mrs. Katz, is a devout Jew. She told me that there's nothing in the Old Testament that would support the things the city officials and the White Citizens' Council are doing in Montgomery."

Brother Calvin Walker, City of Montgomery policeman, music-less song leader, and vice chairman of the Montgomery White Citizens' Council, thought he had finally figured it out. He lit into me like a pit bull at a petting zoo.

"Pip," he screamed, "how long have you been conspiring with these Jews who murdered our Lord and Savior Jesus Christ?"

I was taken off balance and assured him, "Brother Walker, Mr. and Mrs. Katz are some of the nicest people I've ever known. Besides, they're both only thirty-five-years-old, and that fact alone makes them much too young to have killed Christ. Does this mean that you believe in reincarnation? Because as far as I can tell, from my reading about world religions, a belief in reincarnation makes you a Buddhist."

The Sunday School class was abuzz with the information that Brother Calvin Walker was a closet Buddhist. While he was trying to be heard over the din of the class, he was saying, "Pip, you're a sinful boy who's bearing false witness against your elders. You've obviously been influenced by the Christ killers and Yankee carpetbaggers."

"Sir, most of my theological instruction came from Brother Roy Harper Jr., an evangelist-to-be. I'm sure Roy will back me up that a man who believes as strongly as you do that my next-door neighbors, Mr. and Mrs. Katz, helped kill Jesus, must believe in reincarnation and thus be a practicing Buddhist. I'm going to have to leave your class because I don't think my parents want me to become a Buddhist—they want me to be a New Roads member."

As I left the room, the other members of the class began to get up and follow me. I heard my sister remark to Brother Walker that he would do better to agree with me in the future because I had a way of twisting everything around on people.

I made a lifelong enemy out of my Sunday School teacher that day, but this seemed to be par for my new course since I had joined the world of young adults. Being a member of the White Citizens' Council was acceptable amongst most of the New Roaders, but the thought of a closet Buddhist teaching their young was more than the congregation and the minister could abide. So, Brother Calvin Walker was notified that he was suspended from his teaching and song leading duties until he could be examined for his faithfulness to the New Roads religion by Professor Ronald T. Snodgrass, the New Roads School and College Senior Professor of Religion. He was instructed to see the professor that week or have the fellowship of the New Roads Church withdrawn. Calvin had little choice, given his lifelong New Roads membership, and proceeded to make an appointment with the professor for the next afternoon.

When Calvin showed up for the appointment, Professor Snodgrass was clearly upset at having a potential Buddhist on hallowed New Roads soil.

"Calvin," the professor started, "any untruth you tell me in this spiritual inquiry could pose a threat of eternal damnation and even an early death, because I am going to put you under oath and make you ask God for severe punishment if you lie."

If Calvin Walker had been half-literate, he might have thought of the great Inquisition, but these were the days before most policemen or Sunday School teachers had been exposed to a liberal arts education.

Professor Snodgrass asked, "Calvin, have you ever consumed alcoholic beverages?"

Calvin answered, "Yes, sir, but . . ."

Before he could explain the circumstances of what it was like being in the Army in Korea, Professor Snodgrass cut him off, "Have you ever had premarital sex?"

Calvin knew that there was no use trying to explain his life of twenty years ago and answered, "Yes."

This answer brought a visible frown to the professor's face, and the next question took Calvin by complete surprise.

The New Roads Senior Professor of Religion asked the Sunday School teacher, "Have you ever owned and listened to Elvis Presley records?"

Calvin owned every record Elvis had ever recorded but couldn't hold himself to yes and no answers anymore. "Professor, what in the world does this have to do with the charges against me?"

"I'm trying to establish your moral picture, Calvin, and any possession of recordings by the leader of the rock-and-roll, lead-the-kids-to-Hell movement is an important piece of evidence," the professor explained.

"Yes, sir, I do own some Elvis records," Calvin confessed.

"Well, are you, or have you ever been, a member of the Buddhist religion?" asked the professor.

This is when Calvin answered with a resounding, "NO! But I did meet many Buddhists during my two years in the Army in Asia, and I even tried to convert a few."

Poor Calvin didn't know, however, what any first-year law student knows: keep your answers short and to the point. The professor was immediately suspicious of anyone who had spent time with the infidels, and he knew that association leads to conversion. Because of this, the professor determined that Calvin Walker, based on his answers to the preceding moral questions, was a probable infidel.

I knew from my five-percenter spy network that Calvin Walker, accused Buddhist and suspended song leader, had another appointment with Professor Snodgrass the next Monday afternoon. I engaged the services of my friends, Pecker and Archie, for an afternoon project that would add a little excitement to Brother Walker's appointment. The three of us agreed to meet at the Catholic bookstore on Dexter Street in downtown Montgomery at one o'clock on the Saturday before Brother Walker's appointment with Professor Snodgrass. We entered the bookstore and purchased a small statue of The Virgin Mary and a set of rosary beads. We then returned to Archie's house to set our plan in motion.

We gathered at Archie's house that Monday afternoon after school. I asked Archie to get the dust bag out of his mother's vacuum cleaner and a tube of fast-drying model airplane glue. I shook the bag over a piece of paper until I had enough fine dust to serve my purposes. I folded the paper with the dust inside and stuffed it into my pocket along with the airplane glue. We grabbed our Catholic bookstore purchases, and then we headed in the direction of the New Roads School.

We were hiding behind the library when Brother Calvin Walker arrived. As soon as he was up the stairs to Professor Snodgrass's office we set to work. Pecker was on lookout at the bottom of the stairs, Archie was arranging our faked emergency, and my job was to place the evidence in Calvin's car.

Archie brought a length of plastic-covered car wiring that he attached to Calvin's fuse box inside the car so that it would burn through when the ends were twisted together. I was busy gluing The Virgin Mary to the center of Calvin's dashboard, dusting the whole dash and the statue with Archie's mom's vacuum dust and knotting the rosary beads around the mirror, as Archie twisted the wires together and shoved them under the dash. As the burning wire was starting to fill the car with smoke, Archie and I ran for our lookout under the library steps. Pecker went into action as we left the car; he ran up the steps and screamed that there was a blue Chevy downstairs on fire!

Calvin and the professor sprinted down the stairs together and found Calvin's car filled with smoke. Calvin opened the car's driver's side door as the professor opened the passenger's side, and they both saw the smoking wire Archie had planted with enough exposed wire for easy detection. Calvin pulled the wire loose and the car began to clear of smoke, at which point the New Roads Professor of Religion noticed The Virgin Mary attached to the dashboard. Calvin was only seconds behind the professor in noticing the Catholic icon sitting on his car's dash.

The professor reminded Calvin, "You are still under the sacred oath, and I want to know what is the meaning of you having the statue of The

Virgin Mary on your dash?"

Dumbfounded, Calvin replied, "I've never seen that before in my life!"

It was at this point the detective professor of religion pointed out, "That statue is as dusty as the rest of the car, so I know it's been in your car for quite some time."

Calvin reached to pick up The Virgin Mary but she wouldn't move, she was stuck to the dash, which did not escape the professor's attention. At this point, they both noticed the rosary beads on the mirror, which came off along with the mirror as a frustrated Calvin Walker jerked on them.

The professor said, "I've seen quite enough. I'm convinced, Calvin, that you're suffering from a Multiple Religious Personality Disorder. I have no choice but to recommend to the leadership of the First New Roads Church of Montgomery that you start a long-term weekly pastoral counseling process to rid you of your Buddhist and Catholic personalities. Once you've completed the pastoral counseling successfully, then and only then can you resume your duties as a song leader and Sunday school teacher."

11. 1958 Triumph Daytona 500

When school began for the second semester, we worked out our plan for obtaining our Triumph motorcycle but had no plans to deal with Brother Roy Harper Jr. I had seen Roy the first day back at school and there was a marked change in his personality. He wasn't drooling and howling like a mad dog as he had been on the last day I had seen him but was quiet and had a dangerous look that sent a shiver up my spine. I could see the judge's determination in Roy's face—he was a man who was on a mission and was not going to be deterred by a Pecker Devil or his friends. My guess was that Roy had traded in the idea of my spiritual rescue for the sweet taste of revenge, and I knew that hate would out-perform love as a motivator nine times out of ten.

After I shared these suspicions with Pecker and Archie, I said, "We'll both stick close to you, Pecker, because I know that you are going to be Roy's target for destruction."

Pecker said, "Well, boys, the best defense is a good offense, and we're going to have to turn the heat up on Brother Roy to get and keep him off balance. We're going to have to get the five-percenter info network to work overtime on Brother Roy's comings and goings, because we need details and plenty of them if we are going to keep our petards from being hoisted by Brother Roy."

Roy had turned into a loner at the New Roads College, going to class, the Bistro, and back to his dorm room alone. He shunned conversation and stayed to himself most of the time, but we had heard that he was slipping out of his dorm window at night after curfew. We knew we were facing a new and sinister Roy Harper Jr. that would have to be watched carefully but, at the moment, we had a motorcycle to obtain at a good price from our fellow student Jim Bob.

We tried to reason with Jim Bob that his motorcycle was overpriced in hopes that he would have more compassion for transportation-less youths in that new year of 1963. He was still an asshole who insisted on a premium price for his risk in selling the motorcycle to three under-aged teenagers. We had tried my plan of giving Jim Bob one more chance at feeling sorry for us by reminding him of the feelings he had when he got his first motorcycle, but Jim Bob's lack of empathy pushed us on to Pecker's plan. Pecker reasoned that you couldn't cheat an honest man so whatever we did to Jim Bob was divine retribution for his trying to take advantage of our youth and inability to register a motorcycle.

Motorcycles at the New Roads School were parked behind the men's dorm where they would be out of the view of anyone who might have seen a Marlon Brando movie and therefore get the wrong idea about the New Roads School. The dorm sat on a hill above the evil cow bowl barn, and one could quietly push a motorcycle down the hill without detection.

On the second Monday of the new semester, Archie called in sick for school and instead went to the cow bowl barn with his tool kit. At the end of first period, Pecker and I slipped away from the classroom building to the back of the men's dorm to capture Jim Bob's motorcycle and deliver it very quietly to Archie in the barn. Pecker's plan called for Archie to make the motorcycle's engine seem to be on its last leg without actually doing any permanent damage to it. Archie did a masterful job of undoing all kinds of internal parts, so the bike coughed and sputtered, leaked fluids in three places, and made a horrible knock inside the engine when it was started.

Our job was to convince Jim Bob that we had three hundred fifty dollars and would give it to him after we had checked the compression on the Triumph's engine.

"So, Jim Bob," I asked. "What's the condition of the motorcycle? Does it run okay? Have you ever crashed it?"

Jim Bob said, "This motorcycle has been sitting behind the men's dorm in perfect condition and unused since I got my Buick for Christmas. I've got the keys, and I'll be glad to trade them for three hundred fifty dollars."

I explained, "Before we can do that, Jim Bob, we've got to have Archie, our partner and mechanic, check out the Triumph to see if everything is all right. If we think it's okay, then we'll hand over the money."

We set the engine checkup for the next morning before class. Pecker wanted a double score out of this deal and put out the word through the five-percenter info net-work that Brother Roy had been seen sneaking out of the dorm at night and riding Jim Bob's motorcycle to the Spur Club, a local honky-tonk known for fights, fast women, and cheap whiskey.

We all showed up the next day at 7 a.m. to test the engine. Jim Bob turned the switch on and kicked the starter, but nothing happened. After twenty tries, the motor finally started and black smoke billowed out all sides of the engine and oil was dripping to the ground from three places. Pecker asked, "Jim Bob, what the Hell are you trying to put over on us?

This motorcycle is about to fall apart!"

In a calm voice, Archie added, "It appears to me that someone has blown the head on the engine, and it'll cost at least three hundred dollars to fix it."

"This motorcycle ran perfectly when I went home for Christmas break," Jim Bob stammered. "I can't understand how it could have blown its head just sitting there!"

Archie responded, "That's because it couldn't. It's obvious that this motorcycle has been ridden hard in the last few days."

Pecker went over to the Triumph and fumbled through the saddle bags. There he found an empty Early Times bottle, a pair of women's underpants, a handbill from the Spur Club, and a book on coin collecting. From what we could all see, it looked like someone had been having a high old time on Jim Bob's motorcycle.

We agreed on a price of one hundred fifty dollars for the decrepit machine that Archie would have as good as new by dark. We also agreed to see if we could find out who had ruined Jim Bob's bike and would report the results of our investigation to Jim Bob as soon as we knew who had done the damage.

By midday, Jim Bob had heard the rumor that it was Roy Harper Jr. who had been using his motorcycle, but no one could prove it, and Jim Bob wasn't going to cause a fuss with just one semester to go before graduation. Jim Bob had been ejected from so many schools in his academic career that he knew this was his last chance to graduate.

We convinced Jim Bob not to worry about his need for revenge because we would take care of Brother Roy for what he had done to the Triumph Tiger Daytona 500 if Jim Bob would just go downtown to the

Montgomery County Courthouse that after-noon and change the registration of the motorcycle from his name to Roy Harper Jr.'s. Jim Bob didn't know what we were up to but he figured it would be at Brother

Roy's expense and did what Pecker asked him to do.

Where to keep our newly purchased freedom machine was our next problem. We could have left it behind the dorm for the rest of the semester without drawing any attention, but we ran the risk of discovery each time we would try to use it because there were students constantly entering and exiting from the back door of the dorm. Our task was to find the Triumph Tiger Daytona 500 a home in the cow bowl barn, but we had to find a ploy that would satisfy Estill, the maintenance man and guardian of the cow bowl barn.

If we had been any other students at the New Roads School, the task before us would have been easier. However, since Estill had barely escaped his almost disastrous brush with the Pecker Devil and his cohorts, he would not be likely to fall for any idea we cooked up. We needed a story that would hold water and didn't require Estill's approval. We knew that our credibility had been slipping with the school's authorities all year, and this made our task of finding a good cover story extremely difficult. This was the problem with being a five percenter at the New Roads School, we were always perceived to be up to no good.

What we needed was a beard, someone who was accepted by the majority community and would thus shield our true activity. We needed someone with authority and position who would allay any suspicion of abnormality. We needed someone naive enough to buy our tale and who would settle for a story long on promise and short on delivery. There was only one man who fit this bill and that was the New Roads Senior Professor of Religion, Dr. Ronald T. Snodgrass.

Being the quickest of tongue and least known for corruption, I was selected to find the right story and to deliver it in a convincing way to the professor. After reviewing the seven virtues for the answer to my problem of a cover story, I settled on charity as the most salable to Professor Snodgrass. I went to see the professor that afternoon and found him ensconced in his office preparing his lecture for the next day. When I entered his office, he drew back and had a look on his face that said "be gone evil spirit of exorcisms past" but this passed quickly.

He asked, "Pip, can I help you?"

"Yes, sir, I think you can," I said. "You see, sir, lately I've been feeling the spirit of giving and I've got a strong desire to help my fellow man in a material way. I think I've come up with a plan to involve the entire school in a humanitarian effort that will benefit those in need around us."

He lit up like a Christmas tree, and I knew he had taken the bait. All I had to do next was set the hook.

"Sir, what I've done is gotten a small group of mechanically minded students together who have agreed to repair and refurbish broken items for reuse by those with-out the funds to buy them. The best items for repair are small motor-driven items like lawn mowers, but we could also fix bicycles and household appliances.

"There's a lot of extra space in the barn to store and repair these items before they're distributed, and I think the Junior League of Montgomery can help with that part. I think we should call ourselves the New Roads Helping Hands Club. We just need a sponsor. All we have to do is ask every student to scour their homes and neighborhoods for broken and discarded motorized items, bicycles, and household appliances that the mechanical group can repair."

The hook was set; the professor loved the idea. He volunteered to be our sponsor and agreed to get everything set up with the administration. He also offered to make sure Estill would reserve the space we would need in the barn.

When I told Archie and Pecker what I had done, they thought I had lost my mind. "Pip," Archie asked, "what are you going to do when all those broken items start to pour in?"

"Don't worry, boys. I've got a plan," I said. "All we need is enough broken equipment to hide one functional Triumph Tiger Daytona 500 motorcycle."

The U.S. Army Reserve building was six blocks from the New Roads School campus. I had wandered down there a few times when I left my math class via the front porch window and was therefore aware of what they were up to at the armory. The folks who worked there were in a motor pool repair unit, and they had lots of time on their hands because the Russians weren't much interested in a takeover of Montgomery. The full-time staff, with the help of the weekend warriors, had adopted the favorite charity of the commanding major's wife: the Junior League of Montgomery. As the recipient of the Army post's good deeds, the Junior League helped them fill their days with a few productive activities, which kept some of their boredom at bay. The ladies had come up with a few repair tasks for the National Guard armory's full-time enlisted men but not that many.

I left my friends and headed for the armory to find Major John Collins so I could explain my new club and how we would help with their stock of items that needed to be repaired. The major, like the professor, loved the idea but I gave him a little different version of my story.

After giving the major most of the story, I explained, "Sir, the only thing we'd like to ask in return for our club's gathering these very repairable items is to affix a sticker that says, 'These items were donated by the New Roads Helping Hands Club.'" This was fine because the major was walking a tightrope between his wife's intolerance of the relaxed life of the full-time reservists waiting on the Russians to pick Montgomery for their jumping-off point and his own ambivalence at disturbing his place of employment.

The major's wife, who had a private sector upbringing, thought the major's men should be doing something productive while they waited on the Russians and hatched the idea of helping the needy with their repair skills, which would turn unfulfilled, unproductive time to a positive purpose and increase morale. After a few weeks of grumbling, the major's wife's prediction proved true, the reservists began to enjoy their own helping hands effort and found through the experience that their lives were less boring and the time at work didn't seem as long anymore.

The only threat to this newfound purpose to the volunteer activities of the army-in-waiting was for his superiors to find out that they were becoming a Goodwill look-alike repair shop. This could call into question what other civic and governmental duties the full-time reservists could perform when not fighting Russians. He knew that his bosses liked things pretty much like they were, so discretion was critical. The major saw where the merger of our Helping Hands Club with his good deeds program could keep the brass above him from finding out and complaining about the best thing he had ever done to improve the morale and harmonious working conditions of his men. The major thought that affixing our club's stickers to the output of his clandestine military operation was a great idea and a great way to keep his wife happy and his superiors none the wiser.

12. The Helping Hands Club

My Helping Hands Club was invented as a cover for our escape from the world of the walking, but things had a way of getting really strange in those New Roads days. When Professor Snodgrass announced the Helping Hands Club plan during chapel and the fact that I would be heading the club, you could have heard a pin drop. The general feeling among the majority group was that I was lost to the five percenters, and this announcement created a paradox in their highly structured universe of the righteous, and it absolutely befuddled the five percenters. Those of the minority five-percent persuasion were wondering if I had had a New Roads conversion over the holidays.

After chapel, I was confronted by a rush of those who prided themselves on trying to do the right thing and being helpful and gracious to others. I had offered them a way to self-actualize without spending all that goodness trying to convert the ninety-nine percent of the city who were infidels on the road to Hell because they weren't New Roaders. The more suspicious ministers-to-be group saw a hopeful sign in my founding of the Helping Hands Club—they thought I was seeing the light and turning away from my wicked ways and wicked friends.

The Grand Council had a meeting that afternoon to devise a new plan to get me inside the New Roads tent now that my attitude about being involved with the better elements of the New Roads School seemed to them to have changed.

The Grand Council's plan was to support me in my good works because they knew that a failure might drive me back into the arms of the five percenters. They would look high and low for repairable motorized items and broken household appliances and encourage the other students to do the same, thus building a close relationship with me that would lead to my conversion by my attesting to the New Roads articles of faith.

If they had only known about my intense commitment to the proposition that all religions were not created equal and that any religion that had something against saxophones in church, dancing, and drinking beer was not going to make it on my religious preference list.

Brother Stride-X as we called him—a nickname that came from the angry constellation of acne that dominated his face and neck—had been one of the most enthusiastic participants in the effort to reclaim my soul the previous semester. He was a true believer, earnest to a fault, and deeply committed to the idea that anyone outside the New Roads enlightenment was wandering blindly toward eternal damnation. Of all the ministerial students, he seemed the most convinced that persistence, prayer, and proximity could save even the most stubborn sinner.

When the Helping Hands Club was announced, Brother Stride-X took it as proof that the Lord had finally broken through to me. He was visibly elated by the news and told anyone who would listen that our efforts had not been in vain and that God's timing was perfect, even if His methods were mysterious.

Brother Stride-X went to Roy Jr.'s room right after the Grand Council had met on my case to enlist him in winning me over to the New Roads way. Brother Stride-X was very excited about the Helping Hands Club and exclaimed, "Roy, the Lord touched Pip over the holidays! Our work on him last semester wasn't in vain!"

Roy's attitude was a great surprise to Brother Stride-X because Roy said, "I'm not going to be sucked into another plot by the Pecker Devil and his friends. I don't know what they're up to, but I know that whatever it is, it's evil. I'm going to spend my time fighting the Devil, not cavorting with his friends."

Brother Stride-X was shocked at what Brother Roy was saying. Then he reminded Roy, "Don't forget. It's your duty as a ministerial student to bring unbelievers to the New Roads enlightenment."

Brother Roy flew into a rage. "Listen here, Brother Stride-X, I don't need your dumbass telling me my duty. The only duty I have is to catch that damnable Pecker Devil and his friends up to no good and expose them, so the takeover of the New Roads School can be stopped!"

Within two weeks, we filled a quarter of the barn with a variety of discarded motor-driven items and home appliances including a Vespa motor scooter. I had arranged a transshipment system to the National Guard armory. When we had an overflow of broken items, I would go and get the guardsmen after school to come and remove the broken items we had neatly placed outside the closed barn. We always held back enough junk to hide our motorcycle amongst the clutter, including a wide assortment of electrical devices. The only person besides Roy who was none too happy about this new endeavor was Estill.

We had cluttered his barn and had permission to do it. We were in his barn both night and day, and he couldn't run us off because we had the backing of the president. His private refuge from the demands of keeping the old, cheaply built campus functioning was being stolen by young infidels. He needed his alone time in the barn and couldn't abide Pecker and his friends. Estill had decided after his near escape in December that landed Roy Harper Jr. in trouble with the administration to keep his distance from us and wait for this humanitarian effort to wear thin.

The obsession started like most others; we agreed that we would only take the motorcycle out once a week on the dirt road that was on the other side of the cow bowl. This worked for about two weeks until we learned to ride that big British hog. The world opened a little wider for me the day I skipped math class and headed for the barn. I was just going to give the Triumph a short spin down our little lonely dirt road when the next thing I knew I was downtown roaming the streets of Montgomery. The freedom of being able to go anywhere I wanted, as fast as I wanted, was an unbelievably addictive feeling. That day I mainlined the American drug of choice, internally combusted gasoline. There was no going back; I had to have more of this personal freedom to go wherever I wanted to go within a time frame that wouldn't get me in trouble.

Archie went to work on the Vespa and had it running in a week but still looking like it was on its way to the scrap yard. This suited our purposes because, if questioned, we could say that we were holding on to it for parts in case another Vespa arrived through the Helping Hands Club. The Triumph was hidden in the cluttered corner of our repair and storage area where we had cut and hinged part of the barn's back wall for easy access and return from the outside. The freedom of motorized movement was totally seducing; we were consumed with the thrill of being out on the streets and the knowledge that we could go anywhere we wanted to go. Once we got the Vespa running, we could all go together.

As with any tendency, we began to commit almost all our mental energy to finding ways to feed our addiction, looking for ways to spend more hours on the road and less hours in the classroom or at home. I devised a plan that would do just that if we could get the support of Professor Snodgrass and, with his help, get the school's higher-ups to go along with my plan.

"Professor," I said, "I feel like our repair work might be more important than mere schoolwork. I strongly support the goals of modern academics and the curriculum here at New Roads, but practical skills are good, too. After all, there's a private school here in Alabama that has blended the two, and that school has won accolades from a master of academics, John Dewey. What if Archie, Pecker, and I come up with a schedule? One of us could attend all our classes, and the other two of us could continue to work on our Helping Hands project in the barn. Then, we would cover both the practical and educational skills needed. Whoever is scheduled to attend each class can instruct the other two on missed information and any homework that might need to be completed."

Professor Snodgrass began to mull this over and I thought we were home free, but the professor had some doubts that my plan for the blending of academic and practical skills was exactly what John Dewey had in mind. The professor didn't want to derail my enthusiasm for our very positive Helping Hands movement that was sweeping the school, but the thought of Archie teaching Pecker and me algebra was painful to even think about.

"How about this solution instead, Pip?" the professor asked. "I know three ministerial students who are handy with tools, and I'll get in touch with Brother Stride-X this afternoon. I think he can help with the repairs, and I also think he can help persuade the others I have in mind to join the repair group as well."

I was slack-jawed, and my mind was spinning. The plan had not only failed but the presence of the ministerial students in our barn would lead to the discovery of our Helping Hands scam and the eventual transshipment of our beloved Tiger Daytona 500 to the Junior League of Montgomery. The professor had proposed the invasion of our personal space by ministerial geeks. This was WAR! But all I could do was agree to his suggestion and return to my friends Pecker and Archie with the bad news.

After giving them the lowdown on my failure and with the imminent arrival of Brother Stride-X and his repair buddies at any moment, I began to despair for the loss of our newfound freedom that the motorcycle had provided. Pecker's response to my depression was action; he jumped up from his bench and started stalking the barn in search of red paint and a long rubber garden hose. At that point, I knew the devious Pecker had found a way out of this dilemma for us.

"The first thing to do, Pip," Pecker said, "is for you to get up the hill and make arrangements with Brother Stride-X and his pals to come to the barn at about six o'clock when it will be dark outside. You need to tell them that when they get down here, we'll show them how we organize and prioritize our repair operation, and we'll be assigning projects for the week. Oh, and Pip, make sure you are authoritative with them about who runs the Helping Hands repair project. We don't want them to get the wrong idea." Pecker wanted to ensure that the correct psychological mood would be in place by six o'clock.

I did as I was instructed. All systems were go on my end, and it was time to find out what exactly Pecker had planned for the new Helping Hands repair team recruits.

When I got back to the barn, I found Archie and Pecker outside the barn affixing a large rubber hose with holes cut in it around a series of nails in the shape of a pentacle, the sign of the Devil. The barn was old and there were small gaps between each board, which was just what was needed for one of the greatest plans ever hatched by any of the three of us.

Pecker found a ten-gallon bucket of red paint that was left over from the Bistro's last paint job. He put a metal tap on the bottom of the bucket, which he attached to a hand-pull valve that had been left in the barn in years past. I helped Archie and Pecker lift the paint to the side of the barn's roof and helped Archie secure it while Pecker hooked the valve to the hose, tied a string to the valve's handle, and fed the end through a small hole in the roof.

Once inside the barn, I noticed the number 666, another sign of the Devil, written in three places on the walls in rusty brown paint. Each number oozed down the walls and was of a different size with the largest being about a foot in height. Pecker filled us in on our roles, and we waited on Brother Stride-X and his friends like a spider waits on its web for an unsuspecting insect.

They were right on time for our six o'clock meeting, and Pecker took charge. He explained to the ministerial students, "I've been selected as the Helping Hands Club's repair supervisor by the club's founder, Pip Cooper, with the concurrence of Professor Snodgrass. I'm sure you men have heard about the productivity of the repair team, and I'm so glad to have you all on board!"

Then, Pecker proceeded to give a thirty-minute discourse on the way he assigned priority to a disabled gasoline or electric powered machine or appliance that was headed for a needy person after it was repaired. He had these guys thinking that they were back in the Scouts again: the picture of order and authority for a higher purpose he had painted in their minds was sending them into a euphoric state, and that's when he set them to worrying about what they had gotten themselves into.

Pecker then launched into his story, "Boys, the only negative part of being on the repair team is that strange things have been happening in the barn. Voices are heard but no one is there. The foul odor of rotting flesh can sometimes be smelt, but then it goes away as fast as it came. Those aren't the only things. Ever since the Helping Hands Club started its work in the barn, the number 666 has begun to appear on the east wall." While walking toward the wall, he continued his explanation, "We've seen all three numbers appear out of nowhere while working on our good-deed projects. When they first appeared, they were blood red and oozing down the wall. I'm sure the Devil is just trying to keep us from our good works, but I think I can speak for the whole group in saying we're willing to die in a fight with the Devil over the Helping Hands Club."

Terror was on each of the new recruits' faces.

Then Brother Stride-X confessed, "I've never even been to the barn before be-cause it's known all over campus as a place of evil. I don't like getting this close to the powers of darkness."

"If we all stick together," Pecker assured the group of frightened ministerial students, "then we'll be able to hold the Devil off, do our good deeds, and maybe only lose a couple of us in the battle with Satan. Besides, fellas, your presence here will protect the younger three of us because the Devil is bound to choose to do battle with a minister-in-training before going after us."

At that point, Archie quietly and with great aplomb pulled the string that was attached to the paint valve. Pecker was looking past the group when he saw the evidence of his and Archie's planning start dripping down the wall. Then Brother Stride-X saw it, too, and he began to shake like Jerry Lee Lewis playing his piano. In shock, he began mumbling and stuttering about Satan getting behind him. Then, he tore out of the barn and up the hill with the other ex-Helping Hands repairmen right behind him.

The security of our turf was all but assured. We painted over the walls we had messed up to keep the administration off balance in case the ravings of three ministerial students about unholy happenings in the barn caused an inspection. Within an hour, we had removed all the evidence of our trick and had everything looking like a perfectly natural Helping Hands repair yard. We were secure in the knowledge that this was once again five-percenter territory. We knew that no other do-gooders would descend to the cow bowl after they heard Brother Stride-X and his associates testify to the horrors they had endured.

In our celebration of victory, we had forgotten about Brother Roy, but Brother Roy hadn't forgotten about us. Roy had been sporadically hiding in the woods. He had secretly observed us as we prepared for his friends' arrival and had watched their terror-stricken departure from the cow bowl barn.

All Hell broke loose the next morning at school. Archie, Pecker, and I were hauled into the president's office, where we were marched right by the usual authority figures of the principal and the dean, so we knew this meant big trouble. After we were ushered into the president's inner office, we were faced with a man who was looking about as tense as a man could look. He said not a word to us. After about five minutes, the door opened and the principal, the dean, and the three former Helping Hands ministerial student repairmen walked in. The president instructed everyone to sit down. As the president began to speak, Professor Snodgrass entered and took a chair. I knew the odds had changed in our favor when the professor entered.

The president looked each of us in the eye and spoke, "Boys, I've been notified of demonic sightings at the cow bowl barn by three reliable witnesses who are seniors in the preachers' degree program. Right now, the campus is in an uproar and there's talk being instigated by the five percenters of burning the barn. I want some straight talk, right now, before I have a riot on my hands and the whole school gets torched trying to burn out the Devil. So, boys, tell me. What did you three see last night in the barn?"

I spoke first, "Sir, all we saw were three deadbeats who were forced to report for duty or disappoint their professor. I think they're loafers who only have their own interests at heart, and I don't think they could care less about the poor of Montgomery."

President Slim Bailey was flushed with anger and asked, "Did any of you see blood running down the walls in the shape of a pentacle?"

We all gave the president a look like he had lost his mind. I said, "Sir, none of us know why we're here or what this is all about, but I'll tell you what happened in detail at last evening's meeting with these three slackers. First, they came to the barn at six o'clock, and Pecker told them about our procedures for organizing the repairs and the work expectations. After hearing about that, they didn't seem too interested in our Helping Hands work, and then suddenly, they got quiet and were staring at the wall. The next thing we knew, they were hollering about the sign of the Devil and running away. I figured they ran off because of all the work we expected out of them. Right, guys?"

Archie chimed in, "I thought it was a hallucination caused by all the solvent fumes we use down in the barn with our work."

"I thought it was a triple Demonic Possession," Pecker figured.

The president turned to the professor and asked, "Dr. Snodgrass, have you completed your inspection of the barn?"

"Yes, sir, I have. I didn't find any evidence at all of Satanic symbols or blood, just evidence of the good works of the New Roads School's Helping Hands Club," the professor claimed.

President Slim Bailey, the front man who kept the school financially afloat, knew that he was facing a potentially disastrous situation. If word got out that the Devil was living in his campus barn, most of his students would be pulled out of his school by their parents, donation funds would disappear, and his whole life would collapse. He knew what he had to do—he had to get these three ministerial students to recant their story willingly and fast.

President Bailey faced the three divinity students and asked, "Gentlemen, is it possible that you all were influenced by the cleaning solution fumes and had a multiple hallucination?"

Brother Stride-X realized that he had been set up and was about to say some words his mother had told him never to say when his two friends said that that explanation made sense to them. They both knew they had been pulled into a bad situation by Brother Stride-X and just wanted to say whatever the president wanted them to say so they could graduate in May and get on with their lives as New Roads preachers. Brother Stride-X was reticent when the president asked, "Son, do you also think this might be what happened to you three?"

Brother Stride-X was adamant. He said, "No, sir, I do not. This wasn't caused by some bogus theory of solvent fumes. I know this was the work of the Pecker Devil that Brother Roy Harper Jr. encountered last semester!"

After hearing the testimony of Brother Stride-X, the president asked that everyone leave the room except for Brother Stride-X and Pecker. When everyone had left, Pecker and Brother Stride-X saw a side of President Bailey they had never seen. He turned on them like a piranha and shouted, "Let me tell you both something right now! I will not have a bunch of little shits like the two of you ruining my life! I know this business has to do with Pecker and his friends getting up the rear ends of the ministerial students, but that is no reason to destroy my school! Any ideas about getting rid of Pecker and his friends have been dashed by the Helping Hands Club's success, because if I expel these three without solid reasons, I'll have the Montgomery Junior League picketing my school."

Looking then at Brother Stride-X, he continued, "The only solution is for you to tell everyone that you were disoriented by solvent fumes, and you can get even with Pecker after you graduate in May. And if you don't want to go along with this version of what happened, you'll be watching instead of participating in the college's graduation. And I don't want to hear anything else about this."

Brother Stride-X begrudgingly agreed to go along with the story, but on the way out of the president's office, he informed Pecker that he wasn't going to wait until May to exact his revenge. He began thinking of how to get his divine retribution for what we had done to him.

We knew that from that day forward, until summer vacation, we had two ministerial students out for our heads. We were going to have to focus more attention on our defense if we were to survive the double onslaught of Brother Stride-X and Roy Harper Jr. We knew that we had to hone our information networks to keep tabs on what our adversaries were up to and note any changes that occurred in their behavior patterns if we wanted to stay ahead of any plots that they might have in store for us.

13. The Trap Is Set

We decided to lie low again after our encounter with the president because we knew that we would be watched closely by the administration for a while. This was no time to take chances, so we kept our motorcycle fever in check and our profiles minimal. The next month, we went to every class, met at the barn only after lunch, and kept our motorcycle and the Vespa for idol worship instead of riding. When the ruckus we had started with the ministerial students subsided, the time, we figured, would be right to resume enjoying our motorcycle but this took longer than we thought it would.

The rumors in a fundamentalist school last much longer than in a public school, and this is perfectly natural since the vast majority of students at the New Roads School had so little collective sin to make into good rumors and gossip. Any indiscretions were precious and thus savored longer. The signs during the days after our encounter with Dr. Bailey pointed to greater danger ahead, because the thing the three of us noticed and worried us the most was the constant company that Roy and Brother Stride-X kept. When Roy told Brother Stride-X about his observations at the barn of the night before, Brother Stride-X was livid. "We should go tell Dr. Bailey right now, Roy!" said Brother Stride-X.

Roy then said, "We can't do that, not right now. There's no proof left in the barn of what they did. Even my own explanation would be suspect because of my avid pursuit of the Pecker Devil. Just for a while, we're going to have to proceed slowly and carefully if we want to catch those heathens violating the New Roads rules.

"Brother, we are up against the most cunning of foes, so any trap that we set has to be foolproof, well researched and thought-out. From all my spying, sneaking, and snooping, I found out that they bought the motorcycle from Jim Bob Brewer, and they've been riding it all around the cow bowl. When they bought it, it wasn't working very well, and I got blamed for causing those problems. On top of that, there's no rule banning motorcycle riding on campus, and they would just claim it was just being tested as part of its repair. Then they would say as soon as it's fixed that they'll be donating it to the Montgomery Junior League.

"This Helping Hands Club is a fraud, and I think it will eventually take those three boys down. In the meantime, Brother Stride-X, you and I will have to catch them in a definite illegal or immoral act if we want to get them kicked out of our school. If we're going to save the school from being devastated, then we'll have to prepare our-selves like never before. We've got to get ready because we're about to do battle with the wiliest enemy ever known, the Devil. Now, his imp, the Pecker Devil, has the whole school hysterical over hearing about some signs from Satan appearing in the barn. I think that's part of his plan to get most of the students here to withdraw; it's so he and the other five percenters can take over and completely destroy the school!

"Just this morning, Brother Stride-X, I saw all the unbelieving five percenters laughing at the faithful students, trying to talk them into burning down the barn to get rid of the Satanic influence there! If that didn't do the trick, Pecker and his friends could have sanctioned the burning any of the other buildings on campus. Can you believe it has come to this?

"It almost worked, too, because most of our Grand Council was on the way to torch the barn when Estill stopped them. He threatened to beat the shit out of anyone who harmed his barn, so they began to scatter after that. If it hadn't been for Estill," Brother Roy explained, "the whole campus could have gone up in flames while the Pecker Devil sat in the president's office and mused at his success."

Once Roy had finished his long and agonizing story about the events of the last day, he and Brother Stride-X sat around discussing different ideas to try to illuminate the truth about me, Archie, and Pecker.

The plan that evolved was for them to begin with a twenty-four-hour-a-day surveillance of the barn and any activities that involved any of the three of us, with each event duly recorded in a daily logbook.

Roy said, "How about this: I'll sneak out of the dorm each night and sleep in a hidden place in the barn loft if you'll relieve me for breakfast. Then we'll split up the rest of the day with each missing half our classes."

Brother Stride-X agreed. "Then, on the weekends, we can swap out surveillance duty with each of us spending every other weekend hidden in the barn."

This was actually a great plan because our defense systems were designed to handle each of them separately; we had not planned on the synergy factor that would magnify their power to ensnare us.

The barn watching began the next day, a cold Friday in late February, but we didn't find out about the spies in our midst until a warm beautiful day in May. We kept a low profile until the middle of March, and only then did we begin our daily luncheon rides on the Triumph and the

Vespa, which were recorded by our adversaries in their daily logbook of our sins. Roy Jr. recorded our storage of the broken lawn mowers, appliances, go carts, and kitchen appliances that were being brought by the New Roads students supporting the Helping Hands Club. He also noted the monthly pickup by the Alabama National Guard of these same items, still untouched by the teenage repair team of the Helping Hands Club.

For weeks, Roy and Brother Stride-X agonized at their daily debriefing about the meaning of what they were seeing: three kids smoking, cussing, and admiring a motor-cycle. These were all offenses to them but not enough to get the Pecker Devil and his friends thrown out of the New Roads School. Roy Jr. said he thought President Bailey was fearful of any bad publicity that could lead to outsiders and government officials looking too closely at the school's finances and Dr. Bailey's leasing arrangement.

The other thing that disturbed Roy and Brother Stride-X was the fact that we never seemed to be working on any of the donations in need of repair. One day, as Roy observed the National Guard pickup, he finally figured out the mystery of the Helping Hands Club: it was a front to hide the motorcycle we had bought from Jim Bob Brewer. Brother Stride-X was ready to go public with their newly discovered truth, but Roy Jr. had been burned in the past by underestimating the Pecker Devil and persuaded Brother Stride-X that they had to have irrefutable evidence of a severe violation before going to the school authorities.

We, of course, were inadvertently plotting our own demise as the unseen spies listened to our open discussion of plans for future excesses and new unsavory deeds to be accomplished sometime in the future.

Roy Jr. and Brother Stride-X decided on a divide-and-conquer strategy with a decision to turn the heat up on us by reporting any minor offenses we committed that might cause Archie and me to come out from under the Pecker Devil's evil spell. I walked into their trap first because I was the most afflicted by the charm of the Tiger Daytona 500.

It was late March, my senile math teacher had started to ramble on about theorems she had long since forgotten when the urge hit me to jump from the classroom window to the front porch. The next thing I knew, my math teacher had turned to write on the blackboard, and I was out of the window sprinting to the barn to enjoy forty-five minutes of motorized freedom. For some reason, the Vespa that Archie had running perfectly seemed to be the right choice of transportation for my afternoon adventure. As it turned out, this choice proved to be a very wise decision.

When I left the barn on the Vespa, Brother Stride-X came out of his hiding place and went to find Roy Jr. I had been gone for thirty minutes enjoying a beautiful Montgomery spring day while Roy and Brother Stride-X went to get the school authorities. What Roy and his accomplice didn't know about my riding habits was that I would return to the barn from a different direction than my departing path, which allowed me to check the situation before I committed to reenter the barn. I came back to campus by way of the woods above the property and cut the engine before I crested the hill and rolled silently toward the barn. Just after starting my descent, I saw the principal standing in front of the barn with Brother Stride-X and Roy Jr. My heart was in my mouth as I quietly stopped the Vespa and gathered my wits, I had very little time to get out of the trap that had been set for me.

I knew I had to get back to math class before the principal figured out that it might be a better place to look for me because he might want conclusive evidence that I really was AWOL. I pushed the Vespa to the back of the men's dorm, removed the engine skirt, and doused the engine with oil from the scooter's tool compartment. Then, I returned to class through the porch window. The senile teacher was trying to figure out what she had written on the board when I reentered the open window unnoticed and returned to my desk that sat next to the window.

Within five minutes I saw the principal and his spying companions cross the porch on the way to verify my absence from math class. Just seconds before the door opened, I got the teacher's attention and was asking a question about algebraic equations when the principal walked in. He walked up to the dean's great aunt, the math teacher, and asked if I had left the class for any reason, and she assured him that no one had asked to leave during the whole class period. The bell rang during their discussion, and the principal said that he wanted to see me outside.

The principal asked, "Pip, have you, by any chance, been out on the streets of Montgomery on the Vespa from the barn during your math class?"

"Sir, that couldn't possibly be true! You saw me sitting in class and asking a question," I retorted.

Roy Jr. began his own lie to protect his undercover operation, "Pip, Brother Stride-X and I saw you! You were out on the Vespa not thirty minutes ago when we were walking up to the 7-Eleven!"

"Sir," I addressed the principal, "I did ride the Vespa up the hill before class to test the new rings I had put in, but that was way before class. Why don't you all come with me? I'll show you the scooter where I left it behind the men's dorm because it's in such bad shape. It would never make it to the 7-Eleven."

We walked over to the rear of the men's dorm, and I mounted the Vespa. As I began to kick the scooter's starter, I stealthily engaged the Vespa's manual choke about fifty percent. The effect of the extra gas was enough to cause the Vespa to sputter, pop, and skip, which appeared to be a minor problem compared to the billowing smoke that poured from underneath the engine skirt once I got it started. The burning oil that I had coated the outside of the engine with had convinced the principal that I had told the truth.

The credibility of my accusers had deteriorated, and I went after Brother Stride-X and Roy Jr. I screamed, "I'm just being persecuted and lied about for trying to help some poor person who's down on his luck! Someone needs personal transportation to get to a job to support his starving family, and y'all are trying to get me into trouble!"

I looked at Principal Allen, and begged, "Sir, please stop this conspiracy to damage the Helping Hands movement! I don't want to go to the Montgomery Junior League and tell them I'm going to have to call off their most newsworthy project."

This statement gave the principal reason to reassess the situation he found him-self in because the president of the Montgomery Junior League, Mrs. Angus Argon, was the wife of the Montgomery Journal publisher. The principal could see the head-lines in his mind's eye, and it was an awful sight: HELPING HANDS FOUNDER PERSECUTED BY WOULD-BE MINISTERS.

Brother Stride-X was starting to fall apart and go into his famous overcome-shaking routine when Roy Jr. grabbed him and told the principal that they must have seen some-one else on a broken-down Vespa who looked like me. Roy Jr. spirited Brother Stride-X around the corner before the principal could respond to their new story. The principal then turned to me and said that I had better watch my step because he was going to keep a close eye on me.

Brother Stride-X was pissed at Roy Jr. for removing him as he was about to expose the Helping Hands Club to the principal for what it was, a scam by the Pecker Devil to help take over the New Roads School by corrupting other students and getting them involved in the bogus club. The Pecker Devil had the students scouring their homes and neighborhoods for items to support their sinful schemes.

"Now, Brother Stride-X, you listen to me," Roy said. "We are not ready to take on the three of them yet. The experience we just went through should be a lesson in what kind of powers we're facing. We need absolute, undeniable proof, or we'll both end up getting thrown out of the New Roads ministerial program. My plan is to continue with the surveillance until the next Alabama National Guard truck comes. Then, I'll talk to the driver and get the scoop on the Helping Hands repair program."

After reviewing the happenings of the last hour with Roy Jr., Brother Stride-X said, "Roy, you're right. It's not time yet, but after we've watched them a little longer, we'll have enough evidence to bring charges then, right?"

I also had learned a lesson from that same encounter, which was that I needed a stronger hand if I were going to survive the rest of the school year, so I made an appointment to see Mrs. Betty Ruth Argon, president of the Montgomery Junior League. Mrs. Argon was very gracious and a befitting example of the organization she represented: rich, white, maternalistic to the poor, and very well organized.

She started the conversation, "Pip! I'm so glad to see you. Your Helping Hands club is changing lives! Those items are going to individuals who are most in need; even the donated rototiller is being loaned to poor people all over Montgomery to till gardens so their families can eat right during the growing season."

"Mrs. Argon, what will these people do the rest of the year for food?" I asked. "Well, Pip," she said, "if they're frugal and work hard at canning, they should be able to store enough food to last for the winter."

I knew this was not the time for a philosophical discussion on the merits of the richest nation in the world providing food to all its citizens for the benefit of the whole society. Instead, I told Mrs. Argon that we were glad to help such a worthwhile organization as the Junior League of Montgomery.

The response I was fishing for was the next statement out of her mouth. She asked, "Pip, would it be alright with you if I ask my husband's paper to do a story on the Helping Hands Club?"

"Ma'am, that sure would be nice," I told her. "But I'll have to ask the other club members before we agree to it. Some of them have the notion that good works should speak for themselves. How about I get back to you before the end of the school year? Then I can let you know if we want the publicity for our club. While I'm asking the other members about that, though, could you do me a favor? Could you call the president of the New Roads School and College and let him know how you feel about the Helping Hands Club? You could also let him know about the favorable publicity the school might receive when I let you know if the club is okay with publishing a story about our work to help the poor."

"Son, that's the least I can do for you fine boys," she said. "I'll be sure to tell the president that he's got one of the finest Christians I've ever known attending his school, a boy who makes good deeds happen."

14. Panama City Beach, Florida

There was an emergency meeting of the New Roads School and College administrative council the day after my chat with Mrs. Argon. The president asked the group if they had any idea what a terrible situation they could be in if the local press began asking questions about the Helping Hands Club and got into other matters about the New Roads School and College. The other two men, the dean and the principal, knew exactly what the president meant: there were some things that outsiders would not exactly understand if they delved into the school's finances and academic-credit-awarding policies. There was nothing necessarily illegal about these things, but they would rather keep these matters to themselves. Someone from the secular world might view them as living very close to the edge of the ethical academic and financial rules of the game that those in the secular world lived by.

The president told the group about his conversation with Mrs. Argon, the wife of the publisher of the Montgomery Journal, and how she loaded praise on the Helping Hands Club and its founder, Pip Cooper. The president said the danger was in the fact that I, a non-believer, had sway over Mrs. Argon. The group knew that most of the five percenters were there because of the tuition they provided the school, and there was always the slim possibility that one of them might be converted to the New Roads faith one day. We had always been viewed as an irritation but not a real threat because the five percenters were being educated in the insulated world of the New Roads School. Now that one of the five percenters might expose the school to the probing of a reporter for one of the most important newspapers in the state was reason for deep concern.

The president suggested to his administrators that they see what they could find out about the Helping Hands Club and its barn repair team, and what was behind the apparent feud with Brothers Stride-X and Roy Jr. The administrators were to report back before the upcoming mid-April spring break. All that the New Roads administrative council knew about the Helping Hands Club was that Professor Snodgrass had endorsed it, a lot of New Roads students would bring junk to school on Monday mornings, and then Pecker, Archie, and I would transfer it to the barn. From there, it would somehow end up in working order at the Junior League's Warehouse for the Poor. The president said it was time for the administrative council to learn the inner workings of the Helping Hands Club, and I knew that could only mean trouble for the Helping Hands cow bowl barn boys.

Our five-percenter information network was burning up the wires with the accounts of numerous five percenters being hauled into the principal's office and quizzed as to the possibilities of what Pecker, Archie, and I were up to with the Helping Hands Club. The principal found out that we were a secretive subset of the larger five-percenter group and that they were as curious as anyone as to what we were up to. As our spies reported in, we were always asked at the end of the conversation what we really were up to, and we would always answer that "we are just trying to find enlightenment, and thus freedom, which is so vital to the human spirit." They all decided to let the mystery be.

We were just three days away from a week's spring break when most of the students went home or off to the New Roads spring spiritual retreat at their summer camp complex, a dreary group of surplus Quonset huts donated by the U.S. Air Force and dragged to a pine forest forty-five miles north of Montgomery. I knew teenagers should engage in recreational pursuits during the spring holidays, and I figured that if my brother and sister were representing our family at the religious retreat, then we would also need a representative of the family at the beach to monitor the secular world's spring break activities. This was the greatest challenge to my wit and cunning that I had ever faced because under no circumstances would my parents let me go to Panama City Beach, Florida, even if I were accompanied by the whole New Roads School. My parents had learned years before that I had a weakened sin immunity system, and it was best to try to steer me clear of places like Panama City Beach.

Not to be overcome by minor obstacles like parental desires, I began planning my unnoticed escape to, and return from, Panama City Beach. That day after lunch in the barn, I proposed my idea of a road trip on the Tiger Daytona 500 to a real spring break that my friends from my old life in public school talked about. My friend Pogey's older brother had told us all about his incredible spring break trip the year before. He told us about the beautiful teenage girls clad in two-piece bathing suits and he and his friends never being questioned about their age at a beach-front Tiki bar where they drank beer with the college kids. Panama City Beach, Florida—it was all I could think about.

Archie said I should count him out because he had to go with his family to visit his grandmother in Georgia, but Pecker had the grin of a Cheshire cat, and I knew he was up for an adventure. With nine days of holiday, I said we should be able to sneak in a quick trip to the beach without anyone being the wiser. What we didn't know was that Brother Roy Harper Jr. started planning our demise the moment these words left my mouth. From his hiding place in the barn, he was about to explode with joy while he listened to our plan for self-destruction.

Pecker and I spent the last days before spring break working out the details of our beach excursion while Roy Jr. listened and planned our capture and expulsion as we refined our trip and cover plan each day. We decided we would leave Montgomery on Saturday morning, but that would require both of us talking our way out of church on Sunday, so we discarded that idea. It seemed prudent that the conditions be optimal since we had about forty hours of motorcycle riding experience between us. This was a concern but not a major one, because we were great believers in the theory of teenage invincibility.

It was about two hundred miles from Montgomery to Panama City Beach, about five hours if we hit no snags in any of the small towns that dotted the two-lane highway from Montgomery to Panama City. If we left in the early morning, we would be able to spend the afternoon roaming the beach, finding some excitement to get into that evening, sleep on the beach, and be back in Montgomery well before dark the next day. We might even be back to our respective homes for supper. All we needed was a story that would cover us while we were gone and that was the easiest part. Our parents were used to their progeny camping out in a safe location for a couple of nights, and we figured what could be a safer story than saying we would camp in the cow bowl at the New Roads School.

Now at home, I spent some time thinking through the most necessary items we needed to take with us to the beach. At least a dozen times throughout the weekend, my mother asked, "Pip, are you absolutely sure you don't want to spend the week at Camp New Roads with your brother, your sister, and all your friends from school? It might be a lot of fun."

"Mama," I said. "you know better than anyone else that my personality and their routines don't mix. I wouldn't fit in well with all the camp's highly structured activities, and besides, I need the downtime to help refresh my alpha brain waves. I really would rather hang out around the house or kill time with Pecker on campus. I might even get some Helping Hands Club repairs done. If the weather's good, we might camp out a night or two during the week."

"Well," she said, "if you boys decide to camp out, make sure to use your brother's sleeping bag. It's warmer than yours."

At that point, I knew she had bought into my scheme without knowing it, and everything was going to fall into place for my grand adventure. What I didn't plan on was a couple of New Roads snitches, Roy Harper Jr. and Brother Stride-X, trying to spoil my holiday at the beach.

Roy Jr. needed his partner to help him pull off the capture of the Pecker Devil. However, his aide-de-camp, Brother Stride-X, was committed to attending the New Roads retreat trip and couldn't get out of it. Roy Jr. was on his own, but he knew what we were going to do, so all he had to do, as he spied on us from the barn loft, was gather more information and nail down our departure day and return time. Then, he'd call in the school authorities to await our return from Panama City Beach, Florida, and enjoy our capture and expulsion.

The weekend began with cloudy weather and building anticipation of our imminent trip. We pulled the Tiger Daytona 500 out on Saturday and Sunday and cranked it and took spins around the cow bowl as Roy watched from his spy's nest in the loft of the barn.

On Monday, we decided that Wednesday would be our departure day and that nine o'clock a.m. would give us time to get free from our parents without creating any unnecessary doubts.

We stuck to our plans for our trip to Panama Beach, Florida. I left home Wednesday morning before my mother went to work. I had my bicycle loaded with camping and some sports equipment and canned food. My mother gave me best wishes for our two-night campout in the cow bowl. She advised me to have a good time and to watch out for snakes, which was good counsel since that snake Roy Harper Jr. was trying to spoil our camping trip to Florida.

Brother Roy had made a strategic mistake that Monday morning listening to us plan our trip because he thought he knew our plan was to leave Thursday and return Fri-day, so he decided to sleep in his bed at the dorm on Wednesday and be well rested for his big day on Friday. We arrived at the cow bowl at nine o'clock Wednesday morning and proceeded to set up our camp in a hollowed-out dense thicket on the far side of the cow bowl. I was lucky to be the son of a meticulous planner who had taught me the necessity of backup plans and redundancy in doing things.

By nine thirty, our campsite was hidden and looked well used with empty food cans and coke bottles spread around. At that very moment, Roy was resting in his bed like a man who had been sleeping uncomfortably in a barn loft for weeks. By nine forty-five, we were leaving the Montgomery city limits on our Triumph Tiger Daytona 500 carrying two sleeping bags and thirty dollars in cash money.

The trip to Florida was the road trip that all others would be measured against for the rest of my life. We were free on a magnificent spring day, headed south through sleepy Southern towns with the wind in our hair and the excitement of adventure boiling in our veins. We arrived in Panama City Beach at three thirty and found the beach hangout that was most popular with the teenage crowd. We met pretty girls and totally dumbfounded males who couldn't believe what we had done to get there. We were elevated to hero status that afternoon and evening for our daring and insane trip to the spring break Teen Mecca of our time and place. We each had a beer, but it tasted so vile we just pretended to drink it. We were pursued by adolescent girls who thought our unapproved and unsupervised adventure was so cool, and a couple of the girls taught Pecker and me what heavy petting was all about. We were doing things that we had only dreamed about, we were tasting the fruits of the secular world, and we loved it. If we had faced a firing squad when we got back to Montgomery, it would have been worth it; this was the best day of my life, and I was ready and willing to pay the piper if we had gotten caught.

Roy awoke at eleven thirty that Wednesday of our departure and made a quick dash for his hiding spot in the loft of the barn to see if he could get any last-minute in-formation on what he thought would be our last prank at the New Roads School. He crept quietly into his hiding place and stayed until dark, but we never showed up, so he went back to his room to think about the sweet victory that was to be his soon. Roy slept well and was in his hiding place at six o'clock the next morning waiting for our expected departure at nine o'clock.

By noon, Roy began to worry that we had canceled our trip, so he went to check on the Tiger Daytona 500 and to his surprise found it missing. Roy realized right away that he had blown it because we must have left the day before while he slept the morning away. He was furious with himself for not keeping his watch on the barn, but he knew he could still ensure our capture by getting a New Roads official down to the barn for our return that afternoon. What Roy hadn't thought about was the fact that the entire administrative council was up at the New Roads Camp for the retreat and the only official left behind on campus was Professor Ronald T. Snodgrass.

Roy ran to the professor's house and beat on the door until the timid professor opened it. Roy Jr. was wild-eyed and in a high state of agitation and demanded that the New Roads Professor of Religion rush up to the New Roads Camp and bring the president, the dean, and the principal back right away. He said that time was of the essence if they were going to catch the Pecker Devil and save the school.

The professor was not real keen on being drawn back into Roy's delusions again and said, "Roy, the retreat will be over tomorrow morning and then you can see the members of the administrative council when they return on their own to campus."

Roy was not about to let weeks of work and dozens of sleepless nights in the barn go down the tube because the wimp professor would not go get the school authorities, so he announced, "Professor Snodgrass if you don't go and get the members of the administrative council right now you will force me to be the Lord's avenger and the blood will be on your hands."

This threatening attitude scared the Hell out of the professor. He knew he would have to deal with Roy's request before he got completely out of hand and hurt someone. He got Roy to give him the complete story of our plan to go to the Sodom and Gomorrah of the secular world, Panama City Beach, Florida.

The professor couldn't decide if Roy Jr. was telling the story of what we had actually done or if he was hearing Roy Jr.'s created fantasy. Roy insisted the professor leave right away because it was already one o'clock, and he was sure that we would be back before dark. The professor left for the New Roads Camp with a heavy heart be-cause he suspected that Roy had been repossessed by the Devil.

At midnight in Panama City Beach, we ran out of energy and found a beach dune that was hidden from the road where we unrolled our sleeping bags and slept the sleep of the greatest adventurers of all times. We were awakened at sunrise and decided it was time to return and savor the memories of our day at the beach in the comfort and safety of not getting caught. We arrived silently at the top of the hill above the barn and saw a distraught Roy Harper Jr. in the barn. Five minutes later we watched a red-faced Roy Jr. run up the hill at two minutes past noon.

We had cut the engine to make our survey of the situation as was our habit and a damn good one as it turned out. I knew Roy Jr. was on to us by that insane look he had on his face and his manic movements around the barn. I knew we had to move fast if we were to escape the fate he had in store for us. We quickly rolled the Tiger Daytona 500 down to the barn, and I sent Pecker to the creek to get two buckets of water while I looked for the kerosene that was kept in the barn.

When Pecker returned with the water, I cooled the Tiger 500 down with the creek water by pouring it slowly over the engine and drivetrain. Then, I poured two quarts of kerosene in the gas tank. We then wiped up any water that hadn't evaporated and put the motorcycle back in the barn but in a different corner than before and covered it with a tarp. After all that, we returned to our campsite to watch for the fireworks that were sure to follow. At ten minutes after noon, we watched Roy return to the barn and disappear inside.

About every twenty minutes, Roy would make a sentry's round of the outside of the barn trying not to be seen. At three o'clock, we saw the big three New Roads administrators—the president, the principal, and the dean—with Professor Snodgrass, descending the hill toward the barn.

We couldn't hear what was being said when Roy Jr. ran out in front of the barn to greet the four men, but we could see that he was very animated. He showed them the hinged door that we had made for the Tiger Daytona 500 and pointed to the empty space where the motorcycle had lived since January. I told Pecker that we should give them about ten minutes more and then we would break into the field next to the barn, throwing the football we had brought with us. We followed our plan and after two minutes of simulated play, we were intercepted by the principal and told to come to the barn. Roy Jr. was laughing like a madman when we entered the barn and said, "You demons are caught and the best thing you can do is confess and take your punishment for lying, stealing a motorcycle, driving without a license, and going to the spring break sin capitol of the South—Panama City Beach, Florida."

"Boys, have the two of you been to Panama City Beach, Florida, anytime this week?" the president asked.

I looked at him with total astonishment on my face, and Pecker said, "No, sir, that's a lie. How could we be in Florida if we just this morning returned from New York City because we couldn't get a direct flight from Paris to Montgomery?"

The president was not amused. "Pecker, just give me the facts or shut up!" "Sir, how are we supposed to respond to an allegation of such incredible proportions? It's outrageous to think we did that! You're assuming that two teenagers who have been around campus all week went two hundred miles away to Panama City Beach. It's preposterous!" I said.

"I know how it happened," Roy Jr. broke in, "and I can show you all exactly how they did it."

He began throwing broken Helping Hands articles in all directions as he frantically searched for the Tiger Daytona 500. "Sir! They just returned on a perfectly good motorcycle! That motorcycle is the whole reason for the Helping Hands Club sham!" Roy hurled power equipment and appliances out of his way until he spotted the Tiger Daytona 500 hidden under the tarp in the corner. He pushed our motorcycle into the middle of the assembled crowd and crowed, "Now you can see it! You can't be deceived by the Pecker Devil anymore!" He pointed to the Tiger Daytona 500 and said, "There's the proof of their duplicity; it's the sole reason the Helping Hands Club exists!" Then Pecker said, "Professor, I hope you're proficient in the use of electroshock therapy, because Roy is well beyond the reach and limits of any New Roads exorcism treatment."

The president was beyond his tolerance limit of any smart-ass students, and told Pecker, "Boy, you need to shut the fuck up, or I'll turn Roy loose on you!"

This outburst caused a temporary silence from Pecker's corner of the room. The president regained his composure and asked me, "Pip, what do you know about the motorcycle standing here before us?"

"Well, sir," I explained, "it was Jim Bob Brewer's, but it's been destroyed by Brother Roy's sneaking out on it at night. He's been going to the Spur nightclub, and we're merely storing it for him. We're hopeful that Jim Bob will donate the motorcycle to our Helping Hands Club. If he does, some poor person in Montgomery will have transportation once we've repaired all the damage that Roy Jr. has done to it on his sin-filled late-night forays."

Roy Jr. started drooling and cursing. He mumbled, "I've never ridden a motor-cycle in my life! As a matter of fact, I've never even been in a nightclub and never intend to go to one."

Then, he turned the conversation back toward us and said, "These guys are lying about the motorcycle being broken because they've just returned from a four-hundred-mile journey on it."

"If the cycle was driven that far recently," I proposed, "then the engine will still be warm."

I then reached down and felt the engine. Then I looked at the president and said, "Sir, this thing is stone cold."

"That's a lie!" Roy shouted. He felt the engine himself and visibly sagged. "This cold engine is a trick of the Pecker Devil."

"How about this?" I offered. "I'll crank the Tiger Daytona 500 and show you all that it's not roadworthy."

I mounted and kicked the starter of the big British bike, which roared to life.

I explained to the president, "You see, sir, this bike has a blown head. As soon as the engine warms, I think you'll be able to evaluate Roy's story for yourself."

After about one minute, the kerosene hit the engine, and a knocking and clatter began. Black smoke started pouring out the tailpipes. Over the sounds coming from the bike, I yelled to the president, "Sir, do you want me to destroy the engine totally, or I should shut it down?"

The president turned to Roy Jr. "Roy, just how do you explain the fact that this inoperable motorcycle could make a journey of four hundred miles?"

"Sir, this was just more of the Pecker Devil tricks," Roy told him. "They can't prove where they were last night."

I piped up and said, "Actually, we can. We camped out in the cow bowl last night, with our parents' permission, but nobody saw us."

"This can't be," Roy said to the president, "because there's no tent in the cow bowl."

"Would you all at least follow us and see?" I asked the group. Then I led them out to our hidden campsite, littered with the teenage camping artifacts that we had scattered about the day before. The president looked sheepish for having accused us of such an outrageous story and apologized to us for believing the ravings of a student who was known to be unbalanced.

Roy Jr., after seeing our campsite evidence, was starting to make a gurgling sound and fell to his knees. He began to pray in unintelligible words.

Pecker looked at the president and asked, "Sir, has the New Roads faith begun teaching their ministers to speak in tongues, or is Brother Roy just a closet Pentecostal?"

The president didn't answer Pecker, but he did turn to look at Professor Snodgrass.

"Professor, you had better figure out how to cure this son of the largest contributor, or you will be looking for a new job at the end of the semester."

The professor took Roy to his room where Roy stayed under his sheets without moving for the rest of the weekend.

15. The Devil Is Loose on Campus

Close calls have a way of clearing one's mind and illuminating the dangers that await you, and we were sure that we had two preachers-in-training after us. We knew that Roy's bedridden disability would be temporary, that Brother Stride-X would rejoin Roy's quest, and most importantly, that the administrative council was going to continue to dig into our Helping Hands venture until they got the real story. Who we didn't count amongst our enemies was Professor Ronald T. Snodgrass, whose life had been turned upside down and was now facing the possibility of losing his job and career. He was particularly upset with me for getting him involved as the sponsor of the Helping Hands Club, which he now believed to be a diversion tactic by the Devil and, perhaps, his helper the Pecker Devil.

Another enemy who was having to meet with Professor Snodgrass on a weekly basis was Brother Calvin Walker, a sergeant working for the Montgomery City Police Department. Calvin thought that the Devil had invaded my body by using Yankee preachers, Negroes, and the Christ-killing Jewish conspirators who lived next door to me to turn me against my race and my Southern heritage. Brother Calvin mentioned to the professor that my parents—my labor unionist father in particular—had some radical ideas about giving Negroes full freedoms, but he was sure that my troublemaking was the effect of growing up so close to that liberal, Yankee, Jew neighbor of mine.

In the process of trying to rid Brother Calvin of his Catholic and Buddhist influences, the professor recognized that Calvin had no knowledge of these religions but did possess rather strong views about Negroes, Jews, and Communists. Brother Calvin was sure that both former groups were aligned with the latter. He figured Mr. and Mrs. Katz were probably sent here from Moscow to establish an ideological beachhead by fomenting strife in the only true Bible church and school in Montgomery. Once they had a hold over us, he reasoned, the Baptists, Methodists, and the rest of the well-meaning, but theologically wrong, would follow and bring the tide of race mixing and Armageddon down on the Christians of Montgomery.

What Calvin didn't know, or want to know, was that Mr. Katz's family had lived, and been discriminated against, in Alabama for six generations, and his wife was from that breeding ground of working-class revolutionaries, Scarsdale, New York, one of the wealthiest small towns in America, just a short train ride from New York City.

The pastoral counseling sessions with Brother Calvin got reversed after the spring break trouble with Roy Jr. at the barn. Calvin was now advising Professor Snodgrass. "Calvin," the professor said, "I'm actually scared that I'm going to lose my job!

I just know that Roy Jr. is going to make one more attempt to get the Pecker Devil and his friends before the school year ends. The only ending I can see from that situation is Roy ending up in the state mental hospital, and I'll be in the unemployment line!"

Brother Calvin then said, "Well, sir, I've got a score to settle with that scoundrel Pip. In addition to that, I think I can help see that justice is done, that Brother Roy stays out of trouble, and there's even a very good chance that you might get to keep your job."

The professor saw the first ray of hope in his very dark outlook of his future. He was lost in thought for a bit, thinking back on all that had gone on during the school year, how he had been hoodwinked into becoming a dupe in my Helping Hands Club, and had become known as an exorcist to boot because of my pranks.

After a weekend under his bed covers, Roy Jr. emerged with renewed energy and determination to catch us for a serious rule violation within the next three weeks before the semester ended and the summer break began. After trying unsuccessfully to talk to Roy during his under-the-sheets weekend hibernation, Brother Stride-X had begun to have doubts about throwing his career away by following the advice of a lunatic just weeks before graduation.

Roy Jr. was very persuasive after he left his bed and returned to his vengeance planning. He proposed a new plan to get even before the summer recess. Brother Stride-X told Roy that he would help with the watching duties but would do nothing else. What Roy Jr. didn't know was that the president had set up his own surveillance team to monitor our activities and was getting daily reports on our attendance in class and time spent in the barn. The principal and the dean were not as clever as Roy Jr. in their spying because we were on to their game the first day back at school.

We knew we were being watched in the barn and monitored on our attendance in classes, so we changed our ways for the benefit of our audience. We made every class and actually worked on our Helping Hands gifts at noon and after school. We had drained the tainted gas from the tank of the Tiger Daytona 500, and it was back in fine running condition, but we knew better than to attempt an adventure until the summer break had begun. What the spies didn't know was that we had begun to sneak into the barn to watch the watchers and that was very fortuitous because I was hidden in the loft one warm day in May when the dean, Roy, and the suspended song leader, Officer Calvin Walker, discovered each other waiting on us to screw up and get caught.

After their initial shock at finding each other spying on us, the three watchers agreed to share the duties, and Roy Jr. let it be known that he had been watching us for months prior to his bedridden experience of the week before. He explained that the National Guard was picking up the broken Helping Hands donations and he felt that this was where our vulnerability was and that if they could find the National Guard unit in town that was picking up the broken items, then they would have the evidence to prove our duplicity.

The dean was the only one of the three who understood the potential disaster that exposure of the Helping Hands Club could bring on the school and agreed to go along with the plan if it were left up to the president to make the final decision about what should be done if there were any improper activities. The other two agreed to this stipulation and they set up a monitoring schedule as I listened from the loft.

I slipped out of the loft and went to find Archie and Pecker for a council of war. The spring holidays had brought an inordinate amount of motorized and electric junk, and we knew we were going to need a National Guard pickup soon or we'd find our-selves overrun with charitable items. Our power base was making sure that Mrs. Argon had fresh supplies for her Junior League Warehouse for the Poor. This was another reason, besides the Tiger Daytona 500, that we could not shut down our Helping Hands program. We had to risk a pickup, and we decided that it had to be on Roy's watching shift because he was the only one who didn't have a car and would be the least likely to follow the National

Guard truck. When I went to the armory to fetch the soldiers with the removal truck, I alerted the sergeant who drove the truck that we might en-counter a very disturbed student who had been exorcised twice but still had enough

Demonic Possession in him to try to disrupt our good deeds, and it would be best not to speak to him if he approached us.

When we arrived to start loading the broken items, Roy Jr. appeared out of his hiding place wild with excitement. He asked the sergeant for his unit's name and location, at which point the sergeant gave Roy Jr. a knowing look and kept loading his truck. Roy was not accustomed to the working class not giving the son of the most powerful man in Opp an answer and asked if he was a deaf and dumb son of a bitch. That was all the silence the sergeant could give, and he told Roy Jr. that he would beat his Devil-infested ass to a bloody pulp if he said one more word. Roy Jr. considered his position and backed off to the other end of the barn knowing that the truck would be gone before he could get help from the dean.

After they finished their loading and the sergeant left, Roy Jr. ran out of the barn, opened our hinged wall, jumped on the Tiger Daytona 500, fired up the engine, and was gone before I could stop him. As he sped through the campus, the dean, the president, and the principal were walking out of the administration building. The dean said that he had best go see what was going on at the barn and found me pondering what had just happened. He asked me, "Pip, was that Roy riding off on that motorcycle that was in the barn?" I told him that Jim Bob had decided to sell the Tiger Daytona 500 to Roy after Archie had replaced the head, but that Jim Bob was supposed to make a cash donation to the Helping Hands Club for our efforts.

This seemed to mollify the dean, but it was also a cause of worry for him for crazy Roy Jr. to be piloting a motorcycle, but he reasoned that Roy Jr. was an adult and there was no rule against his buying a motorcycle. The dean also realized the upside to this situation: it would keep a functional motorcycle out of the hands of Archie, Pecker, and me.

When Roy returned from his short journey of discovery, he parked the Tiger Daytona 500 behind the men's dorm, took the padlock off his footlocker, grabbed a section of chain off an old swing set on the playground, and padlocked our bike to the water spigot. He then charged over to the dean's office to tell him that the armory they were searching for was a mere six blocks away, and they could go right now and expose the whole mess. Roy Jr. was irate when the dean said that he would have to bring this up before the administrative council the next day. The dean did, however, congratulate Roy Jr. on getting the Tiger Daytona 500 out of our hands because we might have been tempted to make use of it. Roy Jr. couldn't believe what he was hearing—that the dean approved of his stealing our motorcycle to keep us out of trouble. This made Roy wonder if he had done the right thing because the last thing he wanted was for us not to get into trouble.

The next morning, the dean told the president and the principal what Roy had found out about the National Guard pickup of the still broken items that the student body collected for the Helping Hands Club and the subsequent delivery to the National Guard armory down the street. The president said that they would have to proceed carefully if they were going to catch us in a lie and remove us from the school without causing any backlash from Mrs. Argon. He said he would go and have a talk with the commanding officer and see if he could get some incriminating evidence that would get the school off the hook with Mrs. Argon. The president had no idea how tangled a web we had woven with the Helping Hands Club.

When the president arrived at the armory, he was shown into Major Collins's office, and they exchanged pleasantries. The president spoke first and asked, "Major, can you tell me what the relationship is between the Helping Hands Club and the National Guard?"

The major didn't know why the president was there, but he knew that it was a threat to his job if his superiors found out that his men spent eighty percent of their time repairing broken machines and appliances for the Montgomery Junior League.

"My men donate a small amount of their personal time picking up and delivering used items from the Helping Hands Club to the Montgomery Junior League's Ware-house for the Poor," said Major Collins.

The president was enraged that he was being lied to. He told the major, "Don't lie to me like that! If you fear for your soul at all, you should tell me the truth because I'm standing before you right now as one of God's representatives on earth!"

The arrogance of this pretentious hick preacher coming to his armory and making demands infuriated the major, who replied, "I'm not about to be abused by a skinny, pompous, shithead like you in my own office! My soul is in fine shape; I go to mass and confession every week! You are the one who should be worried about his soul. In case you didn't know, my sergeant was informed that one of the New Roads School's students has been exorcised on multiple occasions and that the Devil is loose on your campus over there."

The president turned as white as a sheet when he found out that this Army major and Catholic had knowledge of the New Roads experimental exorcism. He explained, "Major, I don't know what you heard, but the New Roads faith does not practice Catholic rituals. However, we are fighting one case of Demonic Possession with a delivering ministry method developed by our New Roads Senior Professor of Religion, Dr. Ronald T. Snodgrass."

That's when the major knew he had the president hemmed in. He said, "A goat by any other name is still a goat. I don't think you'd like for my friend, Mrs. Argon, to tell her husband, the publisher of the Montgomery Journal, that Satan is on the loose on the New Roads campus."

The president recognized that he had lost. "Major Collins, I think that whatever secrets we know about the other we should keep to ourselves," he said. He left the armory in a hurry.

There was an emergency meeting of the administrative council that afternoon to figure out what to do to keep the pot from boiling all over them. The president made a decision. "Gentlemen, I think the thing to do is to keep a lid on everything for the next few weeks until summer break begins. By then, everything will blow over. It will be natural for the Helping Hands Club to cease operations for the summer, and I'll see to it that it doesn't restart in the fall.

"The greatest danger," he continued, "is Roy Harper Jr. We need to forget about those three main troublemakers and concentrate on keeping Roy in line until the end of the semester. Roy doesn't have enough time to get his grades up enough to pass, which means he'll flunk out of school and won't return in the fall to stir up any more trouble. I'm sure his father would love for him to transfer to his alma mater, The University of Alabama. Dr. Leatherbury, since you are the dean, I need you to instruct Professor Snodgrass to take responsibility for Roy Jr. and make sure he stays out of trouble until exams are over."

We had our own emergency meeting that day to talk about what we should do between now and the end of the school year. Pecker looked at Archie and me. He said,

"I think we should all agree that we need to keep a close eye on Roy and plan a fitting send-off for his summer vacation."

"We should really try to stay out of the administrators' hair," I said, "because they're just doing their jobs trying to mesh two incompatible groups into one institution. How about this? I'll figure out a way to involve Roy Jr. and Brother Calvin in a little adventure that will stimulate them both."

Pecker and Archie thought this was a great idea. We decided to leave the Tiger Daytona 500 chained behind the dorm for the time being. We had a growing acceptance of the idea that we would probably lose our wheels of freedom now that our barn operation was being investigated. In less than three weeks, we would be free for the summer, but some debts had to be collected if we were to feel that the scales of justice were back in their even position.

16. The Spur Nightclub

With knowledge of the ongoing surveillance, we knew it was time to feed our spies some disinformation, as one was always hiding out in the barn every day trying to find out what new devilment plans we had. The dean had instructed Brother Roy to give up on trying to catch us and instead pay attention to his studies because exams were right around the corner. The dean's dropping out of their task force made the job of watching the barn much harder because Brother Calvin had to work, and Brother Stride-X was determined to go to class, study for his exams, and not to get too deeply involved with any more of Roy Jr.'s schemes to catch us up to no good. Little did these idiots know that every word we uttered in the barn after we found out we were being watched was for the purpose of disinformation because we were watching them a Hell of a lot closer than they were watching us.

As the weeks wore on toward summer break, we talked very loudly in the barn about a guy we knew named Pogey who would sell us a complete set of fake IDs so we could go drinking at the Spur Club on Highland Avenue, just four blocks from the New Roads School. I actually did know a boy named Pogey, who went to Lanier High School, and could, for the sum of twenty-five dollars, procure for us a set of five fake and stolen documents that would list anyone's age as twenty-one. So, we anted up the twenty-five dollars, cut four pictures of Brother Roy out of the library's copies of the New Roads School and College yearbooks and ordered a complete set of fake IDs for Roy Harper Jr., who was actually only twenty years of age.

Pogey did great work on his fake IDs for Roy. He included a replica of an Iowa driver's license, a stolen National Guard ID card, a Montgomery cabbie's license, a verified birth certificate filched from a stack of forms at the state Bureau of Vital Statistics when the clerk was distracted, and a simple card Pogey had produced by a local print shop that proclaimed itself to be an Official ID Card. All these items were registered with Roy Harper Jr.'s name and showing him as aged twenty-one. We found an old wallet to put these IDs in and included two Trojan rubbers that we purchased in the Billups service station bathroom along with a business card I had swiped from my father's desk of a man who worked for the NAACP. On the back of the business card I wrote, "Roy, we are so glad you have decided to join the struggle, call me as soon as you have any information on the Montgomery Police Department."

The week before exams, we made sure one of our watchers was on duty and hid-den in the barn before we began to discuss our fictionalized trip the previous weekend to the Spur Club. We bragged about how well our fake IDs had worked and our plans to return the following Saturday night for another visit. Roy was beside himself with joy when he heard what we had done and what we were going to do the next weekend. When he called a meeting with Brother Stride-X and Officer Calvin Walker for the next day, they all knew that they finally had us in the best situation they could think of: not only would we be thrown out of school, but Officer Calvin Walker assured them that we would be arrested for drinking under age, that we would be charged and booked, and be in deep trouble with our parents and the New Roads School. Calvin said that they needed to tighten the security of the barn to try to get our exact time of arrival at the Spur Club so he could be there to arrest us.

The Spur Club was noted for its lax attitude toward enforcing the drinking age requirements and the bar fights that seemed to break out on a regular basis. The Club was a concrete block building with a glass front door and a large plate glass window that were both painted black to keep its secrets locked away from the view of outsiders. Inside, there was a large bar and booths along the walls were surrounded with cloth curtains to let customers drink in privacy. There was a pool table in the middle of the open area and a juke box against the wall. In the back, there were two restrooms with a rear exit door in between, left unlocked for patrons who did not wish to be seen entering from the street side.

The Friday before exams we had several things to accomplish. We had to get Jim Bob in on our plan, we had to find a pair of wire cutters and a motorcycle helmet with a dark screen visor, and we had to detail our next evening's trip to the Spur Club while Roy was hiding and listening in the barn.

We told Jim Bob that we had a strategy to make Roy pay for the damage he had done to his old motorcycle and that our plan was of no risk to him. All he had to say was that he sold the motorcycle to Roy and that was all he knew about it. After we started explaining our intentions, Jim Bob decided he didn't want to know any more about it but would do his part as requested. When I added that a helmet with a dark visor would also be helpful, he said that he would give us his old helmet, which just happened to have a very dark plastic wind screen that snapped onto the front. The last task was accomplished that morning when I snuck into Roy's room and removed a heavy wool coat that he had worn almost every cold day that year.

When we were sure that Roy was hidden away in the barn, we entered and described our plan to meet at Archie's house the following evening at seven o'clock. We would tell his mother we were going to the outdoor basketball court at the school to shoot a few baskets and that we would then actually go over to the basketball courts before we went to the Spur Club for a few beers.

Even Roy could use that information to figure our arrival at the Spur Club would be between seven thirty and nine o'clock. Roy informed Officer Calvin Walker and Brother Stride-X of our plans, but Brother Stride-X was getting cold feet with just a week to go before graduation. His past experience of getting involved with us and Brother Roy's attempts to catch us persuaded him to study that Saturday night and forget he had ever heard of the Pecker Devil.

Meanwhile, Officer Calvin and Roy were hashing out the final details of the ambush.

"Roy, I can be at the Spur Club," Officer Calvin said, "but you and I have to get our plan down so that those Devils don't slip through our net again! I can wait outside the front of the Spur Club in an unmarked police cruiser with my partner if you can wait inside in case they enter from the rear. Then, I'll tell my partner that I've heard about very young teens being seen drinking in the Spur Club. I should be able to talk him into a stakeout between seven and nine o'clock. Now, Roy, you'll walk out front to signal us after you're sure they've been served. That's when my partner and I will bust in and nab them!"

"We're finally going to get 'em!" Roy exclaimed. He was so excited that he barely slept that Friday night.

Roy couldn't wait for the Pecker Devil and his friends to be locked up and thrown out of the New Roads School. He'd be a prize student and get his normal life back just in time to graduate with his class, once the administrative council realized he had saved the college from the Pecker Devil.

We met at Archie's on Saturday at seven o'clock, grabbed a pair of wire cutters from his father's tool shed, and headed for the school. Archie freed the Tiger Daytona 500 from the water pipe and fired it up while I donned heavy gloves, the helmet with the dark visor, and Roy Jr.'s wool coat with the wallet we had put together in one of the front pockets. The three of us loaded on our motorcycle for one last trip and took the back streets to a location about half a block from the Spur Club. We dismounted and went to a nearby pay phone where we called the Montgomery Police Department and reported a break-in at a watch repair shop two blocks from where we stood.

Within three minutes, Officer Calvin Walker and his partner took off in their car to check out the alleged burglary. I jumped on the Tiger Daytona 500, fired the engine, and headed for the Spur Club's glass front door as Archie and Pecker ran to the back door. I hit the glass door at about ten miles an hour and came crashing into the middle of the main room as patrons dived over the bar and under the pool table and looked out from behind the booths' curtains. I put the bike on its side in front of the pool table and headed for the back door, pulling Roy's stolen coat off as I ran for the rear exit just as Roy Jr. came out of the bathroom.

Roy Jr. was right behind me as I made my way across the darkened back parking lot where Archie and Pecker waited. I threw the helmet at Roy Jr. striking his leg and he went down on the grass holding his knee and screaming about the Pecker Devil as we disappeared into a thick hedge. Within seconds, ten people were surrounding Roy Jr. as Officer Calvin Walker and his partner entered through the smashed front door and worked their way to the back parking lot. The bartender had already picked up Roy's coat and was going through his wallet when the officers escorted Roy Jr. back inside the bar.

Roy Jr. was asked for his driver's license by Calvin's partner as Calvin watched the whole scene in disbelief.

The bartender called to the patrolman as he was looking at Roy's Alabama driver's license, he was holding up another wallet and the discarded coat I had taken from Roy's dorm room and said the motorcycle driver had left it behind.

When Calvin's partner looked at both wallets, he realized that Roy Jr. was not only a reckless twenty-year-old motorcycle driver but also the possessor of a wallet full of fake IDs that said he was from Iowa, belonged to the Alabama National Guard, was a cab driver in Montgomery, and was twenty-one years of age.

Calvin finally came back to a conscious state and demanded to see the two wallets. Then, he found the NAACP card with the note on the back and realized he had been duped by Roy Jr. to embarrass himself and the Montgomery Police Department. Calvin slipped the NAACP card in his pocket.

He turned to his partner and the hobbling Roy, and said, "Cuff him, and then take him downtown to lockup. I don't want to see him again."

Roy Jr. couldn't believe his friend was arresting him. "It was the Pecker Devil who did all this!" Then he bellowed, "I don't even own a motorcycle! I've only ridden one once in my whole life!"

Calvin's partner spoke up, "Well, that's believable just from the way you entered the bar." Then, he picked up the bar's phone and called the police department to verify the motorcycle's registration. He hung up the phone and asked Roy Jr., "Son, I've got just one question for you. Why do you own a motorcycle that you don't know how to ride?"

"Sir, this motorcycle is under the influence of the Pecker Devil," Roy said. "And now I know that he's out to take over the entire City of Montgomery. Calvin! Officer Calvin! Why have you forsaken me for the Pecker Devil?"

Roy Jr. was taken to the psychiatric ward of St. Margaret's Hospital instead of the city jail because he began to moan and wail and he was from a very prominent family. Calvin decided that he could extricate himself from this situation with more ease if he treated Roy as a lunatic whose accusations should be disregarded. Calvin explained to his partner, "Let's see if we can go easy on him this time. I know this kid from my church. He's not a bad kid, but he's had a previous history of mental illness. It might be best if we take him to the hospital's psycho ward and call his pastoral counselor, Dr. Ronald T. Snodgrass, in on the case."

The officers escorted Roy to his padded room at the hospital and Calvin agreed to stay with Roy Jr. while his partner went to fill out the paperwork. When they were alone, Brother Calvin flew into a rage. "Roy, you are a spy working for the NAACP so you can bring the feds down on me and my police brothers!"

Roy Jr. was awestruck at this accusation and said, "I have never even met or been within five hundred yards of anyone from the NAACP!"

Calvin was pissed and showed Roy Jr. the card he had pulled from his fake wallet. "Is that so, Roy? Because I've got the proof right here."

The cursing preacher-to-be from Opp then said, "You are an ignorant son of a bitch who fell for another Pecker Devil trick! All you have to do is call the number on the card and ask the guy if he knows anyone named Roy Harper Jr."

After being gone for a few minutes, Calvin came back to the padded room. "I've checked out your story with the NAACP bastard," he said. "He denied knowing you, just like you said. So, I called Professor Snodgrass to get you out of the hospital."

Calvin had also talked to the bar owner who said he would not press charges if Roy would pay for the damage, and they had agreed that he could keep the Tiger Daytona 500 in lieu of cash. The only snag was that his partner had already filed charges on the fake IDs and Roy Jr. would have to go before a city judge now that it was on record.

Another complication was that Roy had a forged Alabama National Guard ID, and his case would have to go before the U.S. Attorney who was appointed by that damned Catholic, President John Kennedy. Calvin told Roy he could help with the city judge, but the feds could be big trouble because he had absolutely no influence with the son of a bitch who was the U.S. Attorney, Ira McDuffy.

When Professor Snodgrass arrived at the hospital and went to Roy's room, he was livid about Roy Jr. getting in trouble again. The professor spoke up and asked Brother Calvin, "Were you overtaken by one of your other religious personalities again? I can't understand why you didn't just bring Roy Jr. back to the New Roads School instead of arresting him and exposing the school to a potential avalanche of bad publicity. Calvin, you're an idiot. I might even lose my job over this fiasco you have created."

Poor Calvin didn't want to admit that he had been pulled into another swamp of deceit. "Professor," Calvin said, "there wasn't anything I could do after my partner had seen the false ID evidence."

Roy Jr. interrupted. He said, "I've never seen those IDs before! I was inside the Spur Club when the motorcycle came crashing through. I know it was the Pecker Devil Pack that pulled this stunt!"

"What in the name of Jesus were you doing in that den of iniquity, Roy?" the professor asked.

"Well, sir," Roy recounted, "I've been spying on the three trouble-makers in the barn and I was in the Spur Club to make sure they were served alcohol before I signaled Brother Walker to make the arrest. My plan was to rid the school of the Pecker Devil and his friends forever. Now, I've finally realized that I'm outmatched. If I ever get out of this mess, sir, I will never cross the Pecker Devil and his friends again."

Professor Snodgrass ordered Brother Calvin to pull every string he had with the local authorities to have any charges withdrawn and that he would go and see the U.S. Attorney to see if he would drop the federal charges against Roy Jr.

Roy began to cry and said if this is what the life of a New Roads minister was all about, he would rather rethink his options and perhaps accept his uncle's offer to manage the Opp Furniture Warehouse. However, this was not going to be Roy Jr.'s option for his near future because this was 1963 and there was a little war heating up in Southeast Asia that needed some draft-age young men for the war machine.

Officer Calvin Walker pulled his strings, and all local charges were dropped. The professor went to see the U.S. Attorney, Ira D. McDuffy, an Irish Catholic Kennedy supporter who was very understanding of boyish pranks and the desire to drink before reaching the age of twenty-one. Ira was known to believe that a boy who was old enough to die for his country should be old enough to vote and get drunk if that was his desire. The professor asked the U.S. Attorney, "What do you intend to do about my student, Roy Harper Jr., sir?"

"My intentions are to do absolutely nothing," Ira said. "I was known to take a drink when I was Roy's age, and I think the federal government would do better to spend the taxpayers' money rounding up and convicting Klansmen and their front men in the White Citizens' Council."

This was not the answer Professor Snodgrass was looking for because he had come to work out an agreement to rid himself of Roy Jr. by getting the U.S. Attorney to pressure Roy to join the Army. Professor Snodgrass had already told Roy Jr. that he might possibly be spending the next ten years in the Leavenworth Federal Penitentiary for forging a military ID. The professor needed Roy out of his life right away before the president found out what kind of trouble Roy Jr. had gotten himself into this time. He wanted to make certain to keep his job.

Roy's running off and joining the Army was the perfect answer, but he needed this Catholic federal official to give Roy the push to join up.

The professor changed his tack with Ira. He asked, "Sir, are you aware of the clinical term, adjustment reaction to adolescence?"

The U.S. Attorney said, "No, I'll admit that I'm unfamiliar with that."

"Roy Harper Jr. is a good kid, but he is suffering from the worst case I've ever seen! This fake ID problem is just the beginning," said the professor, "and I'm sure that unless he gets some strong discipline in his life, he'll be up before the bench of justice again soon."

The U.S. Attorney told the professor, "I don't know much about this psychology stuff, but I'd hate to see a good boy go bad. But I don't see how I can help in providing any discipline for this boy I don't even know, one who's barely brushed the wrong side of the law. What do you expect me to do?"

The professor said, "You could do this boy a great service and help your country at the same time. All we need you to do is concur with my clinical opinion that Roy Jr. should sign up for the Army this afternoon."

Ira said, "I was in the Army, and it did me a world of good. I think every young man could benefit from military service as long as he protects himself in the whore-houses that surround most of the Army bases."

After Roy Jr.'s release from the hospital, he took to his bed and was under the sheets when the professor returned from seeing the U.S. Attorney.

The professor said, "Roy, come on out from under the sheets. You need to accept your fate like a man."

At this point, Roy Jr. pulled down the sheets and asked, "What exactly is my fate, Professor?"

The professor began his big lie. He said, "Roy, I've been able to work out a favorable deal with the U.S. Attorney whereby you will not have to spend ten years doing hard labor in a federal penitentiary. All you have to do is join the U.S. Army for two years. Roy, you'll be paid, get to see the world, learn responsibility, and meet all kinds of nice young people who you can convert to the New Roads faith."

"But, Professor!" Roy protested. "I'm innocent of any charges against me. I don't see why I should have to join the Army! I'm calling my father!"

"Roy, keeping Judge Roy Harper Sr. out of the deal I made with the U.S. Attorney was part of the bargain," the professor said, "and if that forgery of a U. S. Army ID hits the press, you could be charged with treason and might get life in prison without parole because we'll be dealing with Catholic-appointed federal judges."

In the end, Roy Jr. got dressed and accepted his fate. Professor Snodgrass drove him to the recruiting station that afternoon, and he joined the U.S. Army.

When Roy called his father to tell him he had enlisted, the judge was ecstatic that his son was going to serve his country and get away from the do-gooders at the New Roads College. When the judge called his son back later that afternoon, he asked him why he had decided to serve his country. Roy Jr. said that it was a long story that he would rather not get into but that it had to do with the three boys his father had met before the Christmas holidays when he came to get him at the school. After the judge hung up the phone, he made a note to himself to send each of us one hundred dollars for helping his son become a man.

17. Which Side Are You On?

The loss of the Tiger Daytona 500 was deeply felt by the three of us, but the knowledge that it was a sacrifice for the greater good of helping Roy Jr. become a man of the world made it worthwhile. Life has a funny way of turning things around on you if you use too much force trying to get what you want. Roy wanted me to be like him and he ended up being like me. We were catalysts in Roy Jr.'s change of life, but his hand was dealt long before he spotted me. I guess this kind of predestination thinking would make me a Presbyterian of sorts. I remember thinking that if the subject of the Spur Club fiasco ever came up in my discussions with Brother Calvin Walker, I would explain that it was God's will for Roy Jr. to go on a tour of the brothels of Southeast Asia, and God wanted Officer Calvin Walker to sweat a few bullets that May evening at the Spur Club.

After helping Professor Snodgrass save his job, Brother Calvin was rewarded with a clean bill of spiritual health and returned to his posts as the music-less song leader and the teen Sunday School teacher. However, he was viewed with suspicion until the day he left the First New Roads Church of Montgomery during the religious racial wars that were to occur later that summer.

The dissension in the First New Roads Church of Montgomery began in June, when three African Americans showed up at the all-white All Saints Episcopal Church in down-town Montgomery, as a tactic in the battle for civil rights. The All Saints Episcopal church in Montgomery was comprised of many bankers, lawyers, doctors, and large business owners. Having a college degree was commonplace among these Episcopalians. This congregation was prepared for a visit from Negro parishioners and was even ready for progressive change in Montgomery. The Negro delegation was welcomed into the church and seated on the front row without incident.

This event was a call to action for Brother Calvin Walker, and he demanded a meeting of New Roads elders and deacons after church the next Sunday. He wanted the members of church leadership to plan a strategy for dealing with civil rights troublemakers if they tried to defile the real house of the Lord, the First New Roads Church of Montgomery, with their presence.

Calvin already had his hands full that summer because he had come up with a nutso defense strategy to protect Alabama's Southern heritage from the duo from Hell, Martin Luther King Jr. and John F. Kennedy. These two, along with the federal courts, were Calvin's most vexing adversaries, but he was working with the new governor, key state legislators, and White Citizens' Councils all over Alabama to pass a state law to make driving or riding in an unsafe car a felony. This would mean a loss of voting privileges for anyone convicted, and he was sure that everyone rounded up for these crimes would be convicted. Calvin envisioned mass trials held at Cramton Bowl and other football stadiums throughout the state where thousands of voting-eligible Negroes would be convicted, given probation, and stripped of any future chance to vote because of their felony conviction. Calvin was feeling very good about his plan and was getting a lot of support from the racist reactionary community until he and a few more of the plan's ringleaders got a call from

Ira D. McDuffy, the U.S. Attorney for the Middle District of Alabama.

Mr. McDuffy called Calvin one night after Calvin had returned home from whipping up the weekly meeting of the White Citizens' Council about his plan. Calvin was advised by the U.S. Attorney that if such a law was passed and mass arrests began that he had been informed by his boss, the Attorney General of the United States of America, that martial law would be declared, and the State of Alabama would look like one big Army post within a week.

Mr. McDuffy also noted that he would make sure that Calvin would be the first person arrested if martial law was enacted, and he had already made reservations for Calvin at a maximum-security federal prison in upstate New York. This news cooled Calvin's passion for legislative lobbying, and he decided to resign from the White Citizens' Council with the excuse that he needed to pay more attention to his church work and police duties.

When Calvin had assembled the church leadership, he proposed a plan where five of the largest, strongest men of the church be selected to stand in front of the church until services began and then a token force of two men would wait outside until the services were over. Calvin figured that the show of force would keep any troublemakers from trying to praise God at the First New Roads Church of Montgomery.

Unfortunately for Calvin, my father was a deacon, a liberal, six feet six inches tall, weighed two hundred fifty pounds, and he had been made madder than a wet hen by Brother Calvin's plan to keep the church white by force. At the meeting of the church officials that Calvin had called, my father jumped out of his seat and towered over Calvin after he made his proposal to station goons outside the church during Sunday services.

He asked Calvin, in a less than a pleasant voice, "Brother Calvin, have you ever bothered to read the Bible?"

"Mr. Cooper, I assure you that I have an intimate knowledge of the Bible. After all, I am a Sunday School teacher," said Brother Calvin.

"Well, Calvin, that's the thing," my father said. "You're not a regular Sunday School teacher. You're a rehabilitated Sunday School teacher, and as far as I can tell, your pastoral counseling didn't take. Furthermore, it seems to me that the Devil has gotten hold of your soul. Where exactly in the Bible does it say, Calvin, that thugs should keep anyone out of the house of the Lord? And exactly where did you get this power from, to tell the difference between a troublemaker and a peaceful parishioner?" "Mr. Cooper," Brother Calvin said, "You know good and well that the niggers have their own New Roads churches. There's no need for them to come to ours."

My father was a systematic thinker and followed a logical line of reasoning. That's when he asked, "Brother Calvin, don't we both have an obligation to try and convert all humans to follow Jesus? If we do, then shouldn't the church welcome anyone who appears on its doorstep?"

Brother Calvin then launched into the standard line of the era, "Mr. Cooper, you know, and I know, that Negroes have Negro New Roads churches and Negro New Roads preachers! This gives them a separate but equal chance of reaching Heaven, where I'm sure there will be separate but equal accommodation for the faithful."

I should have warned my father about Brother Calvin's Old Testament leanings because the next thing he did was launch into the story of the Tower of Babel to justify his segregationist philosophy.

My father was also a quick-thinking man and began a treatise on loving thy neighbor as thyself, but Brother Calvin cut him off with a personal attack.

He said, "Look here, Mr. Cooper. I know all about your dealings with Northern liberal labor leaders and their efforts to admit niggers to Southern unions! And I know about your friendship with that nigger-loving lawyer, Clifford Durr, who gets nigger troublemakers, like Rosa Parks, out of jail!"

Brother Calvin then addressed the other church leaders. "How can Mr. Cooper's opinions be trusted when his youngest son, who's well past the age of reason, is not a New Roads convert?"

In this instance, my individual pursuit of the meaning of God and life's purpose was a detriment to my father's righteous quest because the accusation turned the tide of Calvin's discourse and his influence that day with his New Roads leadership peers.

The leadership voted, and it was decided to have one person stand out front of the church to guide any Negroes to the nearest Black New Roads church, but there was a growing feeling among many of the elders and deacons that day that this decision was not in the spirit of the teachings of Jesus.

There was no discourse at this meeting from the minister of the First New Roads Church. He was thinking of another minister, who was the Baptist preacher of the Linden, Alabama, First Baptist Church, who had had a cross burned in his yard, the windows of his home broken out, and had been invited to find a new church by his elders for saying that the church should accept any soul in need of nourishment, regardless of their color. This was one of the rare instances in that era when a minister's beliefs were put before his job, but the lesson of this moral act sent most struggling ethical ministers back into their foxholes.

As summer began, the struggle for basic human rights heated to a fast boil in Montgomery, Alabama, when my former newspaper customer, George Corley Wallace, made life tougher for the righteous by setting his sights on bigger game than a four-year term as Governor of Alabama. He wanted to be President of the United States of America. He knew how he would get the name recognition he needed; he told the world that he would block the admission of three black students to The University of Alabama because we had a separate but equal system of higher education in Alabama and everyone, including the Negroes, liked things as they were.

The religious righteousness of this act was liberally applied to all the new governor's acts of oppression. The state legislature even prayed in the statehouse for God to guide the governor's hand in his confrontation with that Yankee Catholic President who promised to make an issue out of Alabama's state right to block black taxpayers from attending the state college of their choice.

As the wheels of justice were put into motion by the federal government to keep the governor from having his way, there were certain procedural rules that had to be followed before he could be stopped. A federal judge called a hearing to deal with the governor, but first Wallace had to be served a subpoena. This was something the lawyer governor of Alabama knew, so to keep the subpoena from ever reaching him, he always installed a protective ring of ten state troopers around him. What George Wallace didn't figure on was U.S. Attorney Ira D. McDuffy and his wily ways of bringing the most powerful to the bar of justice.

The weekend before summer registration at The University of Alabama, an institution that the governor had vowed to keep all white, he was scheduled to appear on "Meet the Press," the national television program aired by NBC in New York. Ira saw his opportunity to serve the court papers requiring Wallace to appear in U.S. District Court the next Monday. On the day of Wallace's aerial departure, Ira drove to the city's airport dressed in a Southern Airways ticket agent's uniform. He boarded the aircraft that was taking the governor to New York City. When the governor ascended the stairs and entered the plane without his massive state trooper escort, Ira—dressed in his Southern Airways uniform—approached the governor from the rear of the airplane and handed him an envelope. The governor said, "My bodyguard trooper takes care of all my flight paperwork so just give it to him."

The U.S. Attorney told the governor, "This is something special. My boss asked me to watch you open it." Governor Wallace placated the fake ticket agent and opened the envelope.

The U.S. Attorney took off his hat and glasses and identified himself. "Governor, you have been duly served. I will see you in Federal Court on Monday at 9 a.m." McDuffy then wished Wallace a pleasant flight to New York and left the airplane.

Back at home, Brother Calvin's wife, Sue Ann, picked up the torch that her husband had dropped after thinking about the cold winters in an upstate New York federal prison. Sue Ann had formed a group called Women For Segregation to support Governor Wallace in his efforts to protect white women from the dark third of the state's population. Her group went en masse to the Governor's Mansion to present their petition of support for the upcoming battle with the federal government over the admission of Negroes to The University of Alabama and the white public schools of Alabama. Their document was a plea for the governor to protect white women's rights to have safe homes and moral schools;

they also respectfully asked for the right to stand with Governor Wallace in his time of peril.

The governor thanked the women for their support. "I vow to you that a political revolution will sweep America in the next presidential election when Southerners and Northerners join forces to roll back what the liberals are trying to do to our country. I will keep standing up for you ladies and America if you will stand up with me against the liberals that want to destroy America and Alabama."

Sue Ann's encounter with Governor George Wallace ignited her enthusiasm for building her Women For Segregation organization, and she thought a natural recruiting ground was the First New Roads Church of Montgomery. She had already talked to many of the church's women when she stopped my mother to see if she might be willing to join. My mother is a woman of few words and has a natural belief in the triumph of good over evil. However, this request to join what she saw as an abomination of the Lord's basic values caused a rare explosion in her normally affable disposition. She said, "Sue Ann, you are a scripturally ignorant woman who will find yourself in violation of God's laws on love and will be rewarded with an eternity in the fires of Hell. I will pray for your deliverance from the influences of Lucifer, but you should spend more time in prayer and less time trying to convert the women of the church to the ways of the Devil."

I figured that I came by making enemies with Brother Calvin Walker genetically since both my mother and father were now topping the list of our music-less song leader's ledger of undesirables. My brother and sister were included on Calvin's enemies list for their close association with the rest of the family, which gave us a one hundred percent level of Christian hate from the Calvin Walker family. The word around the church was that Calvin was secretly meeting with other church members to have my father removed as a deacon. To depose my father would be more difficult than Calvin had ever imagined. He had not thought about what kind of determination and infighting skills it takes to get to the top ranks of a local labor union. My father was quite used to being challenged and thought Calvin was a weak opponent. Eventually, he found that Calvin's message ran deep but not deep enough for Calvin's philosophy to take control of the First New Roads Church of Montgomery.

When my father found out about Calvin's treachery, he did what he did best: he organized a resistance movement. He probed his fellow New Roaders for signs of dis-comfort with Calvin's strong-arm tactics for keeping fellow Christians out of the First New Roads Church of Montgomery and pursued the swing voters for more intense conversation. Within a month, he had forged a coalition against Calvin's pro-violence group that was larger than Calvin's allies, and he was ready for a showdown that would divide the fellowship of the First New Roads Church of Montgomery.

My father had a family meeting to tell us what we already knew through the church's teenage grapevine: that last Sunday's meeting of the church leadership had led to an upcoming vote by the entire membership on the Sunday admission policies of the First New Roads Church of Montgomery. The opposition to open admissions was led by Calvin and the backup lay minister, Layton Chesterfield. My father was heading the open admissions wing and had coaxed Junus Reed, the First New Roads Church of Montgomery minister, out of his foxhole by assuring him that he could live up to the Christian doctrine and keep his job. The meeting would take place immediately after Sunday morning services, and Preacher Reed had taken this opportunity to deliver a moving sermon on loving your fellow man and the penalties God imposes if you don't. This topic infuriated the closed-admission contingent and had them in mean spirits when the group meeting began after the sermon.

Brother Layton Chesterfield began the discussion with a soft-edged appeal. "Brothers and sisters, we live in troubled times when all loyal Southerners find them-selves perplexed when all we need to do is to support the leadership of the state, the people we elected to guide us to calmer waters. Our church, by admitting Negroes, could do irreparable damage by deserting the governor in his hour of need and the church's decision could be the straw that could break the back of our traditional Southern values."

Chesterfield went on. "There are members of the church who come from good Southern families but have been led astray by having to associate, because of their jobs, with secular union internationalists who want to subvert a way of life that has survived Northern aggression and a carpetbagger invasion in my great grandfather's era. We must be firm in supporting our heritage and follow our elected leaders. It is the righteous and Godly thing to do."

My father followed Layton Chesterfield's presentation with an analysis of what the New Testament, and what Jesus in particular, had to say about what the obligations of following God's commandments involved. He pointed out that Jesus was tortured to death for his message of love and if this church would rather stand up for a two-bit politician trying to get himself elected President of the United States than follow the teachings of their Lord and Master, they should all be able to figure out where that would leave them on Judgment Day.

Calvin endured all the mealymouthed dancing around the issue that he could take. He rushed to the podium and declared, "The only issue we need to discuss today is whether the niggers are going to take over every institution in the state, including the First New Roads Church of Montgomery!"

I couldn't stay seated any longer. I stood and stepped in the aisle and innocently asked the congregation, "How can a group who composes only one third of the state take power?"

To be questioned by a fifteen-year-old, who had accused him of being a Buddhist and was the source of his loss of face and influence in the church—this sent Calvin over the edge. He began to rave, "Pip Cooper is a follower of the Pecker Devil! He hangs out in the Spur Night Club! He even attempted to convince my pastoral counselor that I'm a Catholic!"

"Brother Calvin, and everyone else here," I addressed the room, "I'm only a young boy trying to ask a logical question. I'm no doctor, but it seems to me that Brother Calvin needs heavy medication in addition to pastoral counseling."

Calvin leapt from the stage and screamed at me. "That's it, you little bastard!" He came running down the aisle, but before he could reach me, he was gang-tackled by a half dozen men and led out of the building cursing and screaming.

After order was restored, it was time for the vote on open Sunday admission, which passed by a two-thirds vote. As soon as the vote was over, Brother Chesterfield said that he had arranged a plan in case the membership was led astray by misguided liberals who belonged to international unions and lived next door to Jews. He announced that he had rented the basement of the W.T. Grant building where the clear-thinking members of the church could meet until they built their own new church, the Southern New Roads Church of Montgomery. Brother Chesterfield offered to quit his sales job to devote full attention to this new ministry that would stand tall for Alabama in her defense of her state's rights.

18. Very Inept Cross Burners

The breakup of the First New Roads Church went smoothly because the segregationist element just disappeared the next week and the remaining two thirds of the congregation braced itself for the Negroes who never came. Summer was settling into a nice, slow pace when the phone calls began at home. We were getting calls at all times of the day and night that were intended for my father but anyone who answered the phone would do. The general theme of these calls was that my father was a Negro-loving race traitor who would be made to atone for turning his back on his race. The rest of the family just hung up on these American Nazis, but as usual, I loved to mess with them and sport with their dull intellects.

I told them that I was thinking of deserting my family's liberal ways, but I needed more information about the segregationist point of view. This usually stopped them in mid-curse because they figured the way to really get at my father was by subverting his son. I would get them to spew out all their fears and hatreds, and get them to talk about the Jewish, Negro, Communist conspiracy to take over the world. I would engage with them about their idea of the superiority of the white race. After all that, I would cut off the conversation with the same comment, "Sounds like to me what you are selling is just like Hitler's philosophy, and I am not interested in joining up with another group of proven losers." Then I would hang up.

My father was getting worried about violence occurring in Montgomery and that it might be directed toward our family. He drilled us in defensive techniques for the home: all drapes were to be drawn in the late afternoon, and if we heard a loud sound, we were to hit the floor. Most importantly, if we noticed a cross burning in the front yard, we were not to go out of the house until the police arrived. I wondered if we could keep marshmallows on hand for the cross burning, but my father probably wouldn't appreciate my attempt at humor. I wasn't worried about the cross burners because I kept my most recent Christmas gift under my bed, a Remington 30/30 rifle with a fully loaded clip of steel-tipped bullets ready for insertion into the firing chamber.

About the middle of August, my father and I had gone up to Mr. Clifford Durr's cabin in Wetumpka on a Friday night so they could talk about politics, and I could listen and learn. The cabin was only half an hour's drive from Montgomery, so we were there by six o'clock, eating Mr. Durr's wonderful beef stew and cornbread.

The phone rang in the kitchen, and when Mr. Durr returned, he had a serious look on his face.

"Mr. Cooper," he said, "there's going to be a joint meeting of the White Citizens' Council and the Ku Klux Klan in a field about five miles from here at eight o'clock. The Grand Wizard will be naming names of the traitors of the white race, and my source says that you and I are at the top of that list."

Mr. Durr was experienced in the ways of these people because he held the record for the most crosses burned in any yard in Montgomery. He had often remarked that he wished that those "damned Klukker fools" would burn their crosses in the same place in his yard every time because he had very little grass left in his front yard anymore.

"Let's go over about eight fifteen, Mr. Cooper," Mr. Durr suggested. "We'll stay on the darker outer edges of the field and see what these cross burners have to say." My father nodded and said, "Pip, I want you to stay here at the cabin."

I started pitching a fit. "Dad! I should be able to see for myself these people who are threatening us!" I insisted.

"You're right. You can go with us on one condition," he said. "We'll take you with us only if you promise to cut and run if there's any trouble involving me or Mr. Durr if we're recognized."

I agreed and was off to my first hate rally.

When we arrived, Bull Connor, the police chief of Birmingham, was being introduced to the crowd as "Mr. Segregation." He proceeded to make his proposal for a white boycott of any business that employed Blacks in any capacity. He said the way to deal with the Negro problem was to starve them out of Alabama by cutting off their incomes. He noted that real men would use "friendly persuasion" with any businessman who re-fused to fire their Negroes. As he spoke, Bull Connor stood on a platform built up against a gigantic barn with its sides draped in a huge Confederate battle flag and the banners of the Ku Klux Klan and the White Citizens' Council; he was surrounded by some men in business suits and some men wearing bed sheets. At the end of the stage, hanging from a pole rooted in the ground, was an effigy of President Kennedy that I figured was for the grand finale.

Next up was the main speaker of the evening, J.B. Stoner of the National States' Rights Party, who told the assembly, "Forced integration is a Jewish Communist conspiracy. White Christians built this country, and it is time for us to take it back." He concluded with the comment, "There

is no man lower and more despised than the filthy nigger-loving President of the United States, John Kennedy."

At this point, one of Stoner's underlings handed him a lit torch, which
he took down to the end of the stage where the gasoline-soaked President in effigy was set afire. The problem that night was that a bunch of
overzealous and half-drunk Klansmen had doused gasoline not only on
the effigy but also on the platform floor, the wall of the barn, and on their
robes as well. What old J.B. Stoner wanted was for his speech to have a
dramatic ending by setting the President Kennedy effigy on fire, instead
he succeeded in setting the whole end of the stage, the barn, himself, and
his Klan escort ablaze as well.

High comedy ensued for the three of us watching from edge of the
field. First, we noticed the guest speaker's pants caught fire, and he was
tossed off the burning stage to be rolled around in the dirt to extinguish
his burning pants cuffs.

Next, a half dozen Klansmen rushed the fire with blankets, but three
of these fire-fighters had to be tossed off the stage and rolled around
in the dirt because they were on fire, too. Several vain attempts were
made to control the inferno, but the barn was old and dry and went up in
flames very quickly. I have never heard so much cussing and screaming
in my life as those bozos tried to bring order out of their self-created
chaos. As we left, a man ran toward us with a small fire extinguisher;
that was when I said hello to Brother Calvin Walker as he passed. He
turned and cussed me and headed on toward the blazing barn.

We returned to Mr. Durr's cabin where he said that tonight showed
that God does truly work in strange and mysterious ways. Mr. Durr was
one of the few truly religious men I had ever met because he didn't talk
about the Christian life, he lived it every day. He was duly persecuted for

his belief that actions speak louder than words. His oldest child had been driven from the local high school by threats to her well-being and was obliged to attend a private school in Massachusetts on an anonymously funded scholarship from one of Montgomery's closet liberals. Mr. Durr had served in the Roosevelt administration and was appointed by FDR to be an FCC commissioner. He was known for his struggle against the commercial radio giants to secure a frequency space on radios and televisions for non-commercial educational programming.

His wife, Virginia, was on the road most of the time helping in voter registration efforts and fighting to overturn the poll tax. Mr. Durr's law practice was slow and economically unproductive to say the least. When Mr. Durr showed up in city or state court, he was assured of a defeat for his client because of the hostility or fear of the judges and juries to handing Mr. Durr a judicial win. In this time and place, any juror or judge could face the wrath of the hard-core segregationists who ruled a state government that condoned fear and intimidation to oppose integration. Because of his involvement in the civil rights movement in Alabama, Durr's appearance representing a defendant in state or municipal courtrooms unsettled average citizens.

Mr. Durr sealed his fate as a lawyer in Montgomery in 1955 when he and E.D. Nixon went to the Montgomery jail to free Rosa Parks on the day she was arrested for not giving up her seat on a city bus to a white man. His modest resources came from a few large sympathetic corporations that would give Mr. Durr the occasional federal court cases they had in Alabama and the modest fees that the under-funded civil rights community could afford to pay him for getting demonstrators out of jail.

My father and I returned to Montgomery late that night, and I decided to check out this Jewish, Communist, Negro conspiracy to take over the world with Mrs. Katz the next day. Mrs. Katz was one of my best friends, a friendship developed over much of the three years that we had been neighbors, while sitting at her kitchen table trying to figure out the adult world.

Mrs. Katz was never judgmental and never talked down to me but would usually answer my questions about why something was the way it was with another question that would lead me to my own discovery about the truths of life. She had moved to Montgomery from the very affluent suburb of Scarsdale, New York, to be with her husband who was a native of Montgomery and the sports editor for the local newspaper, the Montgomery Journal.

When I told her about my adventure of the night before, she howled with laughter imagining all those hooded figures running around in mass confusion trying to undo what they had done.

"President Kennedy," she said, "had the last laugh on those boys, Pip, because it was his effigy that burned their gathering spot to the ground."

"Mrs. Katz, did you know that J. B. Stoner has a theory that you and the other Jews in the world are in on some type of conspiracy? What do you think of that?" I asked.

Once again, she answered my question with a question. "Pip," she asked, "if the Jews are so powerful, why did six million of them have to be slaughtered in just my lifetime? If the Jews are so powerful, why is it that I'm barred from membership in half the social organizations in Montgomery, and I'm not invited to many of the social functions my Christian friends are invited to, all because I'm a Jew? Son, Jews and Negroes share the most fundamental of all feelings, the desire to belong and participate fully in the larger culture. If this feeling constitutes the conspiracy he's talking about, then I'm definitely one of the plotters to change the world we live in."

The next day at church, the whole congregation of the First New Roads Church of Montgomery was surprised to see the return of Al Smith, better known as The King of Aluminum Siding, from his constant appearance on local television pushing the ad-vantages of never painting your house again. The King of Aluminum Siding had joined Brother Layton Chesterfield to establish the new Southern New Roads Church of Montgomery, and his re-defection was the talk of both churches that Sunday morning. My father kept us sitting in the hot car after church for half an hour while he and Al Smith had a conversation in the parking lot. When he returned to the car, we were all waiting for the story of this prodigal son who had returned to the congregation he had left only weeks before. Even my mother, who was the epitome of patience, was right in there with my siblings and me wanting to know the scoop on Al Smith's return.

As he drove us home from church, my father told us what had transpired between Al Smith and his former preacher. It seemed that Brother Smith had been placed in an untenable situation because of Preacher Layton Chesterfield. Chesterfield had demanded that The King of Aluminum Siding fire all his Negro workers in support of the White Citizens' Council's reverse boycott policy that was now fully supported by the members of the Southern New Roads Church of Montgomery. Al Smith told my father what he said to his new preacher, "Brother Chesterfield, half of my eighty employees are Negros who are skilled in the installation of aluminum siding, and most of them have worked for me for years. You can't expect me to destroy these loyal employees' lives, do you?"

Preacher Chesterfield said, "I know it will be difficult, but I am sure that this is the Lord's will. You had best get on with it if you don't want to face the Lord's wrath both here and in Heaven."

Brother Smith told Layton Chesterfield, "I tell you what I'm going to get on with and that is my return to the First New Roads Church of Montgomery, and you, Preacher Chesterfield, can stick my pledge of ten thousand dollars for the Southern New Roads Church building fund up your butt."

We were all shocked by the story, but we were ready to welcome Al Smith back into fellowship with us.

All this church drama happened toward the end of summer vacation, and I had about a week of freedom left before my re-incarceration in the New Roads School and College. My mother was busy buying school supplies and new clothes for our return to school. My brother and sister were chomping at the bit to get back to their retreat from the secular world, and I was preparing myself by setting my clock radio for every hour of my sleeping time so I would be good and hopped up on alpha waves by the time I returned to school.

This quirk of mine proved to be a good thing because one night that week as I was awakened by my radio clock at two a.m. and was resetting it for the next hour, I heard muffled voices outside my window. I crept over and peeked out through a small opening in the drapes to see three men wearing white bed sheets standing in our front yard engaged in a quiet but heated conversation. I knew then that the Klan had arrived at last. I quietly pulled my Remington 30/30 from under my bed, slipped in the magazine, and crept out the back door and around to the side of the house.

I crouched behind a giant hedge that went down the property line between our house and the Katz property and ended about ten feet from the street. I was so close to these hooded thugs that I could hear them discussing the placement of a wooden cross that was in the back of a pickup truck parked behind a mint condition 1950 Mercury coupe. This car belonged to none other than Officer Calvin Walker, and it was the pride of his life. Calvin was arguing with his thug buddies "that cross should be planted right on the property line so we can send a message to both the Jews and the nigger-lovers with a single burning." But one of his buddies was much more concerned that a very clear message be sent to my father. Calvin won the argument, and as they headed closer to my position to dig the hole, I retreated to the corner of my house with my fully loaded 30/30 rifle in hand.

I stretched out under an azalea bush and zeroed in on the beautifully restored 1950 Mercury's gas tank. I figured I would need three shots, two to make sure I punctured the gas tank and one into the cement curb to set it afire, a process that should take about five seconds. As soon as the Klan boys lit their cross, I fired my two direct hits into the gas tank and then the third that caused the explosion that knocked all three night riders to the ground. I heard Calvin ask, "What happened? What did you numbskulls do to my beautiful car?"

Very quickly his friends loaded him into the truck, and they peeled off down the street as the neighbors were coming out of their houses. I tore around the edge of the house and ditched my rifle in the tool shed and reentered the back door as my father exited from the front door followed by my mother, brother, sister, and then me. The cross was burning on the property line, and the Mercury was blazing in front of the house on the other side of the street. My father shooed us inside, then called the police and his friend Ira D. McDuffy, the U.S. Attorney. That's when I was certain that my father recognized the owner of the car burning out front.

The next morning, my father went to meet with the police chief for the City of Montgomery who was a friend of his walking a political tightrope in those troubled days in Montgomery.

The chief said, "Mr. Cooper, I can't tell you how sorry I am for the incident at your home last night. I want you to know that a full investigation is underway to find the guilty parties."

"Oh, just cut the crap right now!" my father told his friend. "You and I both know it was Officer Calvin Walker who burned that cross in my front yard!"

"There is a small group of radicals in the department," the police chief explained, "and they hold some extremist views. I'm trying to weed them out but it's going to take a little time."

"Let me tell you something, Chief," my father said. "You have exactly twenty-four hours to obtain Calvin Walker's resignation, or you will find this case in the hands of the FBI. Furthermore, the U.S. Attorney is anxious to investigate because it will allow him to begin a probe of the entire City of Montgomery Police Department.

"You see, Chief, there are federal laws against harassing labor leaders. Just this morning I was assured by the AFL-CIO national office that I can count on their full support to do whatever is necessary to stop the attacks on local labor leaders in Montgomery."

Office Calvin Walker resigned that afternoon from the police department with an agreement that no further action would be taken against him. He confessed to the police chief that it was a stupid thing for him to have done, particularly since labor leaders have twenty-four-hour armed guards patrolling their houses. He assured the chief that no one else would try a cross burning in our yard again. Calvin also didn't seem to be upset about losing his job on the police force because he had accepted a new position that morning as the assistant minister of the Southern New Roads Church of Montgomery. He was glad to finally be free of his secular job and the unholy people he had to deal with.

I went over to see Mrs. Katz that afternoon to get her angle on the events of the previous evening.

"Mrs. Katz," I asked, "were you scared?"

She just laughed and said, "Pip, it will take more than a truckload of rednecks burning a cross on part of my front yard to cause me any concern. Besides," she added, "I've got an armed teenage bodyguard that keeps an eye on my family."

I feigned innocence. "What are you talking about, Mrs. Katz?"

That's when she explained, "You know, my husband has access to a newsman's sources, and he was unofficially told that there were two well-placed 30/30 steel-tipped bullets found in the burned-out Mercury's gas tank."

She then did what she always did and posed a probing question. "Pip, didn't you receive a Remington 30/30 for Christmas?" Before I could answer, she said, "What's important is that the word is on the street is to stay out of our neighborhood if you're looking for trouble, or you might find yourself dead. I've even started my own rumor by getting my husband to tell his sources that I'm the granddaughter of one of the leaders of the Warsaw ghetto uprising, and killing Nazis or Nazi look-alikes is part of my heritage."

Incidentally, this part was true.

19. Defenders of Dixie

I had mixed feelings that next week when our carpool of siblings returned to the New Roads School and College for our second year.

On our drive to start the new school year, my sister asked, "Pip, would you mind not driving any ministerial students to the brink of madness this year, especially Mark, the guy I'm dating? I don't want him to break up with me because of you and your insanity-causing escapades."

"I think we can work something out, Sis," I told her. "Let's make a deal. If you'll help me, then I promise I won't come between you and your boyfriend. If you can get him to convince the other ministerial students to leave me alone, then they should all be able to go into the ministry and not into the Army like Roy Harper Jr."

"I'll try, Pip, but you're such an inviting target for a would-be preacher to practice on," she said.

I agreed and said, "Well, it will be dangerous for one of them to try and convert me to be a New Roader, and it should be enough to keep most of them at bay if they are reminded of this fact by one of their own. Just get Mark to let his comrades know that I'm working out my own personal relationship with God. Any more probing of my religious beliefs from any of the other ministerial students, and they'll be met with a similar fate as befell Brother Roy."

The tension in the school was evident that first day of classes. The division in the First New Roads Church of Montgomery over the summer, as well as the escalating civil rights struggle in the world outside the church and school, was beginning to draw lines that made staying in the middle more and more difficult. The basic operating structure of the school, until four little black girls were killed in a church bombing that September in Birmingham, was to just not talk about civil rights and hope that all those worldly problems would go away. I did my part and kept my mouth shut until that heinous, cowardly killing of innocent children in Birmingham stirred my passion to act; I decided to stir the pot in my now normally placid environment of the New Roads School and College.

My forum for increasing the tension around the New Roads School was my first-period class, religion. Because I was now in the high school division, I had the New Roads Senior Professor of Religion, Dr. Ronald T. Snodgrass, for the class. All high school students were in the same religion class at eight o'clock, which was fortuitous because I was full to the brim with alpha waves in the morning and ready for action. This class was not your traditional academic religion class but rather a forum for the reiteration of the New Roads dogma of why they were the chosen sect in all of Christendom.

I remember thinking cynically that first day that there were so many people in so many cultures believing in so many religions with so many subsets of each religion. Wasn't I lucky to have been born into the one, and only one, that would be able to see the face of God? I knew that this kind of random occurrence had to be explored in my religion studies that year. It was time to put these folks' Biblical interpretation to the test by seeing if they could put Jesus's philosophy of brotherly love into action.

The first few weeks of school and religion class, I kept my mouth shut and reviewed my summer with Pecker and Archie at our daily meetings at the barn. The administrative council was relieved to see an end to the Helping Hands Club, and it was forgotten by almost all the other students. I was approached by a few ministerial students who were daring enough not to heed my sister's boyfriend's warning; after all, there were plenty of potential converts who would come over to the New Roads faith without the dire consequences that I presented. I had developed a new technique that sent these would-be preachers running back to their studies after their one conversation about my lack of faithful status in the New Roads religious order.

When approached, I just asked the supplicant to give me about fifteen minutes of the gospel according to the New Roads Church and Jesus. This always brought us around to His love for the lost souls and I then confessed faithfulness to Jesus's teachings. I would then tell the preacher-in-training I needed proof of his commitment and willingness to really follow the commandments of Jesus and suggested that he and I attend the weekly Klan rally, held in Prattville due to a very unfortunate fire that destroyed their Wetumpka location. I told my intended converter, "We will go early and mingle amongst those hooded lost souls and proclaim the message of interracial brotherly love, which is the foundation of Christ's teachings of love for every human. When I see the New Roads faith tested as Jesus had been tested on the cross, I will be ready to consider full membership in the New Roads Church."

I would then quickly suggest, "Could you pick me Friday night at seven o'clock so we can get to the Klan rally early so we can catch as many potential converts as possible? We will together proclaim to these errant sinners what Jesus would want them to do and then we will tell them about the New Roads religion and how belonging was the only way to get into Heaven."

I never had but one conversation with any of the preachers-in-training who tried to convert me, and I never saw any of them on my doorstep on any Friday night after our conversation. The word spread amongst the ministerial students about my challenge to a test of faith, and in a very short time, I wasn't pestered by any ministerial students for the rest of the academic year.

The school's attitude of pretending they were above any secular social movement came crashing down on Monday, September 16th, after the horrible bombing at the 16th Avenue Baptist Church in Birmingham the previous day. The school, as well as the nation, was pushed off the fence with this act of cowardly desperation by the segregationist forces in Alabama. Everyone was discussing the bombing that morning before class, and you could watch as the lines were drawn on the big front porch of the classroom building. The students who thought that these troublemakers had brought this bombing on themselves began to coalesce to the left side of the porch, which I found to be ironic. A substantial majority of the students gathered on the other side of the porch and poured out their heartfelt sorrow for the children and the families of the dead children. My sister, Jen, and her boyfriend, Mark, were talking quietly by the rail about what had happened, and I noticed that they both had tears in their eyes. At that moment, I remember thinking that there really was hope for some of these smug, self-righteous New Roaders if they would quit talking about what Jesus said and start doing something about what Jesus said. Since every fire has to start with the first spark, I knew where my duty lay: to get this fire going and drive a wedge between these two groups who were gathered on the same classroom building front porch.

That morning in religion class, Professor Snodgrass began to drone on about the Book of Revelation and the coming rapture when all the New Roaders would be drawn up into the sky. I raised my hand, which was visibly shocking to the New Roads Senior Professor of Religion because in the first two weeks of his class I had not said a word. With a smile, he called on me hoping this was a sign that a summer of reflection had changed my ways of the previous academic year.

"Professor, do you think all New Roaders will ascend to Heaven at the moment of the rapture or only those who have followed the commandments of Jesus?" I asked. The professor was very pleased with my question and explained, "Pip, any New Roads sinners who have not asked for forgiveness will not be part of the ascension to Heaven."

Then I asked, "Sir, wouldn't it be a wise idea to stay ready and forgiven, since the moment of rapture is a closely held secret in Heaven?"

The professor heartily agreed with this and suggested, "Pip, God looks on the asking of forgiveness in public with much more favor than asking hidden away in one's closet, so is there a sin you would like to confess to our class right now?"

I gave him an answer he wasn't expecting: "Sir, how do you think Jesus feels about killing innocent children in Sunday School or about any supporters of this killing? I bet He thinks that's a whopper of a sin! Maybe several people listening to the lecture right now would do well to ask for forgiveness in front of the whole class in case the rapture occurs before the bell rings for second period."

Pandemonium broke out as the segregationist students began to scream and curse that my interpretation of the scripture was not fair. Professor Snodgrass went into action trying to quiet his audience and return order to his very disorderly religion class. Very quickly, a leader of the

Heaven-bound segregationists, Peedrow Walker, stood and ad-dressed the class. Peedrow was the son of Calvin Walker, former Montgomery police-man and current associate minister of the brand-new Southern New Roads Church of Montgomery, currently meeting in the basement of the W.T. Grant variety store.

Peedrow Walker quieted the others and started babbling. "Negroes carry the mark of Cain, which is black skin and God has assigned those people with black skin, the niggers, to serve whites to atone for the sin of Cain."

I asked him, "Where did you get all this misinterpreted Old Testament lore and how does any of that bullshit fit with the commandments of the New Testament that invalidated any misinterpreted rules of the Old Testament you invented?"

Peedrow looked at Professor Snodgrass for scriptural help because he had run through his one and only Biblical argument for segregation. The professor was in the cross hairs of a divided group of students; he was damned if he said anything and damned if he didn't. He tried to wig-gle out of this religious war by suggesting that they return to his lesson about the rapture. I blasted him with both verbal barrels by asking, "Pro-fessor Snodgrass, exactly what is the official and theological position of the New Roads School and College on Civil and Human Rights?" As the philosophical noose drew tighter around Professor Snodgrass's neck, his face turned bright red, and he began to yell at me that I was not going to make his class Hell on earth and for me to go to the principal's office. There was a low grumble about unfairness from most of my fellow stu-dents and a smile of satisfaction on Peedrow's face as I left the room.

I made my way to the principal's office, and when I got there, I said, "Sir, I got kicked out of religion class and got sent to see you." Then I told him what I'd said in class.

"Pip," Dr. Allen said, "I understand where you're coming from, I really do. But son, these are trying times, and good changes are only going to come about if we all have patience with each other and pray about the situation."

"Yes, sir," I said, "but patience isn't really one of my virtues, and any praying I'm doing right now is for the capture and swift electrocution of the Birmingham church bombers. If Hell really is a place, I hope whoever the bombers are get the white-hot seats closest to the center of the fire."

"Pip," he admonished, "that sounds like an unforgiving heart. That's certainly not the New Roads way to get into Heaven."

"Well, I guess it's okay, then, since I'm not a New Roads member," I reminded him. "And another thing, the complacent attitude that New Roads members have with our modern-day Scribes and Pharisees sure isn't going to encourage me to take a second look at your hypocrite religion."

The bell rang before the principal could respond to my verbal attack on his chosen religion. That week, I began my thrice weekly philosophical discussions with the principal because that was the average expulsions I received from the teacher of my eight o'clock religion class, Professor Ronald T. Snodgrass, for the rest of the year.

As I left the principal's office that first expulsion day, I ran right into Peedrow Walker who informed me that he was going to beat the ever-loving shit out of my nigger-loving, traitor, commie ass. This threat sent shock waves through me because Peedrow was not only a big and mean senior, but he also had a grudge against me for getting his father in deep shit by accusing him of being a closet Buddhist. After the incident in the hall, I remembered that Peedrow had been the tough guy who had been beaten and dragged through a septic overflow puddle the previous fall when he challenged my mild-mannered friend, Archie, and this gave me hope that my even larger friend would do it once again if Peedrow actually tried to harm me.

Peedrow's threat called for a meeting with my buddies in the barn.

When I told Pecker and Archie about my encounter with Peedrow in the hall, they said for me not to worry because the three of us could take on ten of them. The bluster made me feel better, but I knew that I had struck more raw nerves than just Peedrow's with my attack on the school bigots. Archie had a talk with Peedrow that afternoon and explained to him that whatever befell me would be visited upon him three-fold before a week had passed.

When Archie and Peedrow had their little talk, Peedrow asked, "Archie, what about you? Do you support what the niggers are trying to do to our Southern heritage and culture and our states' rights?"

"I support my personal right to be left in peace, and I want you to know that any violence done to Pip will interrupt my peace," he said. "As far as the Negroes go, my dog isn't in that fight, and I think I'll sit this one out on the sidelines."

Peedrow responded, "Archie, you're either with my new club that I started today at lunch, The New Roads Defenders of Dixie, or you are against us."

"Peedrow," Archie said, "I'm not going to belong to any group that includes you, so I guess that makes me against y'all."

Peedrow threatened, "Well, Archie, you need to watch your back. My group is going to beat the Hell out of all three of you race traitors when the time is right."

"That might be true," Archie said, "but just remember, I will still deliver on my promise to repay you by a factor of three for anything that's done to Pip by you or your

Defenders of Dixie." And then Archie walked away.

Back in the barn the next day, after spending most of my first period with the principal, I discussed with my friends our need for a defense strategy to protect us from an attack by The Defenders of Dixie. I noted that the only logical place of attack was the barn where they could assault us out of sight of the other students and administrators. I proposed a fortification of our base of operations and an offensive strategy as our best hope of breaking up The Defenders of Dixie's threat. I suggested that we lure them into our trap and try to deal with them before they got to us first.

Pecker's brain had come to life with the talk of an offense: he suggested that I take care of luring The Defenders of Dixie to the barn, and he and Archie would take care of the offensive counterattack. Once again, the game was afoot, and we concocted our plan. While I reviewed material for tomorrow's class on the Book of Matthew, my friends prepared surprises in the barn for The Defenders of Dixie.

The next day in religion class, we were covering the first book of the New Testament, and I was ready when Professor Snodgrass asked if there were any questions from the reading assignment. I started talking before anyone else and asked, "Didn't our reading assignment show Jesus at his most strident best, taking on the hypocrites and condemning those who took authority and lived by other than God's instructions?"

The professor seemed to agree, and I launched into a lecture on brotherly love and do unto others and ended with the hypocrisy of the New Roads Church for not only not standing up for Jesus's teachings but instead letting a hate cult start on the New Roads School and College campus.

The professor asked, "What cult has been started at our school, Pip?"

And then I told him about The Defenders of Dixie club and its leader, Peedrow Walker. The professor's face hardened. He ordered Peedrow to stand and identify other members of this unauthorized club. Peedrow was staring holes through me as he stood up and identified his secret membership list, which numbered ten boys. The professor demanded that this club be disbanded immediately and that he'd like to see Brother Peedrow after class.

We were moving in our group of three after third period when we ran into Peedrow. He said, "The Defenders of Dixie are going to beat the shit out of you commie bastards and we're going to do it this week."

I obliged him by saying we would meet and kick the shit out of him and all the other Defenders of Dixie in the barn at three o'clock that afternoon. At two thirty, the three of us slipped out of biology lab and down to the barn to get on our stage before act one began. At three o'clock, we saw The Defenders of Dixie coming down the hill toward us as we waited just outside the barn's front doors. When they were about thirty feet away from us, we turned and ran for the other end of the barn with The Defenders of Dixie in hot pursuit.

About halfway through the barn, where two ropes were tied off to a pulley in the ceiling, we came to a sudden halt as Pecker pulled out his switchblade knife and opened it. The gleaming knife blade stopped the group in their tracks about fifteen feet away, but before they got moving again, Pecker cut one rope that was tied to a counterweight. The floor beneath The Defenders of Dixie went out from under them and they found themselves bundled up in a huge fishnet eight feet above the ground. The Defenders of Dixie would have shamed their great-great-grandparents who fought and died mostly for someone else's riches and lifestyle.

Pecker, Archie, and I went over to the shouting, quivering mass of flesh we had caught and began our performance. Pecker said, "Shut the fuck up, or I will cut this other rope that is attached to a barrel of gasoline suspended above your heads, which I will set on fire and burn all of you to cinders."

This news quieted The Defenders of Dixie as Pecker explained, "The rumors about my being a Devil are true, and I have decided to take one of your group to Hell with me tonight after the chosen one's ritual sacrifice. I'm going to let you as a group choose which one of you will have his heart cut out, or I'll just burn you all."

Almost at once, the barn was filled with the sound of Peedrow's name being called out as he whimpered that it wasn't fair and that they should draw straws. Pecker said that now that these boys knew his true identity, they would be marked with the scent of the Devil so he could find them at any time he wished to reap their souls. He then cut the second rope, and fifty gallons of septic-tank cesspool goo, not gasoline, poured through the net. Pecker pulled the fuses on three Army surplus smoke grenades and dropped them behind us as we headed for the side door and cut the last rope—the rope that kept The Defenders of Dixie aloft.

From our vantage point hidden in the woods, we saw and smelled our enemies emerging from the barn. This was one scared, stinking lot who were generally agreeing to give the Pecker Devil and his imps lots of room from then on as Peedrow screamed they had been tricked. One of the former Defenders of Dixie said he didn't know if Pecker was the Devil or not, but he had learned his lesson about messing with us and was going to steer clear of all three of us in the future. Peedrow made one more attempt to hold The Defenders of Dixie together as they neared the top of the hill by appealing to their racist emotions about the righteous fight for the Southern way of life. This appeal drew the comment from one of the goo-covered boys that they should let the adults work that problem out.

The former Defenders of Dixie, except for their founder and leader, were true to their word and moved as fast as their feet would take them out of our way at school.

Peedrow was another matter. He threatened me daily and I knew he would catch me someday without my friends, which he did about a week later. I made the tragic mistake that day of using my window seat in math class to enjoy the nice fall day. I was quick and silent that afternoon, but Peedrow was watching me from his study hall window and had a bathroom pass five minutes after I left my class.

I went to the cow bowl creek first and entered the barn after my nature walk when the lights went out in my head. Peedrow had stepped from behind the barn door and sucker-punched me and I went down. The next thing I knew, I was kicked in the legs and ribs. Peedrow said, "You can expect a beating like this every week and tell your buddies I'm not scared of them or even a hundred Pecker Devils and look here at what I got in my pocket, my dad's .38 revolver that makes me a match for any or all of your buddies."

I was sore and bruised when I finally got up, but I had to think this one out care-fully or my friends could get hurt or killed by this madman.

I knew if I told Archie and Pecker what had happened, a gun wouldn't stop them. I knew that I was dealing with someone on the outer edge of any reality of the repercussions of his behavior, a boy who could actually kill for the pride in his beliefs. If I told my father what had happened, all Hell would come down on the school and I would be saddled with the blame for the ruckus. I decided to pose my problem to my neighborhood teen shrink, Mrs. Evelyn Katz.

When I got to her house, I told Mrs. Katz about what had happened at school that afternoon. "Mrs. Katz, I can't tell my father what happened. I can't tell my friends, either," I said.

"Don't worry, Pip," she assured me. "I'm going to take care of this."

"No offense, Mrs. Katz, but I thought I'd get an engaging question when I talked to you today. I didn't think you'd take this problem on yourself," I said.

Mrs. Katz replied, "Pip, there's an important lesson for you to learn today. When you are in over your head with a situation, you need your adult friends to help you out. And, son, you are in over your head with this one. By this time tomorrow, all your problems with Peedrow Walker and his goons will be over, and no one will ever have to know that happened."

Mrs. Katz set the wheels of justice in motion that afternoon when she called two people: her husband and her very close friend, the U.S. Attorney for the Middle District of Alabama, Ira D. McDuffy. Mr. Katz went to see the publisher of his newspaper, Angus Argon, and told him his wife's plan, which Mr. Argon said he would go along with even if he did have to give up a planned front-page story. Mr. McDuffy told Mrs. Katz that he would be delighted to do his part and would arrange for everything to occur the next morning.

My pain was a lot worse the next day. I had also missed all my alpha charge because my body wanted to sleep without interruption. My father noticed my shiner and asked me what had happened, and I said that I fell down the steps at school. He gave me one of those looks that says, "I don't believe you, but I also don't want to know enough to try and get it out of you." My brother sealed the conversation by acknowledging that he had seen me, and my goofball friends, fall down the steps before, which was true but never with any damage.

When I got to religion class, Peedrow was grinning from ear to ear and kept smiling at me and mouthing the words "again soon." I kept my mouth shut and the period was almost over when there was a knock at the door and the president of the New Roads School and College, Dr. Slim Bailey, entered accompanied by none other than U.S. Attorney Ira D. McDuffy. The president asked Professor Snodgrass if he could see Brother Peedrow Walker. The question was really a command and as Peedrow left the room, he gave me an "if looks could kill" stare, and I just smiled.

Once outside, the president introduced Peedrow to the gentleman with him and said they wanted the gun he had right then.

Peedrow spoke up, "I don't know anything about a gun, and I don't know what you're talking about!"

Then Ira D. McDuffy pinned Peedrow Walker's neck to the wall and began to explain to the boy the way things were. He said, "Peedrow, I will bring a hundred FBI agents onto the New Roads campus and find that gun. And, because you're eighteen years old, you'll be tried and convicted of intimidating union officials through their families, and I'll see to it that you're sent to the damn coldest federal prison I can find."

The U.S. Attorney then said, "Or you can give me the gun right now, and we'll all walk over to the president's office. We can have a chat with your parents about what's been going on; they're waiting for us in the president's office right now."

Peedrow led them to a shed behind the classroom building and removed one of his father's fully loaded .38 specials and gave it to the U.S. Attorney.

All four—three people and one pistol—entered the president's office as Associate Minister Calvin Walker stood. "I think I deserve to know what this is all about!" he demanded.

The president took the floor and explained, "Mr. Walker, I've had a call from Mr. Argon, publisher of the Montgomery Journal, who said your son, Peedrow, had beaten and threatened another student with a gun. This isn't just any boy this was done to, but a personal friend of Mrs. Argon's and the son of a powerful labor leader."

On that note, Calvin knew his son, Peedrow, was in big trouble, and he sat down knowing that President Slim Bailey would cover up his son's indiscretions. As soon as Calvin sat down, Sue Ann Walker, Chairman of the Women For Segregation movement, rose to her feet. She spoke up and said, "I am sick and tired of being pushed around by federal bullies! If it takes a gun for my son to defend his birthright, I will support him all the way to prison!"

"Mama, I don't want to go to a Northern federal prison or any other prison!" Peedrow cried out. "I was only trying to scare him with the gun!" Then Peedrow began to cry like a baby and said, "I promise I will never cause any more trouble again at the New Roads School!"

Calvin jumped back to his feet and told his wife, "Woman, you need to shut the fuck up!" Then he turned to the U.S. Attorney and asked, "What do we need to do to end all this trouble my son has caused?"

McDuffy fixed a long silent stare on Calvin Walker before he spoke, and then he said in a voice that was almost a whisper. "I'm so tired of dealing with you and your whole family. If I have to deal with you all one more time, I will have a list of things that I'll do. On that list," he explained, "will be two indictments of a father and son team who both attacked the same family and a full-scale investigation of every member of the Women For Segregation movement."

Calvin said, "Sir, you can count on us. There won't be any more trouble from our family."

"Calvin," McDuffy said, "I want one more thing from the three of you. I want each member of your family here to apologize to Pip Cooper, and I want you all to promise that you'll never bother him again."

The president got me out of my second-period class and asked, "Pip, why didn't you ask me for help? We see each other around campus almost every day."

"Yes, sir," I agreed, "we do. But, by now, you should have figured out that I have my own way of dealing with things."

And he agreed.

When we entered the president's office, all the parties were standing, but only the

U.S. Attorney spoke. "Pip," he stated, "that's quite a shiner you've got there." "Sir, if you like bruises, you ought to see my ribs," I told him.

"Now that you're here, Pip," Mr. McDuffy said, "each member of the

Walker family has something they want to say to you."

"I'm so sorry, Pip! I won't ever bother you again," Peedrow blubbered.

In a wooden voice void of any emotion, Calvin Walker said, "I'm sorry, Pip. I promise I'll never get involved with you or your family again." He sounded like he was reading cue cards.

Next up to bat was Sue Ann Walker. "I'm sorry, Pip. We'll leave you alone. But I'll pray daily that the Devil will turn loose of your soul."

I looked at the Walker family gathered there in the president's office. "I appreciate what you've all said. Thank you," I said. "I think this is a perfect opportunity for you all to consider the importance of nonviolence. You all should study Dr. Martin Luther King Jr. as an example to follow. If you do, you'll be able to stay out of legal trouble and probably lead productive lives."

Then I left the office, and I didn't look back.

20. The Private White School System

As October and early November wore on, my energies were spent reading the Bible and preparing myself for the confrontations with Professor Snodgrass in our morning religion class. This served two purposes: I almost always got ejected from class when I confronted the professor with his own Savior's words, and I had wonderful and insightful religious and philosophical conversations with the principal, Dr. Allen, once I had been ordered out of religion class and into the principal's office. In a thirty-minute discussion of Christian principles laid out in the Bible, the principal said, "Pip, I am trying my best to be a good Christian and stay out of trouble at work at the same time, but it's getting harder and harder to do that because of the civil rights struggle."

He knew that he was going to have to choose very soon, a choice between his faith and his job. Outsiders were approaching the school and the president to see if the New Roads School and College would uphold its whites only regulation for admission. He told me what he knew and said, "Pip, this is ironic because the school has no policy on admission by color and that issue has never come up because no Negroes have ever applied to the New Roads School and College."

He added, "The president has visions of becoming the largest private school in the city once court-ordered integration begins in the public schools. I know that the envisioned increase in attendance will only happen if the school adopts a whites-only admission policy, which I find to be a direct contradiction of the teachings of Jesus."

The principal had plenty of right to worry because President Slim Bailey had been having secret meetings since late summer with Dr. Bobby Ray Frazier, a bigwig in the White Citizens' Council and the 1960 National States' Rights Party's vice presidential candidate. Dr. Frazier was trying to build a compact with every private school in the city so he could establish a private, all-white school system. He had described his in-tended role to be that of Superintendent of the Private White School System of Montgomery and to be its chief fundraiser and chairman of its board of directors. He painted a picture in the president's head of a sprawling upgraded New Roads School and College campus with hundreds of employees and more compensation for the president for having all this added responsibility. Dr. Frazier knew he needed the already accredited existing schools in on his scheme if he was going to accomplish his goal of a unified, all-white, private school system.

The board of directors of the New Roads School and College was composed of New Roads ministers who were long-term friends of President Bailey, preachers who had developed large and successful New Roads churches in various parts of Alabama, and wealthy supporters of the school. Five of the twenty board members were filled by individuals of this latter category. They were all men who could be counted on for a sizable donation from time to time. Additionally, one seat on the board was reserved for one of the male parents of anyone attending the New Roads School and College, which that year was Layton Chesterfield, former ladies' underwear salesman who had recently become the minister of the new Southern New Roads Church of Montgomery. Layton Chesterfield had been meeting with Dr. Frazier prior to the board meeting that was scheduled for the first Tuesday in November.

Chesterfield assured Dr. Frazier that he would get the New Roads School and College board to adopt an all-white admission policy and become the founding member of the Private White School System of Montgomery if Dr. Frazier would guarantee him the job of designing the school system's curriculum and choosing its books.

Preacher Chesterfield had been upset by what school children and adults had access to in the American marketplace of ideas and was very excited about the possibility of turning off the spigot on any idea that struck him as liberal or indecent. He had led the drive three years before to have a children's book removed from every grammar school and library in Montgomery.

The offending book was geared to small children and was about two rabbits get-ting married and was entitled The Rabbits' Wedding. Preacher Chesterfield had succeeded in having the book removed because the graphic artist who had drawn the pictures for the book had made one rabbit white and the other one black, thus offending the sensibilities of Layton Chesterfield and his rabble of followers. He had been further enraged that school year by the McMillan Publishing Company of New York City, which had stopped issuing special textbooks for the Southern market. The result was that there were photos of Negroes and Whites playing on a school playground together in their nationwide editions as well as a modest amount of positive Black history.

The situation in the secular world was becoming more tense as the side effects of the church bombing and the tirades of states' rights demagogues began to be felt by everyone who lived in Alabama. The governor was intent on resistance to any integration of the public school system, but the federal court forbade him or his state troopers from interfering with the court-ordered desegregation of the public schools in Mobile and Birmingham.

The point man for the governor and the head of the Alabama state troopers, Al-Lingo, said that if the feds wanted a police state, the State of Alabama would have one, too. He had every trooper car display a Confederate battle flag tag on its front bumper and had each car mount a visible riot shotgun next to the driver. After a widely quoted comment about using his troops to resist the federal courts, Colonel Lingo received a call from the U.S. Attorney for the Middle District of Alabama, Ira D. McDuffy.

The U.S Attorney asked, "Colonel Lingo, are you and your state troopers ready to take on the 101st Airborne of the United States Army?" The U.S. Attorney suggested that the storm trooper colonel tone down his public remarks before he created a situation that would cause him and all the rest of his troopers to spend the winter in a federal prison in upstate New York.

Colonel Lingo told the U.S. Attorney, "I will not buckle to you or that renegade government in Washington D.C. If you want to test my mettle, you Catholic Whore, then bring it on."

The tension in Montgomery was palpable as the New Roads School and College board met to discuss a whites-only admission policy. Amongst those attending the New Roads School and College November board meeting were the dean, Brother Bob Leatherbury, a noted white supremacist sympathizer; the principal, Dr. Allen; Professor Snodgrass; Al Smith; Layton Chesterfield; a bevy of New Roads preachers; and the newest board member, Judge Roy Harper Sr., from Opp, Alabama. The president, Dr. Slim Bailey, introduced his special guest, Dr. Bobby Ray Frazier, who, he said, would make a fantastic presentation to the board about the future of the New Roads School and College.

The presentation by Dr. Frazier was wisely delayed until after a prayer that asked for the Almighty to guide the board's decisions. My father always believed it was that prayer for guidance that turned the school away from an evil path on that day in November of 1963.

After the prayer, the president turned Dr. Frazier loose on the New Roads board. He told them, "Ninety percent of all white students in Montgomery will leave the public school system over the next two years as a few Negroes are admitted to each of the white public schools. The good news is the New Roads School is already accredited by the Southern Association of Colleges and Schools and will be able to transition these kids immediately and become the largest school in the state of Alabama if this board will seize this opportunity to become the lead institution in a new Montgomery Private White School System." Dr. Frazier said that he had a donor committed to giving five hundred acres of prime Montgomery real estate to the New Roads School if the school would join this burgeoning white private school system movement. He added, "I have national contacts who are willing to aid in the funding of this pilot venture in Montgomery to overcome the intrusive powers of the federal government."

After the presentation, Layton Chesterfield jumped to his feet and said, "Every-one, this is the offer of a lifetime! We should vote now to accept Dr. Frazier's offer and any procedural changes to the school that will clear the way for the large new New Roads campus."

"Chesterfield," Judge Roy Harper asked, "what procedural changes do you have in mind?"

"There will just be some minor formalities, a few changes to adopt our member-ship contract with the new school system, that's all," Dr. Frazier interrupted. "This will bind New Roads School and College to the new private school system about to be set in motion. It will include the adoption of a whites-only policy, which shouldn't be a problem since there have never been any Negroes admitted to the school in the past." The judge spoke up again, "I don't really care what the school does at this point, because this is my first and my last board meeting. But, as a lawyer, I will remind this group that you are about to sign over your school to an unknown entity run by a failed political extremist. Dr. Frazier doesn't have a chance in Hell of pulling off such a crazy scheme."

"Now wait just a minute, Judge," Dr. Frazier objected. "I think you need to justify your statement if you're going to besmirch my name like that!"

The judge then addressed the entire group. "Gentlemen, Dr. Frazier has, in the past, run for Vice President of the United States on an ultra-right-wing political ticket. That fact by itself probably makes him a fringe lunatic. This proposed contract he's talking about today will probably give him complete control of the New Roads School. If that's not enough, he's so dumb that he doesn't recognize that resistance to civil rights has become futile ever since one of his mad bomber friends killed a bunch of children in Sunday School."

The judge was getting worked up. He continued, "Most of Alabama's citizens would rather accept the inevitable change in their school systems than ante up the extra money for a private white school system. You know, I don't care one hoot about what happens to the New Roads School and College now that my son is safely in the Army and out of your hands, but I can smell a bad deal. And this one is a real stinker." He then got up and left the room and vowed to never set foot on the New

Roads School and College campus again.

After the judge left, the president said, "Gentlemen, I hope you won't hold it against Judge Harper knowing that mental illness runs in his family. Anything he said should be viewed as the possible ravings of a very sick man."

"Yes, it's easy to see that the judge has very little faith in the Lord," Preacher Layton Chesterfield agreed with the president, "because God obviously gave dominion over the black man to the white man for his sins against God."

When Preacher Chesterfield made this statement, the principal knew that his time to choose between his beliefs and his job was at hand. He asked Layton Chesterfield, "Preacher, where in the world did you ever get such a stupid theological idea?"

"Why are you attacking a board member?" the president jumped in and asked.

The principal said, "I think I've heard enough unholy talk from this neo-Nazi would-be superintendent of the Montgomery White School System, the pastor of the Southern New Roads Church of Hate, and you as well, Mr. President. You three are trying to lead the New Roads School to the den of the Devil, and I'll resign if the policy of admitting only whites passes."

Layton Chesterfield chimed in. "Great! Go ahead and resign. The school is going to need strong leadership for its future, and any principal who'll turn his back on his own race won't have the moral strength to do the job."

The room was filled with the rumble of low conversations as the board members discussed quietly what was going on before their eyes until The King of Aluminum Siding, Al Smith, stood and began to address the group. Al said, "I have been tricked once into following Layton Chesterfield and his extremist ideology, and it would have cost me my business and probably my soul if I hadn't come to my senses. To follow these three men's ideas would be tantamount to turning over twenty years of work by thousands of New Roads followers to a violent, hateful, secular minority. If we follow these men, we would be turning our backs on the very purpose of the New Roads School, which is to provide an environment of Christian love, not to become the largest and most hate-filled school in the state."

The King of Aluminum Siding then called for a vote on this proposal and the out-come was nineteen to one against it. Dr. Frazier told the board, "You assholes will be Goddamned sorry you have made this decision." He then turned to Al Smith and said, "Your fucking aluminum siding business is finished, because I will make it my solemn duty to ruin you. We will boycott you into bankruptcy."

Al Smith, The King of Aluminum Siding, said that he couldn't have made his point any better than the would-be superintendent had just done. Dr. Frazier stormed out of the room with Preacher Chesterfield right behind him as the president tried to repair the damage he had done to his career. However, this was a futile effort because the president of the New Roads School and College would not be president for much longer.

The next day, the strain on the administrators' faces was evident to the students who had all gotten the gist of the board meeting. Revolution was at the gates of the New Roads School and College, which had always been a port that could not be disturbed by the events of the outer secular world. Lines were being drawn, and common philosophies were not so common anymore; discomfort between brothers and sisters in Christ was a new feeling sweeping the campus. In retrospect, I realized that institutions experience the pain of change just as individuals do, and that was what I was in the middle of during that November of 1963.

21. Kennedy Assassination Riot

I was not ready for the second most emotional and long-lasting negative experience of my life, but you don't get to pick those times. They're on you and inside you before you can prepare yourself for the shock and then the grief. I was cutting history class and listening to the radio we kept in the barn on November 22 when I heard that President Kennedy had been shot and probably would not survive. I sat there by myself and cried for thirty minutes before I started breaking every bottle in the barn as I wailed at the top of my lungs.

When I returned to the top of the hill, the news had already swept the school, and no one was going to their next class. The scene in front of the classroom building is frozen in my mind for all time. The front porch and the sidewalk in front of the building were covered with students: about a third looked like zombies staring off into space, a third were crying and hugging, and a third were yipping and yelling in glee.

What ensued is still lore at the New Roads School and College. I began a fast run toward the biggest and loudest reviler, Peedrow Walker. I put him on his back when I rammed my head into his stomach and then started to pound his face with my fists. When Peedrow's joyous network of hoodlums realized what was happening, they joined us. I was thrown around like a rag doll until my friends came to my rescue.

Archie and Pecker came out of their trances of shock over the President's death and joined the melee on my side. Archie waded into the enemy with his fists flying while Pecker was leveling the mob attacking me with a swinging book bag. From my viewing place flat on my back with Peedrow on top of me, I watched the book bag do its damage as Pecker swung faster and faster in an arcing motion that felled everyone in his path. Just as my large opponent, Peedrow, was about to pound me into the ground, I saw the book bag connect with the side of his face and heard his jaw crack.

The sounds of revelry about President Kennedy's death turned into the sounds of a MASH hospital on the front lines in Korea during the war; there were moans, groans, and the hysterical screaming of those with broken bones. Pecker and Archie had taken their toll on these sorry bastards, and I was finally on my feet again ready for action when those who remained standing began to back away from the three of us. Archie and I grabbed our book bags and joined Pecker that day in clearing the New Roads School of the sick, evil scum I had to share my life with.

The teachers and administrators began to pour out of the classroom building like ants at a picnic. Professor Snodgrass was the first on the scene, and he asked Brother Mark, "What in the Sam Hill happened here?"

"As far as I can tell, Professor," Mark said, "the anti-Kennedy element at our school decided to beat Pip to a bloody pulp when his friends Archie and Pecker came to his rescue. Those boys really should know from past experience who they're dealing with when they decide to take Pip on. The other thing I know is that there's a lot of truth to the rumor of a Pecker Devil's existence, because I just watched Pecker cut down ten strong boys in a matter of seconds."

Archie, Pecker, and I were ushered into the principal's office as ten of the New Roads anti-Kennedy students were driven to St. Margaret's Hospital for repair. There were three broken jaws, four broken ribs, two broken arms, and various minor cuts and abrasions. We were grilled about how this incident happened, and for once in my life, I told the truth: I was beyond my breaking point with grief and charged the joyous and loud Peedrow Walker. Archie and Pecker saw a mob starting to beat the Hell out of me and made like the Lone Ranger and Tonto; they jumped in to save the good guy who was their friend Pip.

Given the political climate at the New Roads School, the last thing the principal wanted was an incident where the segregationists were given an opportunity to exploit this situation. The principal suggested, "Pip, maybe things were just so highly emotionally charged in this situation that perhaps you just ran into Peedrow accidentally? Is that when Peedrow took umbrage and struck you, and then your friends joined in? Is that the way it happened?"

Pecker picked up on what the principal was trying to do and said, "Sir, Archie and I were watching and that was exactly what happened."

Then Archie said, as he stared hard at me, "Pip is just confused by the blows he received to his head, but I know what the truth is because I was right there."

I responded, "Well, if Pecker saw it like that, then that's how it must have happened." "Personally, I'm just glad the truth has been discovered," Archie said with a sigh of relief, at which point he knew that, finally, the punishment of the bad elements in the school could begin.

Later that afternoon while addressing a very tense administrative council, the principal reported his findings that exonerated us.

The president said to the council, "I heard it was Pip Cooper who started the whole fracas, and I can only assume from his past behavior that he is to blame. I'm going to investigate the whole matter, but I'm sure Archie, Pecker, and Pip will be found guilty and expelled."

"I've already investigated the matter," the principal replied, "and the truth is obvious."

The president said to the principal, "Listen! I've had all the back-stabbing I'm going to take from you. You are fired!" Then he turned to the dean and said, "You'll take control immediately of the lower school. I want you to have Archie, Pecker, and Pip in my office next Monday morning at ten a.m."

The principal turned to leave and said to the president, "Sir, I believe you've bartered your soul for earthly power, and I hope God will have mercy on you." Then he walked out the door.

The principal caught me as I was leaving the school with my siblings and relayed to us what the president had said. Then he told me that I had best tell my dad what happened before he got a call from the president. On the way home, my sister said, "Pip, I've talked to everyone at school about what happened. You should never have been attacked by that gang, and except for the known segregationist students, everyone is going to tell the same story, including most of the ministerial students." I knew I could always count on my sister in a pinch, but I still had to tell my dad. When he found out what happened, all I could think was that the conversation would bring the incident at New Roads School to a fast boil.

When I got home, I went immediately over to see Mrs. Katz for some badly needed advice and stimulating questions. When I related my story of the incident, and the story we had cooked up with the aid of the prin-cipal, she began to cry. She sniffled as she said, "Pip, the loss of President Kennedy and the reaction of the thug element at your school breaks my heart! It makes me ashamed of the human species." She asked, "Aren't you a friend of Mrs. Argon, the publisher's wife?"

"Yes, I am, and I think she likes me," I told Mrs. Katz.

As she dried her eyes, she suggested, "You know, newspapers like to report stories of victims' eyewitness accounts. You might want to start by calling Mrs. Argon at home and telling her the story of what your friends saw happen when you accidentally bumped into Peedrow." She then dialed Mrs. Argon's number and handed me the phone.

After hearing my story, Mrs. Argon was outraged that ten boys had tried to beat me because I bumped into one of them while crying over our fallen President. She told me, "Pip, you wait right there at Mrs. Katz's house. I'm going to send my favorite reporter over; he'll be there in about thirty minutes."

Mrs. Katz said she knew who was on the way, M. Brandy Lane, the best and bright-est news reporter at the paper. She explained, "Pip, Mr. Lane grew up in Montgomery, but he's spent ten years as a Washington correspondent for the AP news bureau. I think you'll like him because he's always in trouble with the segregationists for his coverage of their events and the Civil Rights Movement. You see, thugs don't like to be portrayed as they are, a bunch of savages, but prefer the mantle of Southern culture defenders."

Within thirty minutes, I was sitting across the table from M. Brandy Lane, a man in his mid-thirties with the most intense blue eyes I had ever seen. Excitement was all over his face when he asked me to relate the whole story to him in detail. When I had finished the principal's version of the story, I added, "Mr. Lane, the beating I got could be related to the last New Roads School and College board meeting."

M. Brandy Lane jumped on that bit of information with both feet and asked, "Pip, what do you know about the last New Roads board meeting?"

I recounted the attempted school takeover by Dr. Frazier, but I also suggested that he talk to Judge Roy Harper Sr. in Opp, Alabama, for the details, or to Al Smith, The King of Aluminum Siding. We ended the interview, and I knew I would read about it on the front page of the morning edition. Mrs. Argon would hear from him that her favorite contributor to the Junior League's Warehouse for the Poor looked just fine, a bit bruised but basically unhurt.

M. Brandy Lane went back to his office and called the fired principal of the New Roads School. This is when Mr. Lane found out all about the fight, the attempted take-over of the school by Dr. Frazier and the president, and the outcome of the board's vote. He called The King of Aluminum Siding and Judge Harper before he called Dr. Slim Bailey, President of the New Roads School and College.

When Mr. Lane asked for an explanation of the riot that took place on the campus that afternoon, the president said, "The melee appeared to be started by three trouble-makers with whom I've had problems for over a year. They started the fight that involved numerous students."

"Were these three troublemakers, as you call them," M. Brandy Lane asked, "the same three who founded the very successful Helping Hands Club? A club which, by the way, did such laudatory work the previous academic year?"

The president sensed danger in this question and didn't answer for a moment. Then he decided that he was fenced in and had to play it out with us as the villains. He said, "Oh yes, Mr. Lane, those are the same students, but apparently they have lost their way since they left the New Roads School for summer break. They seem to have been influenced by outside agitators over the summer."

Mr. Lane then asked the president, "Sir, does the attempted takeover of the New

Roads School by you and Dr. Frazier have anything to do with a purported gang-beating of the student leader opposing the takeover?"

Slim couldn't keep his composure any longer. "Mr. Lane, are you implying that I had that boy beaten in revenge for the failure of the New Roads School to join the Montgomery Private White School System?"

"That could certainly be a possible explanation for a disturbance that left so many injured," M. Brandy Lane said.

President Slim Bailey hung the phone up in the middle of the reporter's next question, but it rang again thirty minutes later. Judge Roy Harper Sr. was calling and told the president, "Well, Slim, I've got some good news and some bad news. The good news is that I've decided to stay on the New Roads School and College's board. Unfortunately for you, the bad news is that I've talked to all the other board members in the last hour, and they've decided by a vote of nineteen to one to fire you."

President Slim Bailey shouted into the phone, "They can't do that!"

"It's already done, and the principal will be replacing you at once," the judge said as he hung up the phone.

That's when ex-president Dr. Slim Bailey knew that there was no way to beat this powerful man.

My father didn't return home until ten o'clock that night due to the day's events in Dallas. He was haggard and very distraught over President Kennedy's death and wanted to be left alone. However, I knew I had to tell him that he would probably get a call from President Bailey of the New Roads School and College informing him that I was getting booted out of school. In a voice that seemed very far away, he asked me what this was all about, and I told him the true story and the cover story. Animation re-entered his body as I told him what I had done, and he jumped up and grabbed me. He held me to his chest and said he was proud to be my father. He made me tell him three times about Pecker mowing down the gleeful crowd of segregationists and Archie's broad swings that took out two at once. My father was not a man prone to violence, but it seemed the vicarious experience of the brawl displaced his anger at what had happened to his beloved President Kennedy.

He said, "Pip, I want you to know that I'm not worried about Slim Bailey. From everything I hear from my sources around the school, you can take care of yourself pretty well."

"What sources are you talking about, Daddy?" I asked him.

"Son," he said, "I've always kept up with some of your shenanigans at school, but I let it go because I was up to the same tomfoolery when I was your age. Since you've already decided to return to public school next fall, the worst thing that can happen would be an early return. Just don't clean out your locker just yet, because I'm going to investigate the situation in the morning."

We hugged, and that's when I knew that he was sorry for the loss of our President and the loss of my innocence and the loss of my belief in the goodness of my fellow man.

22. New Road for New Roads School

The next day, the Montgomery Journal was full of news about President Kennedy's assassination, but on the lower right-hand side of the front page was an article headlined PRO-KENNEDY YOUTH BEATEN IN NEW ROADS SCHOOL RIOT written by M. Brandy Lane. The article reported that a group of students associated with a New Roads School segregationist club, known as The Defenders of Dixie, had jumped a crying student who was distraught by President Kennedy's death. He noted that the student who was attacked was also known to be the student leader of the open admission movement on the campus. The article went on to say that I was best known in the charitable community as the founder of the Helping Hands Club that had done so much for Montgomery's poorer residents. Mrs. Argon was quoted as saying, "Pip Cooper's Helping Hands Club at the New Roads School has done more for the city's underprivileged citizens than any other group who have worked with Montgomery's Junior League's Warehouse for the Poor."

She added, "The hooligans who attacked Pip got exactly what they deserved be-cause only The Defenders of Dixie club members were taken to the hospital."

M. Brandy Lane described the attempted school takeover by the president, Dr. Slim Bailey, and the noted segregationist and Vice Presidential candidate, Dr. Bobby Ray Frazier. He recounted the events of the last school board meeting and the circumstances of the previous evening that led to the ouster of Dr. Bailey as president and the selection of Dr. Paul Allen as the interim president. He reported the speculation that my beating might have been supported by the previous president as retribution for opposing a proposed whites-only admission rule for the school that had caused an erosion in the board's support of the president.

I was quoted as saying, "I am unsure of the reasons for the attack on me by The Defenders of Dixie students, but I have been informed that I will probably be expelled along with my two friends who beat back the attack by The Defenders of Dixie club members." The article ended with the assurance from the new president of the New Roads School and College that the three of us would not be expelled but instead that he would discipline all those who engaged in the attack on one of the school's most outstanding students.

My father woke me at five thirty, before my nightly alpha infusions were over, to read the article to me. He then laughed and said it seemed wrong to him for one of the most outstanding students in the New Roads School to transfer at mid-year to the public schools. This statement and the new president's published comments assured me of my continued participation at the New Roads School, but given the turn of events, I was not disappointed. I knew that I had a lot more pot stirring to do at the New Roads School before my departure to Sydney Lanier High School the next fall.

We began our morning breakfast at home with a prayer for President Kennedy's family, the country, the new President of the United States, and for the safety of our family as we followed the teachings of Christ and risked any retribution that might follow. My father offered a special prayer for his youngest son who he said was guided by righteousness but would need the Almighty's help to survive these times of peril. I never was one for praying, but that morning's prayer went skyward with my full support. I knew that my notoriety in the morning paper would put me on a bigger enemies list than the one The Defenders of Dixie kept, and I was going to need all the help I could get to survive the revolution that surrounded us.

My siblings and I were apprehensive on our drive across town that Monday because of the riot, the change in the New Roads administration, and the death of our national leader. When we arrived at school, students were talking quietly, milling around in tight groups and looking very serious. We found out that there would be a meeting of the entire student body, faculty, and staff of the New Roads School and College at eight a.m. in the gym. When the whole school was assembled, the new president, Dr. Paul Allen, walked to the podium and began a process of change that was long overdue.

Dr. Allen began his talk by saying, "It is important to remember why the New Roads School and College was founded, which was to create a community of Christian love that would make the philosophy of agape a reality and not just a concept."

He went on to say, "I understand the pressures of the secular world surrounding this Christian community but as followers of Jesus we are committed to following His teachings on love and brotherhood.

"From this day forward, any student who follows the teachings of hate groups will no longer be welcome to attend the New Roads School and College. We carry a special responsibility as Christians to accept into our midst anyone who would follow the ways of the Lord, regardless of their skin color.

"I don't know of any Negroes who want to attend school at the New Roads School and College at the present time, but if any do, the school's policy will be to admit them. The student body is responsible for making them welcome as Christ would if He were standing at the school's entrance."

The segregationist element, some known by their bandages and new casts, were none too happy to hear of this turn of events in their school, but they finally realized that they were the first new minority since five percenters were accepted at the New Roads School ten years before. These people were driven underground that day, but their hearts were still as soiled as week-old underwear, and they would pursue their hate and defense of the white man's supremacy in private with their closest friends. There was general agreement amongst this evil lot that Archie, Pecker, and I would be made to pay for our anti-white attitudes before the school year was over in May.

The new president asked that all faculty and administrators stay seated and then he dismissed the students and told them to return for a prayer service for President Kennedy and his family at nine o'clock. He then said, "I expect full attendance at this special chapel service, and I will take a dim view of anyone who is not back in the chapel at nine a.m."

After the students had gone, the former principal and now interim president ad-dressed his employees. He noted that most people in the room were loving, Christian individuals confused by the events surrounding them in the City of Montgomery. He wanted them to know that he understood the impact of values that had been held in their families since before the War Between the States. As Christians, however, their values went back almost two thousand years, and these were the values that must be followed. He said, "Anyone who has a problem understanding what behavior Jesus wanted of His people should come see me night or day, and we will study the scriptures together to find the answer."

His last comment took the group by surprise, though, when he made it known that any employee associated with any hate group would be dismissed from employment at the New Roads School and College as of the next day. That day there were three resignations from the White Citizens' Council and one maintenance man quit the Ku Klux Klan.

The service for our dead President was a moving experience as the New Roaders put aside their prejudice about Catholics and every other religion as the new leader of the New Roads School and College said: "God will take care of this young man who has died for his beliefs and for our country. We must remember that scripture tells us that God works in mysterious ways and that the life of President John Kennedy may have been taken, as was our own Savior's life, for a greater good."

He added that "big changes are coming to America, and the blood of the Negro children in a Birmingham Sunday School and the blood of our President may be a part of the purchase price of bringing us as a people back to the philosophy of agape, Christian love."

As I left the chapel, I ran into a very bruised Peedrow Walker who was talking really funny because his jaw was wired shut.

I told him, "Peedrow, I'm glad to see you're going to be all right. It sure was nice to be with you for the memorial service for President Kennedy." My sarcastic mouth knew no bounds when talking to him.

Peedrow's face turned bright red as he tried, inaudibly, to cuss me, which made his jaw hurt like Hell. He then mumbled, "Pip, we're gonna get you. There are others, adults, who are going to take care of you."

"That's fine, Peedrow," I said, "but try to do it away from my house because our night guard is a dead shot with his 30/30, and my next-door neighbor has Nazi-killing blood. She's just itching to find one of those hooded boys creeping around her back-yard."

"You're gonna pay for all that has happened to my family and our Southern way of life," Peedrow mumbled again.

"If you keep up this grudge," I retorted, "I will personally turn the Pecker Devil loose and what has happened so far will seem like a summer picnic compared to the full wrath of the Pecker Devil!"

The myth of the Pecker Devil was enough to slow his threats down because he was not completely sure that Pecker wasn't the real Devil given all that had occurred over the past year and a half.

Nothing was ever the same again. My father had been right, I had let go of the innocence and trust in my fellow human beings, which I now know to be part of the evolution to adulthood. To grow and move forward on this journey of life, we have to give up the mythology of universal goodness and begin to dream the plan for our lives to change things for the better, a commitment to a philosophy that defines our lives on the planet Earth. In those few days I was transformed, my view of the world went from playground to battlefield, the leader of what I believed in had fallen. I felt scared for the first time since I had entered the New Roads School. I realized that my willingness to take on my Southern culture was linked to the will of President John Kennedy to provide the example and the security that his people would protect me when times got rough.

When I got home, I went over to Mrs. Katz's house to figure out what was happening inside my head. After I explained my new-found fear, Mrs. Katz told me, "Pip, given the environment you are growing up in, it's time to accept the reality of life amongst our fellow humans, including our racist governor, is going to accelerate the loss of your childhood innocence. You are lucky to have lasted as long as you have growing up in Montgomery before realizing that this can sometimes be a very evil world."

Mrs. Katz then explained her philosophy of change and living amongst the good and the evil. She said, "We have an obligation to the most sacred of God's gifts to man, freedom, and that one must take the long view but temper it with action. When this thesis is applied to our current situation, it means that you must push the fear aside but keep an eye out for the immediate dangers. Pip, you have an obligation to work to change the environment that you find yourself in but, at the same time, you should be keenly aware of the dangers and be alert for those who would really hurt you."

She then said, "Pip, I know you like a son, and I know there is no way for you to stay out of the middle of things, but this wake-up call from the assassins in Dallas should make all of us aware of the dangerous people we live around every day." Once again, I was renewed by the philosophical powers of Mrs. Katz, and it all seemed to make sense again. I had moved further down the road of life that requires one to face one's fears if any advancement in our society is to happen.

When I got home, the television was reporting the day's episode of the continuing saga of the death of our President and our national innocence. My house felt like we were living in a funeral home. We all tried to act normal occasionally, but it seemed so false to our feelings that it didn't last for very long. I retreated to our neighborhood drainage ditch that was my oasis for contemplation to try and hold on to the long view that I had been told about by Mrs. Katz. With the help of my faithful radio alarm, I was able to wake every hour on the hour for maximum alpha power to sustain me through the transition from an innocent into a cynic.

23. Segregationist State Troopers Hospitalized

November was an intense month of wins and losses on both sides of the human rights struggle. I looked beyond what I felt was a devastating blow to the civil rights movement because of the death of President Kennedy and reviewed the month for confirmation that there were changes set in motion that would survive his loss. My father stored all the month's back issues of the Montgomery Journal newspaper, so I re-read all of those trying to fix in my mind the political situation in Montgomery and the State of Alabama. What I needed most in conducting this mind-absorbing task was relief from my fear that I was not going to be able to do anything, that I was a kid, and what could I do to prank and destabilize the most vicious segment of our society that now controlled our state government.

After thinking about it, the words and wisdom of Mrs. Katz came to the center of my thoughts: "Pip, you have to use the skills God gave you to confront evil and do your part in making sure those skills help improve the world God gave us." I realized I really didn't have a choice, and I was a champion prankster. I could make a difference, but I would have to proceed with caution.

In my review of the news for November, I noted that the momentum was with the forces for good: the largest private sector employer in Alabama, U.S. Steel, merged its white and black personnel systems and promised no more hiring discrimination to ensure they would remain eligible for federal contracts. Also, picketing ordinances in Mobile were used to arrest members of the White Citizens' Council, and the state's first Black police officer was hired in north Alabama. On the debit side of the ledger, the Klan was growing in boldness and intimidation was rampant, state government had been taken over by rabid segregationists, and the judicial system had fallen victim to violent extremists with their intimidation of jurors.

I was consoled by the fact that the New Roads School was headed in the right direction with Dr. Allen as the new president. The segregationist element would be muted under his administration, so I felt it was time to use my prankster skills to improve the City of Montgomery. I scanned the newspaper every day for any hint of information that could lead to an undercover prankster mission to hamper or disrupt the segregationist powers now controlling the city and state government. I found what I was looking for in a small article on the front page of the Montgomery Journal, a story about ten horses being donated to the Alabama State Troopers to be used for crowd control, which really meant control of civil rights demonstrations.

The horses had been donated to the Alabama State Troopers by an arch segregationist Mississippi rancher who said he wanted to do something to support Governor Wallace. The head of the Alabama State/Storm Troopers told the reporter that the horses were the first the State Troopers had ever had, but that competent horsemen in the State Troopers were ready to use these animals to help quell any disturbance that might occur anywhere in the state of Alabama.

The New Roads School closed for Thanksgiving holidays after Wednesday classes, but I had a plan of action that I thought might make for an interesting Thanksgiving Day. I pulled Pecker and Archie in on my scheme to disrupt the Alabama State Troopers' newest weapon, horse-mounted troopers. Archie agreed to provide technical advice but said he would not be operational for my Thanksgiving plot. On the other hand, Pecker was raring to go and ready to participate in disrupting the head-busting fun of the Alabama State Troopers.

Every Thanksgiving Day, the annual football game between rival Tuskegee Institute and Alabama State College was played in Cramton Bowl, a legendary football stadium in Montgomery. Colonel Lingo, the chief of the Alabama State Troopers, had alerted the press that he would not put up with any civil rights demonstrations after the football game. He said that ten mounted State Troopers would be stationed in the parking lot to break up any groups that formed, and he advised the spectators to go home quietly after the game if they wanted to avoid trouble. What Colonel Lingo didn't know was that the Pecker Devil and his boy, Pip, would be paying a visit to the colonel and his troopers.

The day of the football game, I borrowed the family Ford after Thanksgiving lunch and headed for Pecker's house where we checked the supplies we had purchased the previous afternoon at a local ranch and farm supply business and headed for Cramton Bowl. We parked on the outer edges of an almost full parking lot and spotted the horse trailer and twenty State Trooper cars right away. We stuffed one pocket of our jackets with sugar cubes and another with three tubes of Blood Stock Herbal Paste and headed for the State Troopers' horses. There was one trooper assigned to watch the horses that were tied to the sides of the horse trailer, and he greeted us when we walked up. "Hey, boys, are y'all here for the game? Did you have a good Thanksgiving with your families?" he asked.

"Yes, sir," I said, in answer to both his questions. "But we were wondering if it would be okay for us to pet the horses. We brought some sugar cubes with us."

He said, "Son, I don't see any harm in that, but y'all be quick about it. There's probably gonna be trouble when the game lets out, so y'all need to get on out of here in the next thirty minutes."

"Thank you, sir," I answered. "We'll only pet the horses for a few minutes, and then we'll be heading home."

As we petted the horses, we gave them a tasty handful of Blood Stock Herbal Paste, which Archie assured us would wind up these horses like a speed freak on a Saturday night. We thanked the trooper for letting us pet the horses and departed to hide in the bushes that fronted the parking lot. As we crossed the parking lot on our way to our hiding spot, I was spoken to by none other than M. Brandy Lane, star reporter for the Montgomery Journal who was there to cover the riot that he was sure Colonel Lingo would incite. When the fans departed the game and headed for their cars, they saw the State Troopers in the parking lot and the whole crowd began to sing "We Shall Over-come," which provoked the colonel to order his horsemen out.

What ensued was a wonder to behold. The troopers mounted their hopped-up horses and headed at a fast charge toward the singing crowd. The first horses to reach the crowd reared back and deposited three troopers on the ground, which caused the other seven horses in the rear formation to dump their riders as well. Wild horses were running off into the night as ten previously mounted state troopers wiggled and squirmed on the ground in pain. The crowd stopped singing and started laughing and then dispersed to their cars still chuckling. Colonel Lingo cursed and sent his unhurt troopers to try to catch the horses that were headed in all different directions at full speed.

Colonel Lingo made the headlines in the morning paper: SIX OF COLONEL LINGO'S TROOPERS INJURED AS THEY ATTEMPT TO START RIOT AT CRAMTON BOWL.

The colonel called M. Brandy Lane that morning. When Mr. Lane answered the phone, the first thing he heard was the colonel's bellowing.

"Lane," he screamed, "your story makes the Alabama State Troopers look like clowns and fools! I won't stand for this defamation in your paper!"

M. Brandy then asked, "Colonel, did I miss anything? Can you point out any place in the article where there are errors? Because if you can't pinpoint anything, I'd advise you to create a better plan for your hare-brained schemes. If you can't do that, then you're going to find yourself in the paper even more, probably becoming the biggest laughingstock in Montgomery."

Colonel Lingo was not used to being treated with such a lack of respect, so he sputtered, "Lane, if you keep up this one-sided reporting, then you just might find your-self tarred and feathered."

"The press," M. Brandy said, "will not be frightened by any redneck yahoos, even those who head the state police. Colonel, you can just go fuck yourself." Then, M. Brandy Lane slammed the phone into the cradle.

The reporter then called the honorable Ira D. McDuffy, United States Attorney for the Middle District of Alabama.

After a brief greeting, M. Brandy said, "Mr. McDuffy, the reason for this call is because I just spoke with Colonel Lingo from the Alabama State Troopers. He threatened me, and to be honest, sir, it has made me a little frightened. I was wondering if there's anything you might be able to do to help."

The federal representative of law and order in Montgomery did his best to assure the reporter. "Mr. Lane, I don't want you to worry one bit about Colonel Lingo. You are going to be safe from any harm. As a matter of fact, I will personally deal with the colonel on this matter."

Before hanging up, the reporter asked, "Mr. McDuffy, do you happen to know Pip or Pecker from the New Roads School?"

"Mr. Lane, I sure do know both of those boys. I think very highly of them," Mr. McDuffy said.

"Well, Mr. McDuffy," the reporter said, "I don't know how they did it, but I saw those boys with the horses in the parking lot before all the troopers hit the pavement, and I'm convinced that they're somehow involved in the incident."

"Well, Mr. Lane, from what I know of them," the U.S. Attorney said, "it's probably true that they were involved." He laughed and said, "I've even heard rumors of Pecker having magic powers, but as far as I can see, those powers are being used to good ends, if he is, indeed, endowed with special gifts."

The U.S. Attorney called Colonel Lingo as soon as the reporter hung up and began his conversation with a question. "Colonel, how many of the runaway horses that you acquired from Mississippi were caught overnight?"

The colonel said, "Only three horses are still missing. But why is that any of your Goddamned business?"

"Well, sir," the U.S. Attorney said, "I've just gotten off the phone with M. Brandy

Lane, and I was quite disturbed to hear that the head of the Alabama State Troopers was threatening a representative of the free press in Montgomery." He then added, "Did you know, Colonel, that there is an obscure federal law from 1872 that forbids the transportation of horses over state lines for acts of cruelty? Let me tell you something right now. If one hair is harmed on that reporter's head, you, Colonel Lingo, might find your-self arrested and charged with violation of that obscure law. Just for the record, Colonel, I feel that a fair trial in Alabama might be impossible. So, if I decide to pursue charges, I've already arranged with my superiors in Washington to change the venue from Alabama to New York City. That way, we know you'll get a fair and impartial jury. You know, there might even be a few whites on the jury in New York. Oh, and by the way, that Horse Cruelty Act of 1872? It carries a maximum penalty of ten years in a federal prison."

Colonel Lingo replied, "Yes, sir, I understand what you're saying. I can promise you that there will be no trouble with the newspaper reporter."

Ira McDuffy said, "And Colonel, if I see any more stunts like the set-up at Cramton Bowl on Thanksgiving Day, I will come after you, and, in case you're wondering, the new President of the United States, Lyndon B. Johnson, has sent the word down to all the U.S. Attorneys to turn the heat up, not down, on anyone who resists federal laws and federal court orders."

This bit of news spread throughout the Wallace administration that day and the hope of segregation being saved by a white Southern President was stillborn.

The wicked influences at the New Roads School were in disarray and demoralized the Monday after the Thanksgiving holidays. They were now living under the threat of expulsion for espousing their philosophies of hate, white supremacy, and violence. The talk of the day, which only caused the forces of evil to grow more hostile, was that Baylor University in Waco, Texas, had voted to admit Negroes to their all-white university. This was a major blow because Baylor was the largest and most respected Baptist university in the world and a Southern university to boot. The members of the New Roads faith had always envied the size and power of the Baptists and were theologically similar in their approach to the interpretation of the teachings of Christ.

The segregationists were taking it on the chin almost every day as the pressure from Washington and the guilt over the President's death changed institutions and individual hearts. The most important event in Alabama between the death of the President and the New Year happened on the Saturday after Thanksgiving. Judge Roy Harper Sr., Judge Probate for Covington County, originator of the batting-average-of-sin thesis, and vice chairman of the State Democratic Party, gave a speech that Saturday that filled Alabama newspapers for the whole holiday season.

That night, I went with my father and his group of union leader friends to an emergency State Democratic Party meeting, which was being held in the ballroom of the Jeff Davis Hotel in downtown Montgomery. The meeting's purpose was to calm the big party supporters about the new administration in Washington and assure them of the Johnson administration's continued support for defense, highway projects, food aid, and other subsidies to Alabama. My father always found amusement in the fact that Alabama, which fought the federal government tooth and nail, got two- and one-half dollars in tax money for every dollar Alabamians sent to Washington, and he noted that the vast majority of that money ended up in the pockets of white business owners. The judge was the last speaker of that very somber evening where all the previous speakers noted that they didn't agree with President Kennedy's domestic agenda but that they were sorry he had to die. They all began by distancing themselves from the fallen President before they extended their heartfelt condolences to the Kennedy family and the gathered family of Alabama Democrats who had lost their disagreeable President and party leader. Each speaker in turn said that we had to get behind the new President and support what they were sure would be a more moderate domestic agenda that would allow the South the time it would need to make whatever changes would be required for the future.

As Judge Roy Harper Sr. rose to give the final speech, I noticed that the governor slipped out of the meeting without taking the podium. It may have been that Governor Wallace knew what the judge thought about him, which the judge never tried to hide because he had begun referring to the governor as "that pint-sized demagogue." The judge minced no words. He did not ease his audience into the stream of his fury; he began his speech by noting "we have a special responsibility that we as Alabamians must shoulder for electing a state leader who has created a climate of hate and violence and that can only infect the sickest and darkest souls in this entire nation. We must look inside ourselves and see if this is the kind of life we want as Alabamians: bombings, business boycotts, beatings, economic stagnation, anger, and suspicion growing in every heart, black and white alike. The killing of President Kennedy was the last straw for the rest of the nation, and it is time for Alabama's resistance to integration to be over."

He continued, "For Alabama to become a martyred state in the last battle of the civil war would doom our state's children to a legacy that would not be overcome in their life-times. We will be yoked with an image of violence and backwardness if we choose the 'Wallace Road,' which leads to the philosophical dump where National Socialism and Hitler wait for the broken dreams of any new master race."

When the judge finished his speech, you could have heard a pin drop. Then, my father began clapping and was joined by his union brothers and me. Most of the remaining audience did not applaud, and the meeting broke up with low rumblings as the crowd got used to an Alabama politician challenging the governor in public.

Everyone was steering clear of the judge except my father who walked to the stage.

My father spoke up, "Thank you, Judge. Your courage and vision are exactly what we needed to hear."

Before my father could introduce me to the judge, he grabbed me and gave me a hug. He asked my father, "Sir, is this your son?"

My father looked quite perplexed, and then the judge explained, "This boy and I are old friends. He helped my son get his life together. Sir, my son, Roy Jr., was losing his mind until he found himself, with Pip's help, in the U.S. Army. Now, his mom and I are so proud because he is a soldier serving in Vietnam. And it's all because of your boy here."

I felt a lump rise in my throat as I realized that I may have sentenced Roy Jr. to his death, and I asked the judge, "Sir, is Roy in any danger since he's in a war zone?" The judge smiled and replied, "No, Pip. Roy is fine. I pulled some strings, and

Roy Jr.'s job is as a driver for a one-star general who heads the army's legal division in Vietnam, miles and miles from any fighting. As a matter of fact, Roy Jr. plans to re-turn to south Alabama and go into the furniture business with his uncle when he finishes his hitch in the army. You know, I'm sure Roy Jr. would let you have furniture at cost when you grow up, considering what you've done for him."

We were interrupted by M. Brandy Lane who wanted to talk about the implications of the judge's speech.

On the way home, my father and I talked.

He explained, "Pip, you have just been with a great man who can see the future, and he has the courage to spell it out in public." With great sadness in his voice, he said, "The judge will probably have to pay dearly for his courage, but history will remember the clarity with which he could see through the fog of change. So, Pip, is the judge's son the ministerial student that you drove to the brink of madness last year?"

I was shocked. Before I could stop myself, I asked him, "Sir, how did you know about that?"

My father smiled and said, "I have my ways. I heard you're given wide berth around the New Roads School about anything you consider your personal space and ideas. Sometimes I wish you were some things that you aren't, but on balance, you've done fine so far. But I want you to know that I'll feel a lot safer in four years when you've reached the age at which testosterone levels drop in young men."

The next morning, the Montgomery Journal news article was filled with the de-tails of Judge Harper's speech and numerous people were quoted as saying he should step down from the bench and as vice chairman of the State Democratic Party. The judge was not a fool. He coolly responded to the call for his ouster with a statement that he had recently been reelected to both of these posts, and that there were rules and procedures for removing a person from either office, but as far as he could tell as a lawyer, speaking out against the governor was not one of the grounds for dismissal.

The judge weathered the storm better than my father had anticipated. When he came up for reelection as probate judge five years later, he won by the largest margin ever. The overwhelming majority of his votes were from a large number of Negroes who had registered over that five-year period.

24. The Liberty Library

The three weeks between the Thanksgiving holidays and the Christmas holidays seemed to last forever. Things were quiet and somber around the New Roads School and College, and Pecker, Archie, and I were not interested in stirring things up after the riot we had caused earlier in the school year. I think we knew we were treading dangerous waters with our silenced segregationist fellow students, so I decided we should turn our energies outward. Peedrow had been handing out flyers to several students that advertised his mother's latest project, The Liberty Library. This project was operated by The Women for Constitutional Government who were affiliated with the John Birch Society.

The flyer indicated that The Women for Constitutional Government had set up a library of books that were difficult to obtain because the publishing industry was controlled by liberals who were committed to a world government dominated by Communists and Jews. The flyer called on all young people to come investigate the truth and check out one of their Liberty books to learn what was really happening in America. I knew it was time for Archie, Pecker, and me to visit The Liberty Library and stir up some mischief.

We planned to go to The Liberty Library on a Saturday afternoon. Because I needed the morning to prepare for our visit, we decided to meet at Archie's house at one o'clock. I spent that Saturday morning scouring every thrift store and used book-store in Montgomery looking for as many copies of a particular book that I knew should be featured at The Liberty Library. When I picked my friends up, I had found and purchased six copies of Mein Kampf, the mad ravings of these folks' natural spiritual leader, Adolph Hitler.

When we got to the storefront building in downtown Montgomery that housed The Liberty Library, there were three women sitting around a table with no customers in sight. We each stuffed two copies of Hitler's book under our coats and headed for the front door. The plan was to wander around the shelves and insert our book additions into their library when we were not being observed and then get the Hell out of there. What I didn't plan for was the fact that we were immediately surrounded by these three lady zealots as soon as we walked in and were each escorted to the bookshelves by an ardent Bircher who wanted new young recruits for their right-wing cause.

Archie, who really hated to go operational, had a cut-and-run look on his face, and I knew that I had to act fast. I stepped on the edge of a small area rug and went into a controlled fall, clutching the Fuhrer's books under my coat. I hit the floor with a thud, which brought all three women running over, freeing up Archie and Pecker from their watchful eyes. Pecker and Archie inserted their books on the shelves during my distraction and then Pecker moved in close to me and told The Liberty Library women not to move me until he got a closer look at my pupils to ensure there was no concussion.

Pecker told the women to stand back as he lay on my chest and looked in my eyes, at which point he transferred the books under my coat to his jacket. He pronounced me well and I jumped up. I told the women I was sorry for my clumsiness as Pecker moved behind a bookcase and inserted the last two copies of our donation stealthily into The Liberty Library's shelves. Pecker came around the bookshelf and said,

"Pip, I'm going to be late for my grandmother's visit. We have to leave right now, or I will be in trouble with my mom." We told the women we would come again when we had more time. As we got in the car to leave, I noticed Sue Ann Walker observing me as she pulled into the parking space next to mine. This didn't change my plan, but it did increase the danger of repercussions from our adventure.

I took my friends home and headed for my own residence because I had used up my day's allocation of the siblings' Ford Fairlane 500 time. I also needed to talk to Mrs. Katz. I took my place at her table and pulled out the flyer Peedrow had been distributing at school.

"Mrs. Katz, what do you think of this?" I asked as I handed her the paper. "Well, Pip," she responded, "I agree with Harry Truman."

I was confused. "What do you mean, ma'am?"

"Pip, Harry Truman said that the John Birchers were nothing more than the KKK without their nightshirts. Their leader even accused General Eisenhower of being a Communist! Can you believe that? I'm just sorry that these bigots are trying to recruit children with their library of hate here in downtown Montgomery."

I then put part two of my plan into action. I said, "Mrs. Katz, I went down to The Liberty Library earlier this afternoon. I was surprised to see that one of the books they have available is Adolph Hitler's book Mein Kampf."

This information jolted Mrs. Katz, and she shot out of her chair. "What did you just say, Pip?"

I recounted our visit to The Liberty Library with a great deal of embellishment about their saying every young person should read the plan of the misunderstood German leader Adolph Hitler.

She told me not to move and picked up the phone and called M. Brandy Lane. She explained to the reporter what I had just told her. Then she asked, "Mr. Lane, would you mind walking across the street to The Liberty Library and see if they have any copies of Hitler's book on their shelves? When you get back to your office, please call me here at home."

Ten minutes later, M. Brandy Lane called back. He reported to Mrs. Katz, "Ma'am, I looked through their collection of about two hundred books and I was shocked to find seven copies of Mein Kampf. I called you now because I came to get my tape recorder from my desk drawer, but I'm going back over there to get some solid answers about why they are pushing the works of this despot that our heroic troops defeated less than twenty years ago. Mrs. Katz, do you think Pip would mind if I interview him for the story?"

She covered the receiver and asked me. Then she got back on the phone. "Mr. Lane, Pip has agreed to the interview if you promise not to use his name."

The front page of the Sunday paper had an article entitled "NEO-NA-ZI GROUP TRIES TO RECRUIT AREA CHILDREN" by M. Brandy Lane. The reporter explained that the newly opened Liberty Library had many copies of Hitler's famous book Mein Kampf and that its members had been soliciting local children to come in and borrow the fascist books. The article noted that Mrs. Sue Ann Walker, volunteer director of The Liberty Library, was unable to explain why they had even one copy, much less seven copies of such a noxious un-American book on their shelves. The article continued with several scathing denunciations from the commanders of the local American Legion and VFW posts. It ended with a warning that parents should supervise their children's reading material before they end up with a house full of little storm troopers. I went next door Sunday afternoon to get a Mrs. Katz reaction to the day's news, but she said she had something else to discuss with me. "Pip," she said. "I want you to be honest with me: did you plant those books in The Liberty Library to close them down? And did you involve me in this prankster plot without my knowledge?"

I felt as low down as a boy could feel. I had used one of the most important people in my life in a scheme to disrupt evil. "Mrs. Katz, I did plant those books in there!" I confessed. As I began to cry, I said, "I'm so, so sorry for lying to you."

Mrs. Katz then put her arms around me and told me, "I forgive you, Pip. It's going to be okay. Besides, if you had told me what you were up to, I would have gladly helped. The big lesson for you today is that you learned not to use your friends. The secondary lesson is this: if you trust me, then we can do more damage to the forces of evil that are all around us if we work together."

That night, I was feeling quite smug over my successes when the phone rang and my sister called out to say that it was for me. I took the call in my bedroom and was surprised to find a very pissed off Sue Ann Walker yelling at me on the other end of the phone line. She said, "Pip Cooper, I know it was you behind the book planting at The Liberty Library! And I know you're responsible for the broken jaw of my son, Peedrow. And I believe you're somehow behind the problems my husband has faced at church and at the Montgomery Police Department! Son, you are a piece of work, and you are going to pay for what you've done to my family!"

As I flipped on my bedside reel-to-reel recorder and attached my suction recorder device to the phone handset, I said, "Mrs. Walker, my allowance is small, but I'm willing to work out a payment plan if you'll tell me what the going rate is for a broken jaw, a broken husband, and a broken library."

She retorted with a string of profanities that included something about my being a smart-ass little son of a bitch who would wish he had never been born.

I then asked the Wicked Witch of the South, "Ma'am, would it be okay if I call the U.S. Attorney and give him the gist of our conversation?"

She sputtered, "Pip, you can't prove anything. And I'll deny the conversation ever took place!"

"That wouldn't be too smart, Mrs. Walker," I said, "since our conversation is being recorded." There was a hush on the other end of the line as I rewound a few seconds of my reel-to-reel tape recorder and began to play back Sue Ann raging into the phone.

She screamed out, "What kind of Devil are you?"

I replied, "I guess I'm a Pecker Devil, and if anything ever happens to this Devil, the tape of our conversation will end up in the hands of the United States Attorney, and you'll end up in a federal prison in Montana."

I heard her crying softly on the other end of the line as she realized she had lost the confrontation. I said, "Mrs. Walker, you and your family should give up the hate in your lives because it's going to consume you like a cancer, if you allow it to grow."

Then there was a long pause, and the phone was gently hung up on the other end of the telephone line.

The next day in the barn, we dissected the events of the weekend and the resulting havoc we had wrought on the forces of evil. I asked my friends if they were ready for further hijinks in the outer world, and to my surprise, they said that they preferred to wait until a new year had begun. Our adventure at The Liberty Library and the subsequent threats by Sue Ann Walker had caused my friends to doubt my leadership abilities, and after considering how I had treated Mrs. Katz, I had to take their lack of trust with my own dose of self-doubt and guilt.

It was the phone call from Sue Ann Walker that really scared my friends because Archie said he would rather have a wild boar after him than that devious woman. Pecker said that he was all for any plan I might come up with, but his senses told him to give our pranks a rest for a while. I knew any other actions over the rest of the holiday season were going to have to be on my own.

I spent the next few weeks before our Christmas break reading every word in the daily newspaper for any chinks in the segregationists' armor that might lead to a prank that I could carry out alone.

I was successful in my review of the newspaper to find a prank project in the days before our holiday break. The Montgomery Journal reported that NBC television had canceled the telecast of the Blue-Grey football game because of segregation. The Blue-Grey bowl game featured graduating seniors. Northern and Western college players would play football against Southern and Mid-Western college players. The game was scheduled to be played just after Christmas and had always been for only the white seniors because the Montgomery service club that sponsored the contest refused to invite any Negroes to play in the all-star event. This caused the governor to go out of his way to be nice to all the white boys who decided to play in the now non-televised game.

As part of this showering of attention from the governor, the newspaper said he was going to make each player an honorary colonel in the Alabama State Troopers at the game's halftime ceremonies. This was the break I had been looking for because another neighbor who lived across the street, Mr. Rodham, was the assistant director of the state printing office and had been after me for a couple of years to visit and tour the state printing plant. My plan was going to be a long shot for stirring up things, but I didn't have any better ideas, and I had the whole holiday break to burn up with no excitement in sight.

Late that very afternoon, I went to see Mr. Rodham at his home and asked if it would be all right if I visited the state printing plant during my holiday break. He said that he would be delighted to give me a tour and launched into a speech about the art of printing the myriad of state documents that kept our government running and preserved the history of our times.

I remember thinking that day that the world was full of zealots for some cause or other, and the cause of government printing seemed to be the least dangerous to other people of any that I could think of. The plan was set for me to come to his office at mid-morning the following Monday and get a tour to watch the operations of the state printing plant.

Monday morning at ten o'clock I showed up in Mr. Rodham's office and was whisked away for a tour of the state printing office and plant. I was introduced to dozens of people and saw every section including the calligraphy office that attached the names and titles to awards, proclamations, citations, and other official state documents including those certificates that make one an honorary member of the Alabama State Troopers. When I returned to Mr. Rodham's office, I asked if I could go back to the layout room, which was across the hall from the calligraphy office, and watch the layout people work. He agreed to call down and see if they would mind and noted that they might let me do a little printing layout myself. Mr. Rodham was so pleased with himself; he could envision me growing up, joining the state printing business, and saving our governmental processes for posterity and assuring the orderly state government recording for a life-time career.

When I arrived in the layout room, I was greeted by three enthusiastic layout workers whom I had met on my tour earlier. They were anxious to get me involved in the hands-on process, but I demurred and asked if I could just sit by the door and watch. They agreed but added that any time I wanted to help, I should just ask, which I assured them I would do as I placed my chair where I could watch them and the calligrapher across the hall. My luck was holding because the calligrapher was an early lunch person; at eleven thirty, he picked up his hat and coat and departed. I announced to the layout workers that I had to go but would like to return the next day and try my hand at layout if that was all right. The group assured me that it was, and they would be glad to see me the next day.

I left the office and walked halfway down the hall, then I crept back and discreetly sneaked into the calligraphy office. I quietly pushed the door closed and began my search, which took only seconds. The calligrapher was working on a certificate to make Thomas Godwin of the University of Southern California, an honorary colonel in the Alabama State Troopers. He had only completed ten certificates, and most of the certificates were still awaiting the calligrapher's pen. This is when I helped myself to one of the blank certificates. I slipped out unnoticed and into my sibling Ford Fairlane 500, and I was off to find the greatest fake ID man in Montgomery, Pogey Wilson, a junior at Sidney Lanier High School.

Pogey was a boy of many talents, and he loved intrigue. I explained my plan and said that I would need the completed certificate first thing in the morning, but I was as-sured he could do it right then. We went up to his room where he had all the implements to create and change IDs, as well as a set of calligraphy pens. Pogey gave me a calligraphy style book and told me to find the print type they were using on the other certificates. I found the style that was used, and he flawlessly inscribed the certificate with the following words, "Martin Luther King Jr. — Boston University."

"Thanks, Pogey!" I said. "What do I owe you?

Pogey looked at me and said, "Are you kidding? You don't owe me anything. I'm descended from a long line of Republicans, and any trouble I can cause for the Democratic Governor is reward enough for me."

I returned the next morning with the certificate carefully wedged into the lining of the back of my jacket. I hung it gently on the back of my layout room chair so I wouldn't bend the award. It seemed we spent an eternity covering the intricacies of state document layout as I waited for the calligrapher to go to lunch. As soon as he grabbed his hat and coat, I told my layout teachers that I had to go but I might return one day as an adult, which seemed to please them.

I retraced my steps of the day before, and after I had closed the door to the calligrapher's office, I went to his worktable and was relieved to see that he had just finished making William J. Morris of the University of Mississippi a colonel in the Alabama State Troopers. I tore the thread from my jacket lining and placed my doctored certificate in the correct alphabetical place in the finished certificates but only after writing, "KILROY WAS HERE," on the back of the certificate.

Back home I waited for the Blue-Grey Classic football game to roll around a few days after Christmas. My father had tickets for the game, and the plan was for me to go with him and Mr. Durr, who was an avid football fan. I was sure Mr. Durr would be a great fan of my plot to disrupt the honorary officer corps of the Alabama State Troopers if he had known. I was filled with doubt about my plan working because I figured that some fool in the governor's office would check the certificates against the football roster before the governor bestowed State Trooper colonel status upon them in front of twenty thousand people.

As the days grew closer to the game, I had convinced myself that I had failed in my adventure. Even so, the burning ember of hope in my prank's success still survived my adolescent self-doubt that was endemic in that period of my life.

On the day of the game, my belief in the power of good over evil had me in high spirits and ready for the best halftime show I had ever seen. We picked up Mr. Durr and made our way to a packed Cramton Bowl, half full of hard-core racists who were going to show the liberals at NBC that they didn't need their network coverage or any non-white players. The Sidney Lanier High School band played "Dixie" five times before the game started, and the bleachers were red with Confederate flags of all sizes being waved. The spectators couldn't wait to display solidarity with the governor who was the head segregationist of the nation and the day's main attraction for the national news media.

The air was electric with the passion of hate, and Mr. Durr told me that what I was experiencing was going on in Germany thirty years ago. "The Germans," he said, "also had a short, demagogue leader who was quick to stir emotions, and I assure you, Pip, that we will follow them down the same road of death and destruction if we, as a people, chose to follow a power-mad, would-be little Napoleon."

Governor Wallace took to the field before the game began to play to the network news cameras that followed his every move for the evening news. As he walked out, the stadium exploded in cheers and waving Dixie flags. Half the crowd seemed over-come with a madness that one sees only on the back ward of a mental hospital, raw human emotion stripped of any cultural insulators that protects us from each other. The governor thanked the crowd for coming and said, "Today we are show-ing the liberal national media that Alabama doesn't need their network football coverage, but I see the NBC news cameras are here to defame our way of life and our standing up for states' rights."

He then asked that everyone stay for the halftime show because he had a special present for the boys who would be playing in that day's game, especially those boys from Northern schools who were ridiculed for standing up for their right to play football with people of their own race. As the crowd yelled and screamed, I heard my father say something about that "no good little son of a bitch."

The next hour seemed to last an eternity as I waited for the half-time extravaganza that would elevate me to the status of a professional prankster. My father and Mr. Durr droned on about football tactics and the individual players' accomplishments over their college careers. From time to time, they even watched the game. I observed the audience, which was juiced up on hate and Civil War football gladiator symbols. They waved their flags and yelled rebel yells after every minor advance by the Grey team. By the end of the second quarter, the crowd had a very mob-like feel to it as the band played "Dixie" and much of the audience yelled out, "Wallace, Wallace, Wallace" in unison.

The governor walked out on the field, and we were hidden in a forest of standing, cheering spectators who were brought to a frenzy by the governor's presence. A man standing next to my father asked him why we weren't standing and my father explained that we were monarchists and stood only for kings and queens but never for would-be emperors. This explanation confused our states' rights neighbor enough for him to drop the subject and return to waving his rebel flag and screaming Wallace's name.

The governor roused the crowd with a whites'-only patriotic speech about standing up for Alabama and the Constitution of the United States by keeping the traditional values of the Southern way of life alive and well. He predicted dark days ahead as the federal government tried to force liberal social planning down the throats of all Southerners. Mr. Durr almost blew my plan by asking my father if he wanted to sit through anymore of the governor's verbal crap. I chimed in and said that I really wanted to see the second half of the game, which threw my father off because I hadn't paid much attention to the first half. Both men acquiesced to my wishes and the countdown continued as Wallace worked the crowd for another twenty-five minutes. As the teams returned to the field, the governor called all the players to mid-field, and I knew that it was showtime.

The governor announced that all these young men would be given the rank of honorary colonel in the Alabama State Troopers for their service to the state of Alabama. A rather serious-looking young man started handing the governor certificates one at a time, and then he read out the player's name and school. Each player advanced and was handed his certificate by the governor, which was just the way I had envisioned the process. The crowd had seated itself for the graduation-like exercise that the governor had embarked on, but I was on the edge of my seat as the names slowly crept up the alphabet. Each player stepped out of the crowd for a handshake and his certificate as the governor continued to read out names until he called out the name Martin Luther King Jr., and his school, Boston University. As soon as the name was out of his mouth, he knew he had been set up. The hesitation in his awarding ceremony was enough to cause a gasp from the crowd and laughter from several brave souls, including the two grown men with me.

Governor Wallace regained his composure and then launched into a ten-minute tirade on the traitors and saboteurs who would be found out and punished for their treachery of trying to embarrass the people of Alabama. He finally calmed down and continued his award program, but the damage was done, and he knew it. The cameras that were there to record his staged event recorded him making his symbolic foe an officer in the armed forces of integration resistance in the state of Alabama. The irony of this act was front-page news across the nation the next day and spurred an internal investigation of the state bureaucracy. No culprits were found, but there were lots of questions about how the Martin Luther King Jr. certifcate ended up in the governor's hands.

Given the stir that my prank caused, I decided to confine the secret of my ploy to my friends, Archie and Pecker, because even a foolhardy kid knows when to lay low. The emotional experience of being in Cramton Bowl with thousands of whipped-up segregationists was enough to sober my judgment about spreading the news of my triumph over the governor. The feeling of living in a pressure cooker had been growing all year, and 1964 held out no promise of a de-escalation of the tense emotions which surrounded those of us who lived in the geographic center of the Civil

Rights Movement. I was sure that the winds of change were blowing through Montgomery, Alabama. I also knew that they would be accompanied by storms of violence and hatred, which escalated my personal feelings of fear.

25. Mrs. Katz Wakes Up

With the holidays beginning, I had a feeling of apprehension hanging over me, and I knew I needed to go next door for a sit-down with Mrs. Katz to figure out where my anxiety was coming from. Having a stay-at-home neighbor and Yale-trained psychologist only steps away was a stroke of luck for a rambunctious teen. My father bought a vacant lot in 1960 to build his dream home, a totally uninspiring brick ranch that was the popular trend in mid-century Montgomery. The bonus was that Evelyn and Sonny Katz lived next door.

I gave her kitchen door three knocks and barged right in as was my habit when visiting Mrs. Katz, but the always upbeat and helpful Mrs. Katz was sitting at the kitchen table crying her heart out. I was completely flummoxed and at a total loss seeing the strongest woman I knew in a full meltdown. She looked up and pointed at the chair next to her and continued to wail. My heart seized up with pain, and I asked her so many questions: "What is wrong Mrs. Katz? Are your children okay? Did your mother die? Has your husband been injured?"

She raised her hand in a signal for me to wait, and slowly, her crying tapered down to quiet sobs. Then she dried her eyes and said, "I hate for you to see me like this, but living in Montgomery is sometimes overwhelming, especially for a woman like me raised in the shadow of New York City."

She said, "The hate and bigotry of the ignorant who make up the voting majority is mostly tolerable because I have my kids, my husband, and my Jewish temple family, and, of course, my teenage friend who lives next door. I have built a cocoon around my life as most Jews in Montgomery have; we keep quiet about our opinions and focus on making a living and raising our families.

"Last night the veil was ripped away and the ugliness of my new hometown was on full display. Sonny and I have been shamed and embarrassed, and it breaks my heart to see my husband humiliated in front of his friends and colleagues."

Every year at the beginning of the Christmas season, the newspaper would have a black-tie dinner for the senior staff and their largest advertisers. The party was usually held at the Elite Restaurant, which would close to the public for the paper's annual party. This year, however, the publisher had decided to move the party to the Montgomery Golf Club where he was a member. Mrs. Katz knew that Jews were not allowed to join the club, and that the Jewish community had built their own country club, the Standard Club, not far down the road from the Montgomery Golf Club. Gentiles were welcome to come to the Standard Club with their Jewish member friends. Mr. and Mrs. Katz were members, and she occasionally invited some of her Christian friends to lunch at their club.

Mrs. Katz had always enjoyed the newspaper's holiday dinner and had bought a new dress for the event. The dinner was at 7 o'clock in the evening and the guests began arriving at six thirty for cocktails before dinner. She knew most of the attendees and enjoyed seeing the old colonial mansion that served as the main clubhouse for the Montgomery Golf Club. As the publisher asked everyone to take their seats for dinner, the manager of the club appeared and approached Mr. Katz.

"Good evening, sir," he addressed Mr. Katz, "my name is Josh Applewhite, and I am the chief executive of the Montgomery Golf Club. Sir, may I ask, are you Jewish?"

Mr. Katz looked confused. "Why, yes, I am Jewish, but I don't understand why that makes any difference tonight. I have no intentions of applying for membership; I'm just here for the party this evening."

In a loud voice, the manager said, "Sir, you are going to have to leave because the rules of the club don't allow Jews on the property! Is your wife also a Jew? Because if she is a Christian, she can stay."

Mrs. Katz told me that at that moment she had endured all the exclusion and bigotry she could take and blew her top! She said she moved in front of her husband, about six inches from Josh's face. She announced, "Mr. Applewhite, I'm his wife, and yes, I am indeed a Jew! Not only that, but I'm also a Jew from New York where my father is the managing partner at Lehman Brothers Investment Bank on Wall Street in New York City and he makes more money in a week than you do in a year! You, sir, are an ignoramus. Do you even have a high school education?"

This accusation really got to Josh who proclaimed, "Yes, and I also hold a degree from Auburn University in history. Most Jews that I know in Montgomery are aware of their place in the social order, and my job is to make sure that Yankee Jew interlopers in Montgomery know it as well."

Red-faced, Mrs. Katz loudly asked, "Sir, with your history degree from Auburn, do you have any idea who the first European settler and business owner was at this spot, the now City of Montgomery, which is perched on the high banks of the Alabama River? No, you don't know, do you? You poorly educated, redneck historian and religious bigot. It was Abraham Mordecai, a Jew from Pennsylvania, who opened a trading post in 1785 just a few miles from where we now stand. For twenty years he traded with the Indians and opened the door for racist Gentiles to make their fortunes here. He also brought the first cotton gin to Alabama. You know nothing, you pathetic ass-kisser!"

This pissed Josh off, and he started yelling, "If you Jesus killers don't leave immediately, I will call the Montgomery Police and have both of you arrested for trespassing on Montgomery Golf Club property, which is the domain of the white Christian upper class of Montgomery!" The crowd went totally quiet as the Katzs headed for the door.

Mrs. Katz told me that Sonny couldn't apologize enough to her; he just assumed that the rules had changed since he was a child growing up in Montgomery. Mrs. Katz spoke again, "Pip, I'm tired. I'm tired of hiding out and the election of Governor Wallace in November has emboldened his racist followers. They've taken control of the courts, the police, and the public square. Violent behavior in defense of segregation is being condoned, and only the rare person of conscience seems willing to challenge this thug culture. Do you remember the brave Freedom Riders who were beaten at the Montgomery Greyhound bus station two years ago? My hero, Floyd Mann, who was the director of the Alabama Highway Patrol under Governor John Patterson, was there and saw it in person. When he heard about the riot at the bus station only blocks from his capitol office, he rushed the few blocks and waded through idle Montgomery city cops watching the Klan beating the Hell out of the brave Freedom Riders they were pulling off the bus. He pulled his pistol out of his shoulder holster and fired one shot in the air. He demanded that the crowd disperse, or he would shoot the first person he saw wielding a club. Did you know, Pip, that fully a third of the Freedom Riders that day at the bus station were young Jewish students from Northern universities? That's the kind of courage I want to have, but it's going to scare the Hell out of a lot of people I love when I openly choose sides. But I'm determined to be one of those people who stands up for what is right! I'm going to find their office on Monday and join the NAACP."

The holidays were busy and most of my time was taken up with my Blue-Grey Bowl Game prank I devised for Governor Wallace. I hadn't checked in with Mrs. Katz since her golf club humiliation and until my football prank had made the national news. I knew she was ready to step out with her own resistance to discrimination, so I went next door to see if she had heard about the governor inducting Martin Luther King Jr. as an honorary state trooper. When I walked into her kitchen, she had already figured out that somehow I had manipulated our neighbor Mr. Rodham, who worked at the state printing office, to get to the certificates that Governor Wallace handed out at the Blue-Grey Bowl Game.

She howled with laughter at the expression on George Wallace's face when he announced Martin Luther King Jr.'s name at the halftime ceremony. She told me that she and her husband, Sonny, always had front-row seats on the 50-yard line because he was the sports editor for the Montgomery Journal. She said this gave them a great view of the governor's meltdown after his segregationist faux pas. She told me that she told Sonny right then that she didn't know how, but she was sure I was behind this prank.

After we laughed about that prank, I asked her, "So, Mrs. Katz, how did it go when you went to sign up for the NAACP?"

She started laughing again. "Pip, I couldn't actually join. Our last governor, John Patterson, outlawed the NAACP from having a branch in Alabama, although employees from the national office still show up here from time to time. I found out from Sonny that the NAACP was outlawed after the bus boycott in 1956. Ralph Abernathy, Martin Luther King Jr., and E.D. Nixon got together and created the Southern Christian Leadership Conference, better known as the SCLC, to do the work of the outlawed NAACP. I knew that the SCLC had an office in downtown Montgomery, so I headed for it. I was thinking about how ironic it was that I, as a non-Christian Jew, was about to join a Christian organization. Then it hit me, Jesus was a Jew as well!"

The SCLC office was in an old, cotton warehouse building close to the Alabama River in downtown Montgomery. The building had been converted into a large-scale office space in the 1920s and featured sweeping open areas with a few small offices at the rear of the building. Interestingly the building was still owned by the Lehman Brothers In-vestment Bank on Wall Street in New York City, which was where Mrs. Katz's father was the managing partner.

The building was built by the original Lehman Brothers cotton bro-kerage business in 1855 by two Jewish brothers who were the owners of the brokerage business in Montgomery prior to moving their business to New York City and eventually becoming an investment bank. The investment bank had received many written complaints from segrega-tionists about renting the offices to the SCLC, but the only answer they ever got was a form letter from the bank stating that the bank didn't discuss any business matters of their customers or lessees. Even Gover-nor Wallace got one of these form letters when he complained about the bank renting office space to the SCLC.

When Evelyn Katz walked into the office, she was greeted by an older Black woman who asked her how she could help her. The office was buzzing with activity with over fifty people working around several tables set up all over the huge room. Mrs. Katz was overwhelmed with the activity and the people she saw before her. They were mostly Black, but seven or eight were white. To her surprise, she even saw an elderly Jewish woman at a rear table with two Black, college-aged young men, and she recognized her as member of her synagogue. She told the woman who greeted her, "My name is Evelyn Katz, and I want to join the SCLC, but I am a Jew and not a Christian."

The woman at the desk introduced herself as Bertha Thomas, who said, "The SCLC has many fine members who are Jewish. You are welcome to join and volunteer in our efforts to make Montgomery a city that respects all its citizens, white and Black, Jewish and Gentile."

Mrs. Katz asked, "Can I join and begin volunteering today?"

"You sure can," Bertha said. She gave Mrs. Katz a membership application and introduced her to E.D. Nixon, who had just come out of one of the small offices at the back of the room.

Mrs. Katz knew who Mr. Nixon was from reading about the Montgomery bus boycott seven years before. He had been the state president of the NAACP before Governor John Patterson and the Alabama Supreme Court outlawed it. He was the head of the Railroad Porter's Union in Alabama and had selected Martin Luther King Jr. to head the bus boycott in Montgomery. When Bertha introduced him, he told Mrs. Katz, "Ma'am, I'm very glad to meet you. Are you, by any chance, related to the sports editor of the Montgomery Journal?"

"Why, yes, Mr. Nixon, Sonny Katz is my husband," she replied, "and I've lived in Montgomery for ten years. Sonny and I moved here after we had both had finished college, and we got married."

"Mrs. Katz," he asked, "why are you here today?"

That's when Mrs. Katz told him, "Mr. Nixon, I have recently discovered some-thing about myself. I have decided that I can no longer sit on the sidelines, and I want to be active in ending discrimination. I thought that coming here and joining the SCLC was a good place to start."

E.D. Nixon was a shrewd judge of character. He asked, "Mrs. Katz, would you step into my office so we can talk further about how your talents can best be used at the SCLC of Montgomery?"

E.D. Nixon was sixty-four years old and had a second-grade formal education but held a Ph.D. from the school of hard knocks. He was a natural leader and superb organizer who worked his way up as a young man working for the railroad from a baggage handler to a porter on the overnight trains that crisscrossed America before the advent of commercial aviation. When the first all-Black union was formed, The Brotherhood of Sleeping Car Porters, he was one of the organizers. The union was recognized and admitted to membership of the AFL-CIO where E.D. Nixon made valuable friends whom he called on for help in the 1950s' boycott of Montgomery buses for discriminating against Negroes.

Martin Luther King Jr. may have been the face of the bus boycott, but E.D. Nixon was the man who planned the boycott and used his influence to help fund the boycott. Amongst his close friends was Eleanor Roosevelt, the former First Lady of the United States of America whom he met on a Pullman car when he was working. They developed a lifelong friendship that opened doors and wallets for funding anti-discrimination initiatives.

After closing his office door, E.D. Nixon got down to business by having Mrs. Katz give him her complete history. "Mr. Nixon," she replied, "I'll be glad to tell you a few things about myself. I'm a Jew who grew up in Scarsdale, New York, and graduated from Scarsdale High School. I followed in my father's footsteps by attending Yale University and majoring in Psychology for both my undergraduate and master's degrees. My father is the managing partner of Lehman Brothers Investment Bank on Wall Street in New York City."

Mr. Nixon said, "Mrs. Katz, here at the SCLC, we are working on a very secret project. Your father's influence could be very beneficial to what we have going on. Did you know the building we're sitting in is owned by Lehman Brothers?"

"No, sir," she said. "I did not know that."

Mr. Nixon replied, "Mrs. Katz, most of the SCLC higher-ups are concerned with planning sit-ins, marches, and boycotts, but I know that one of the most important things we need is money to keep the SCLC operating at full steam ahead. However, the state government is trying to dry up all our funding. What I'm trying to do is set up a money laundering operation that will bamboozle the governor's revenue agents and increase the funding for the SCLC of Montgomery. Mrs. Katz, would you be willing to volunteer for this top-secret operation?"

"Mr. Nixon," she said, "I would love to use my skills and networks of family and friends to help fund the boots on the ground in Montgomery, Alabama."

Mr. Nixon had friends at the Anti-Defamation League national headquarters in New York City who had volunteered to take any contributions that had verbal instructions for the donation to be used to fight discrimination in Alabama and forward the money in cash to the SCLC in Montgomery. Mr. Nixon had recruited loyal Pullman car porters from Montgomery to bring the cash back on their regular train runs between

New York and Montgomery.

Mrs. Katz's job would be to work with her father and her friends and her contacts across the Northeast to raise funds for the Anti-Defamation League with instructions to indicate that the funds were given to fight discrimination in Alabama. She knew where her father and her friends up North stood on civil rights, but she suggested that she could also work with the rabbis in Alabama to go to the potential donors they knew who would be receptive and get some Alabama money flowing to New York to be returned in cash to propel the work of the SCLC.

Mrs. Katz told me she had started to build her network of donors, and they included both Gentiles and Jews. She said that she knew that she was going to make a difference. She just wished she could tell that little shit of a manager at the Montgomery Golf Club that he was responsible for waking her up to the fact that no one can be free unless we are all free.

26. Justice

I returned to school after the Christmas break with a new feeling of freedom because I knew that I had only one more semester to endure at the New Roads School. I also felt an impending loss because Archie was quitting the New Roads School after spring semester to go to trade school, but Pecker said he was going to stay on at the New Roads School, a place that I had no desire to return to once I extricated myself from its clutches. I also knew from my own past experience that our friendship would drift quickly into other peer groups and that my friends Pecker and Archie would disappear from my life as quickly as they had come into it. They knew and felt this as well, and the process of distancing ourselves from each other was a new and disconcerting feeling as I waited for my new life to begin at Sidney Lanier High School in the fall.

The New Roads School and College was an enthralling place to be in the spring of 1964. New Roads' social evolution was running ahead of the Southern curve of adaptation, and the ideas of tolerance and moderation were reinforced from the top down by the new school president. Dr. Allen succeeded in driving the hard-core bigots under-ground and changing the moderate bigots into a non-infectious strain. However, Peedrow Walker and his friends weren't transformed, just silenced, and I knew that there were scores that these boys wanted to settle with Pecker, Archie, and me. The growing distance among the three of us complicated our ability to develop mutual defense strategies to protect ourselves from the certain retaliatory strike from Peedrow and his friends. I knew we would take losses due to our lack of unity, and I hoped I would survive the onslaught and get on to my life in public school without too much psychological damage.

We returned to our routine of school and cow bowl breaks without interruption or threats from Peedrow, but the look he gave me when our paths crossed said it all. I knew he was waiting for his opportunity to get even with us. I knew that his plan would have to be one where we would walk into a trap that would get us in trouble with the school authorities because he wouldn't risk the wrath of the U.S. Attorney if we were physically injured. I tried to warn my friends that we had to be very careful about every-thing we did, but my warning fell on deaf ears and the only option I had was to concentrate my energy on self-protection and let my friends take care of themselves.

January and February slipped past without incident, and an unwarranted feeling of security overcame me as I envisioned the summer break and a change of life that comes with a change of environments. My vigilance was seduced by the desire to believe in my great new future away from the New Roads School. The lesson I learned that spring was that you have to be mindful of the present if you wish to get to your imaginary future. Peedrow Walker lived those days on his vengeance clock, knowing that his time-line was defined because after May, his chances of getting us would be greatly diminished with Archie off to trade school and me to Sidney Lanier. The emphasis on tolerance and Christian love that was instituted by Dr. Allen added to the feeling that a smooth sail to May was probable, but at the same time a bit of wary cautiousness remained alive and well within me. Turns out, it was just enough caution to keep me out of the Elmore County Jail.

It was late February when Pecker began to disengage his friendship from his two best friends, Archie and me, and move on to developing new friendships with other five percenters who would be around the next year. Archie and I talked about Pecker's withdrawal from us and decided that it was what he needed to do because we were leaving him behind as we ventured off to our new lives in the fall. Pecker had taken up with Moose Malone, a very big and very hostile associate of Peedrow Walker's and one of the recipients of a Pecker bookbag broken arm in the November New Roads riot over President Kennedy's death.

I tried to warn Pecker that Moose was not the forgive-and-forget type, but Pecker didn't receive my advice with much enthusiasm. He let me know that he was getting on with his life without us and he said, "Moose has gotten over being mad at the three of us and he wants to be friends with all three of us." I smelled a rat when Moose began to show up at the barn and talk nonstop about his uncle's lake cabin that he had access to any time we wanted to use it.

Moose said, "The bar at my uncle's lake house is always stocked with beer and liquor and my uncle lets me and my friends drink as much as we want. Not only can I get us free booze, I also know several local country girls who live in the area and who love to party."

My resolve to stay away from Moose Malone faded as I thought of finally having sex for the first time in a beautiful and isolated cabin.

As March arrived, Moose's stories about his adventures with loose girls and free booze at the lake cabin had us begging to be allowed to go with him. After building our expectations for a couple of weeks, Moose told us one Monday that he had arranged to pick up four local girls that Friday night for a wild party at his uncle's cabin at eight o'clock and that the three of us were invited. He said, "I will arrive early and make sure the front door is unlocked, and the booze is out for y'all to warm up with while I go pick up the girls." We were almost sick with excitement as the first Friday in March approached.

Pecker had procured his family's car, and we were on our way to party at the lake with purportedly loose country girls. Our imaginations danced with thoughts of this being the night we would lose our virginity and actually be able to boast of our con-quests for real. The most likely outcome, we knew, was that we would drink some booze, flirt with girls, and chalk it up as one more signpost on the way to adulthood. The excitement of the imagination clouds the reality receptors. What we should have sensed was the danger and duplicity, but it slid right past three of the best pranksters the New Roads School had ever seen.

When we arrived at the cabin, the lights were on and the bar was stocked, so we made ourselves at home, put some records on, and began to explore the cottage to make sure there were enough bedrooms to serve all of us in case it was the night of our fantasies. In the very back bedroom, I noticed a curtain blowing and found a broken pane just above the window latch. That's when my heart leapt into my throat as I realized we had walked into a trap. I told my friends what I thought, and Archie was ready to get the Hell out of Dodge.

However, Pecker didn't buy my logic or my distrust of his new friend, Moose Malone; he thought it was just a broken window that had not been repaired. We argued with him for ten minutes, but he would not be moved, and this presented a big problem because we were in his car. The bad feeling in the pit of my stomach was too great to ignore, so Archie and I left the cabin on foot having decided to hitchhike back to Montgomery. Pecker stood his ground and ended up in the Elmore County Jail for his belief in Moose Malone.

Archie and I worked our way back to the main highway by way of the woods that ran along the county dirt road that led to the cabin. We saw a sheriff's car headed at breakneck speed for the cabin where Pecker thought he was waiting for us to come to our senses and return, but he was actually sitting there waiting for the Peedrow Walker trap to close around him.

Within minutes of reaching the highway, we caught a ride with a trucker into Montgomery, and when we arrived at Archie's house, it was a little past eight o'clock. We had worked out our plan and went to the workshop in the back of Archie's yard and turned on the radio, got out some power tools, and placed several cut boards on a workbench. We made a trip to Archie's kitchen after we set up the workshop and Archie told his mother that we had fixed a sandwich, and we were going back to the workshop. He let her know that we would be outside in the workshop laboring on the task we had been working on all afternoon since school let out.

Two Montgomery city police officers arrived at Archie's house at eight forty-five and were escorted to the backyard workshop by Archie's mother who assured the officers that we had been at the house since school was out. One of the policemen began an intense questioning of our movements that evening, a policeman that I recognized from the night I crashed the Tiger Daytona 500 into the Spur Club, none other than Calvin Walker's old partner.

We explained that we had been in Archie's workshop since a little after four o'clock working on a hobby horse for my next-door neighbor's daughter. The officer wasn't buying our story. He said, "I have information that you boys were seen breaking into a cabin at Lake Martin not two hours ago."

I asked, "Who witnessed our breaking into a cabin miles away when we were here with no transportation other than our bikes and with Archie's mother as a witness?"

I was sure that Pecker had not ratted on us, so there had to be a conspiracy of the law enforcement establishment to snare the three of us. The officer said, "Son, our sources of information are confidential but I can tell you that it was a very respectable citizen who was absolutely sure that he had seen both you boys in Dr. Bobby Ray Frazier's lake house with Pecker Turner, who is currently in the custody of the Elmore County Sheriff's Department and will be charged with breaking and entering."

The setup was beginning to become clear in my mind as I reviewed the data: Elmore County officials were noted for their support of the Ku Klux Klan, the lake house be-longed to none other than the former national vice presidential candidate of the National States' Rights Party, and the policeman before me was Calvin Walker's old partner. I knew it was time for a little bravado, or I was going to find myself behind bars and in very deep shit with my father.

I took a hostile psychological posture and told the policemen, "If you have an eyewitness to our crime, you had better be ready to produce them because my first phone call is going to be to my friend Mrs. Argon, the wife of the Montgomery Journal publisher. My second call will be to the United States Attorney for the Middle District of Alabama, Ira D. McDuffy. If there is a conspiracy to frame us for something we didn't do, I can assure you that it will all come out before a federal grand jury that is sure to be called once the story of our arrest is front-page news."

I painted a hypothetical picture of one of their conspirators, and I suggested Moose

Malone turning on the rest of them when faced with the possibility of five years in a New York federal prison for lying to a federal grand jury. The result was exactly what I wanted: Buddy, Calvin Walker's old partner, asked me, "Are you threatening me, boy?"

I said, "This is no threat as long as you officers have nothing to hide but if y'all arrest us, everything will come out once the U.S. Attorney gets involved." A twitch began to occur in the officer's left eyelid as he pulled his partner aside for a very heated and muffled discussion about what they should do. The officer returned with an admission that the Elmore authorities might have made a mistake in their identification of Pecker's accomplices, but that we had better be careful because they were going to keep an eye on us.

Archie was scared to death by the visit from the Montgomery Police Department. He decided from that moment on, he wasn't going to do anything but go to class and come home while he waited for trade school to begin in the fall. He reiterated his philosophy of wanting to be left alone to do his own thing and that having a police tail forever didn't fit with the way he wanted to live his life. I knew that Archie would be of no use in the rescue of Pecker from the hands of law enforcement, that this operation was mine to figure out on my own; but with the help of my seer and advisor, Mrs. Katz, I knew that justice would prevail. After my painful attempt at deceiving Mrs. Katz in The Liberty Library affair, I knew she would help me figure this out if I was straight with her, gave her the facts, and asked for her help.

Pecker spent Friday night in the Elmore County Jail in Wetumpka and was allowed to call his father the next morning after ten hours of the sheriff trying to get him to name the others who were with him when he broke into Dr. Frazier's cabin. Pecker said he was at the cabin alone to meet Moose Malone, but because of his embarrassment about being there to possibly have sex with loose country girls, he made up a story about meeting Moose to buy a quart of moonshine whiskey. As it turned out, Pecker invented the perfect lie to get him out of the soup and on to a new life in Huntsville, Alabama, instead of spending a two-year stretch in a youth reform school. Pecker had kept the faith with his friends, and I was determined to find a way to get him free of the well-conceived Peedrow trap that had him by the leg.

Pecker was back at home by eleven o'clock the next morning, and I had the details of what had happened by eleven thirty. He was badly shaken by his experience and ashamed of himself for letting Moose pull the wool over his eyes but full to the brim with the desire to get even with Peedrow and Moose. After I got him to tell me what he had told the sheriff for the fifth time, the lie about meeting Moose to buy moonshine surfaced with the comment that he just couldn't tell the cops that he had been lured to the cabin with the hope of losing his virginity. As soon as I heard this part of the story, a plan began to take form that might free Pecker from the grasp of the Elmore County Sheriff.

I went next door to talk with Mrs. Katz. I laid out the whole story for her, including the outline of a plan to get even with the plotters and spring Pecker free from a term in the kids' pokey, Mt. Meigs Reform School. I figured that the best way to end this charade was to break one of the conspirators who would then spill everything they knew. "Mrs. Katz," I started, "the logical target would be Moose Malone, because he is already allegedly running illegal whiskey according to what Pecker told the deputies that arrested him. This offense obviously falls under the jurisdiction of the federal revenue agents and its law enforcement representative in Montgomery, Ira D. McDuffy."

She knew where I was headed with my plan. She said, "Pip, I'm sure that I can persuade Mr. McDuffy to send federal revenue agents to any place I might suspect untaxed liquor is being manufactured, sold, or transported for sale." Then, as an after-thought, she added, "For that matter, agents might even be sent to any lake cabin where federal law is possibly being violated. Come back to my house later today, and I'll let you know if the feds would like your help in searching for any bootleggers who might be operating in the Middle District of Alabama."

When I returned several hours later, Mrs. Katz told me what she had found out. "Pip, I'm sure the government will appreciate any help they can get in rounding up any purveyors of illegal whiskey. All you have to do is call me with any information that you might uncover, and a car full of federal revenue agents will be dispatched within ten minutes. I'll tell you something I bet you don't know, Pip: I have the location of an active still that was abandoned earlier today because federal agents were staking it out and scared off the bootleggers. Any car flying an American flag on its antenna that enters the woods where the still is located will be allowed to come and go from the still location undisturbed. I also understand this site has several full ten-gallon cans of moonshine that were left behind by the former owners as well as lots of distilling equipment."

"Mrs. Katz," I said, "I feel it would be my duty as a junior G-man and loyal American to go out there after church tomorrow and familiarize myself with the tools of this Devil-inspired moonshine trade, and I'm going to do my part to help stamp it out."

I procured the family Ford the next afternoon, attached a small American flag to the antenna, and drove to a dirt road fifteen miles north of Montgomery. I took several twists and turns, which were indicated on the map that Mrs. Katz had provided for me, and ended up right in front of a still perched on the side of a small creek. I wasted no time and loaded six ten-gallon cans of homemade whiskey along with various pieces of copper tubing and pressure gauges into the trunk of the Fairlane 500.

I left the woods without incident and drove very carefully to a certain lake cabin where I had been to once before that weekend. I crept up to the cabin and was relieved to find no cars parked in the drive. I entered the cottage through the window with the broken glass, opened the back door and unloaded all the distilling equipment and three ten-gallon cans of white lightning into a closet. At this point, I noted to myself that there was now irrefutable evidence that something illegal really was going on in Elmore County.

I left the lake and drove to the New Roads School where I deposited my remaining three cans of moonshine in a well-hidden place in the barn. When I returned home, I went next door and told Mrs. Katz to expect a phone call from me the next day after school because I was sure that I had a nose for sniffing out illegal whiskey makers and distributors. She said that she had faith in my abilities to do anything I set my mind to do. She could think of no finer tasks than making sure that every dollar in revenue due the federal government was collected, and catching those individuals who tried to thwart the laws of the land by making and selling illegal whiskey to teenagers would be brought to the federal bar of justice.

I went home and called Pecker and gave him the lowdown on what I had done and the steps we needed to take the next day. Pecker was fearless and as mad as a wet hen about being set up by his new friend and even newer enemy, Moose Malone.

Moose and Peedrow Walker were beside themselves with glee when we saw them the next day. Peedrow asked Pecker, "Did you like your blind date with the sheriff Friday night? Do you think you'll like your new school, the Mt. Meigs Reform School for Way-ward Boys?"

I had to restrain Pecker and moved him down the hall by the arm to keep a fight from breaking out and perhaps spoiling my plan for revenge that would accomplish much more than a satisfying punch to Peedrow's ugly face. As I was calming Pecker down, the president of the New Roads School and College appeared and said that he wanted to see Pecker in his office immediately. This is when Pecker and I both knew that the Friday night arrest news had reached the New Roads administration. Pecker re-turned to class about an hour later and told me, "The president told me that I would have to leave the school if I am not cleared of the charges against me by the end of the week." We knew we had to get moving on our plan to reverse Pecker's troubles, or Pecker might beat me to the public school system or even perhaps find himself digging potatoes in Mt. Meigs, Alabama.

On Monday, we were lucky that Moose had parked his car under the trees at the end of the parking lot above the barn. We commented on what a nice guy he unknowingly was to make our task of loading his car so much safer and convenient. We got a coat hanger out of the classroom closet and proceeded to Moose's car where Pecker opened the locked car door in under a minute. We removed the back seat and went to the barn to fetch the thirty gallons of untaxed whiskey that I had hidden on Sunday. We loaded the three cans in the trunk and then put the back seat back in place, locked the car, and headed for the pay phone over at the

Bistro dining hall.

I called Mrs. Katz to alert her about a rumor I had heard about a blue 1954 Chevy that would be leaving the New Roads School at about three o'clock, loaded down with illegal liquor destined for sale and distribution to the youth of Montgomery.

Mrs. Katz complimented me on my detective work and mentioned that she had heard a rumor herself about a well-known citizen of Montgomery and a former National States' Rights Party candidate for Vice President of the United States who was purported to be making moonshine at his lake cabin in Elmore County to sell to support his political activities. She said that, as an upright citizen, she felt that it was her responsibility to report these rumors to the U.S. Attorney and M. Brandy Lane, star re-porter for the Montgomery Journal.

Pecker and I returned to class and waited for Moose to depart the campus at three o'clock, but when the awaited hour arrived, we were rewarded with a bonus on our plan. Peedrow Walker was crossing the parking lot with Moose Malone, and they were headed for Moose's blue Chevy. Moose called out to Pecker on the way to his car that his name should be Pecker Head because that's probably what he was thinking with Friday night. Once again, I had to physically restrain Pecker to keep him from prematurely springing our trap just as our prey was about to enter

Moose and Peedrow spun out of the parking lot, laughing and yelling "pecker head" at the top of their lungs. We waited about five minutes and began to search the streets near the New Roads campus when we came upon four agents of the federal government. They had surrounded two very disoriented New Roads students standing be-side a blue 1954 Chevy with its trunk open exposing three ten-gallon cans of illegal whiskey.

As we passed the car and the federal agents, Moose bellowed out that he had been framed and it was the two of us who had done it. I stopped and asked one of the federal agents what the problem was, and he asked me if it was any of my business. I said that my friend and I were just walking home after school, but these two young men in the blue Chevy had been trying to sell us moonshine for weeks, but that I never considered it because New Roads students are not supposed to drink alcohol. The agent asked me if I would be willing to testify in federal court to the solicitation to sell illegal liquor, and I responded that I felt that it would be my civic duty to give evidence about any illegal activity. This comment brought a howl of anger from Peedrow who was pushing agents aside trying to get to me, but these men were trained to respond quickly, and they had Peedrow handcuffed and on the ground before he was close enough to grab me. Peedrow was cursing and rolling on the pavement with his hands cuffed behind his back as I bent down and said, "Peedrow, you should ask us for our forgiveness for the sin of trying to lead us into a life of alcoholism and despair."

Peedrow looked like a shark out of water flipping and flopping, trying to get close enough to bite me, but I just moved slowly back as he wormed his way closer. The agents broke into laughter at the sight of Peedrow acting like Flipper on drugs as Moose leaned against his car fender and started to sob.

That afternoon, a federal search warrant was issued for Dr. Bobby Ray Frazier's lake cabin in Elmore County where agents found thirty gallons of illegal whiskey along with various pieces of equipment used to manufacture distilled alcohol. Later that day, a warrant was issued for one of the country's most noted segregationists. Dr. Frazier was indignant when the federal agents and M. Brandy Lane showed up at his Montgomery residence and began questioning him in his front yard.

The agents showed Dr. Frazier the warrant and gave him the opportunity to get anything before they took him to the Montgomery City Jail for booking. Dr. Frazier launched into a string of profanities about the Goddamned federal government framing him so they could continue their oppression of Southern whites unopposed.

M. Brandy Lane broke into the doctor's tirade to ask, "Dr. Frazier, where did you learn to make moonshine? Were you using the proceeds from your illegal liquor business to fund the state chapter of the National States' Rights Party?"

Dr. Frazier quieted at this question and turned a cold eye on the reporter. "Mr. Lane," he told him, "you better keep a close eye on your family if you print a word of that accusation."

"Was that a threat, Dr. Frazier?" asked M. Brandy Lane. "Because if it is, I don't want to misquote you in my front-page article about the possible link between boot-legging profits and the National States' Rights Party."

Dr. Frazier stared for a full minute at the reporter and quietly said, "Boy, you better watch your ass, because you don't know what powers you're messing with."

Dr. Frazier was booked that evening along with Peedrow Walker and Moose Ma-lone, and the three were then transported to the federal building for a meeting with the

U.S. Attorney, Ira D. McDuffy. They were each brought in one at a time for their in-formal, off-the-record discussion about the serious charges they faced. Moose cried and asked the U.S. Attorney what was going to happen to him. Ira D. McDuffy responded that nothing would happen if he told the whole truth about what had been done to Pecker the previous Friday night.

Moose began to bawl and say that he could be hurt if he told the U.S. Attorney about what had happened, at which point Ira D. McDuffy said that he could get hurt in a federal prison in upstate New York as well. Moose then told the whole story of the plot to frame Pecker, Archie, and me for the trouble we had caused Peedrow, Calvin Walker, Sue Ann Walker, and Moose's uncle, Dr. Frazier. He said that the five of them had thought up the fake break-in, and there were law enforcement officers from several departments involved with the plot, too. Ira D. McDuffy said that all the charges against Moose would be dropped when the Elmore County charges against Pecker were dropped.

Peedrow was absolutely hostile in his interview. "Mr. Attorney, sir, I didn't know anything about the moonshine found in Moose's car or the trouble Pecker is in in El-more County!"

Ira D. McDuffy told Peedrow, "Son, you had better get with your father and figure out a way to get Pecker off the hook in Elmore County, or your father won't be seeing his son in the sunny South for about five years. I have no authority to investigate Pecker's frameup, and I doubt that the Elmore County authorities have much interest in keeping Pecker out of reform school. However, I am sure the judicial universe will demand balance, and if Moose and Dr. Frazier spend some hard time in prison, that would probably balance the scales if this innocent boy went to reform school."

Peedrow got the point and said, "Sir, I'll talk to my father right away to see what can be done to get Pecker out of trouble."

The last person to meet with the U.S. Attorney was Dr. Bobby Ray Frazier who knew exactly what was going on when he walked into the office after seeing Peedrow leave.

He started the conversation with the U.S. Attorney. "Mr. McDuffy, I have no ability to stop the prosecution of that troublemaker, Pecker Turner, for breaking into my cabin and you have no jurisdiction in a local county break-in."

"Dr. Frazier, you're exactly right," the U.S. Attorney agreed. "You know, it's possible the search warrant issued for the illegal manufacture of untaxed liquor that was used to search your cabin might have had a minor flaw in it, and that flaw might allow me to drop the charges on you if Pecker has his charges dropped."

"That's blackmail, Mr. McDuffy, and you know it!" Dr. Frazier said. "I'm going to alert your superiors at the Justice Department in Washington and the national press as to your motives in arresting me!"

"Well, doc, it's a free country, and you can do what you want with that information," Mr. McDuffy said, "but I don't think the press is going to believe a bootlegger white supremacist radical who was selling whiskey to teenagers to support his group of adult thugs. As far as my superiors are concerned, they were fully apprised of the discovery of untaxed alcohol on your property."

Dr. Bobby Ray Frazier thought about this for a minute. Then he replied, "If all the charges are withdrawn, and the government apologizes for accusing me wrongly, I will see if the charges can be dropped against Pecker."

Ira D. McDuffy laughed out loud at that suggestion and said that his only bargain was that if Pecker had the charges against him dropped, then the two bootleggers he had caught would also have their charges dropped. If Pecker went to reform school, Dr. Frazier could be damn sure that he and his nephew, Moose Malone, would spend at least five years as guests of the federal government. Dr. Frazier said that if his arrest was thrown out on a technicality, his reputation would be ruined if people thought he was selling whiskey to teenagers. The U.S. Attorney told him that he should have thought about that before he tried to set up an innocent teenager on a burglary charge. Bobby Ray Frazier left the federal building defiant. He was unwilling to help clear Pecker and sure that he could turn this incident to his advantage by making himself into a martyr in the cause of states' rights by proclaiming himself a victim of federal oppression and dirty tricks. The public reaction to the front-page article about the arrests was not what Bobby Ray expected; instead, he was roundly denounced for using evil methods to fund his political organization.

The article further noted that most of the local funds raised by the Alabama States' Rights Party went to pay their director's very high salary. M. Brandy Lane painted a crystal-clear picture of a man who lived very well off his nonprofit organization that had been losing members and contributions over the last year. He even intimated that the anonymous cash donations claimed on Dr. Frazier's tax forms might have come from the sale of moonshine liquor to teenagers.

When Friday rolled around, Pecker had been cleared of all charges against him in Elmore County but he had also received two dozen death threats. Pecker's father was a civilian employee at Maxwell Air Force Base and one call from Mrs. Katz to her well-connected father was all it took for Pecker's father to be transferred, with a pro-motion, to the U.S. Army's Redstone Arsenal in Huntsville. Moose and Peedrow were expelled from the New Roads School for selling alcohol even though the federal charges had been dropped against them and Dr. Frazier.

I received a few death threats but warned the callers that the union provided our family with around-the-clock, dead-shot protection, and all our phone calls were traced, which usually unnerved the callers and caused a quick disconnect. I knew I would always miss Pecker, but our paths were destined to diverge anyway, so I figured it had all worked out for the best. I thought that my time and troubles at the New Roads School were over. Little did I know that I had started a chain reaction, which would end in the deaths of my best friend and my worst enemy.

27. Changes

What I learned of the events that happened after the ill-fated attempt to send Archie, Pecker, and me off to reform school at Mt. Meigs, I gleaned from newspaper reports, FBI informants' reports that Ira D. McDuffy shared with me, and my own very painful memories of the night of May 25, 1964. In our reversal of the frame-up plot at Lake Martin, I had created an adult enemy who had become psychotic from the changes that swirled around him. He was a man so filled with hate and moral indignation that he saw nothing wrong with using one child to kill another child ensuring a message would be sent to any young person who dared confront the racial traditions of their Southern heritage.

I was the perfect choice for a retaliatory example, a boy who deserved to be punished for my traitorous actions. Dr. Frazier had found out about my anti-segregationist deeds because Pecker had shared all the details of my successful plots against Governor George Wallace, Colonel Al Lingo and his storm troopers, as well as The Liberty Library episode, with Moose Malone. Moose then told Dr. Bobby Ray Frazier, and Frazier was determined to make me pay for what I had done.

Dr. Frazier received mounds of publicity after his arrest for selling moonshine to Montgomery's teenagers. His donations to the Alabama chapter of the National States' Rights Party dried up, his open invitation to the Governor's Mansion was withdrawn, as well as his invitations to speak to such august organizations as the White Citizens' Council and the Ku Klux Klan. The long and short of it was that Dr. Bobby Ray Frazier had fallen from grace, and his whole life was coming apart at the seams. Just six months before, he had envisioned himself as the superintendent of an interstate private white school system that would be perfected in Montgomery and recreated in every city, town, and county in the South. Now, he was shunned by his peers and even the most ardent segregationists didn't want this moonshine peddler within ten miles of their kids.

Dr. Bobby Ray Frazier wanted revenge, but it wasn't his style to do the dirty work himself. He needed an accomplice who would buy his line of striking a heroic blow for the Southern way of life by teaching other white boys to stick to their traditions. He didn't need to look further than his nephew's friend, Peedrow Walker, who was out for revenge for all the havoc I had caused his whole family as well as being dumb enough to trust a dangerous psychopathic segregationist.

In early May, Dr. Frazier called Peedrow and asked him to meet him at his lake house to discuss getting even for what had been done to both of them by those race-traitor boys at the New Roads School. Peedrow was instructed to tell no one that they were going to meet, especially his nephew, Moose Malone.

Peedrow followed Dr. Frazier's instructions except for one thing. He did tell Moose about the first meeting as well as all the subsequent meetings with Dr. Frazier, including all the plans and details to keep me out of future mischief forever. These de-tails were given to the U.S. Attorney Ira D. McDuffy by the FBI and made available to state prosecutors but were later excluded from Dr. Frazier's murder trial because the state court judge decided that it was hearsay evidence and not admissible in court even though the outcome of convicting a segregationist leader was predetermined. If you sat on that jury and delivered the wrong verdict, it could threaten you, your job, your family, and even your life.

Bobby Ray Frazier invited Peedrow Walker to come his cabin on Lake Martin but to keep their meeting a secret. When he arrived at the lake, Dr. Frazier welcomed into his cabin a very dejected Peedrow who was not going to graduate from high school and would have to repeat his senior year at another school. Peedrow had lost almost all his friends at the New Roads School and wasn't making any new ones. He was bitter and lonely for his past, which created a natural bond between him and Moose Malone's uncle. Dr. Frazier also missed his previous life and began their first meeting by reciting the litany of crimes I had committed against my race including making a national laughingstock of the leader of all honorable white Americans, the Governor of the State of Alabama, George Wallace. He reminded Peedrow that I had been responsible for his broken jaw, which was wired shut for six weeks, because I had objected to the elimination of the Papist traitor, President John F. Kennedy. Peedrow added that I had ruined his father's career as a policeman and had been instrumental in the closing of The Liberty Library, which was started by his mother.

At this point, Dr. Frazier launched into a discussion of honor and the duty of white men to strike a blow for their families and their Southern culture. Peedrow was on the slippery slope to Hell and being pushed over the edge by a man with a smile on his face and a song of the South in his heart. He was ready to do whatever was necessary to salvage his family's honor and please his new mentor.

Dr. Frazier laid out the plan, which was a lot easier in 1964 than it would be today. In 1964, a person could go to any hardware or general store and buy as much dynamite as he wanted without any identification and with only a cursory explanation, like to blow up stumps back on the farm, as to why he wanted dynamite. Peedrow was sent to a small general store twenty miles south of Montgomery to buy ten sticks of dynamite and three blasting caps, which he did without hesitation. Peedrow had visions of being a hero to his family, his culture, and his mentor dancing in his head all while implicating himself in an innocent human being's murder.

Dr. Frazier had succeeded in convincing Peedrow that the task that lay before him was divine retribution and that no state jury would ever convict him for standing up against a homegrown race traitor to the South. The plan was in motion, and there was no turning back. Peedrow was sure he was headed for an honored place in Southern history, and Dr. Frazier was sure that he would have his revenge without getting his hands publicly soiled in the process.

When Peedrow delivered the dynamite and blasting caps to Dr. Frazier, he was told, "Peedrow, I have a friend who will fashion a bomb into an innocent looking radio case out of these supplies over the next week. Then it will be up to you to deliver God's answer to Pip Cooper, who is one of the worst race traitors I have ever seen." Dr. Frazier quizzed Peedrow again on the secrecy of their plan, and Peedrow assured him that he had told no one, a lie that would send his mentor to a federal correctional facility for seventeen years.

Peedrow was not the only liar in that evil duo of hate and destruction; his partner and new friend in the revenge plan was lying when he assured his young follower that he would be acquitted by any Alabama jury. Dr. Frazier convinced Peedrow that he would never see more than one night in jail if he even got caught at all. He would be a hero to his race whom people would fear and admire.

After their first meeting at the lake, Peedrow and Dr. Frazier met often to plan their attack on my home. Peedrow spent two evenings in the bushes at my house and reported to Dr. Frazier that the rumors of an armed guard were erroneous. This removed one of the major obstacles to carrying out their plot: to make an example of the parts of me that could be found after their plan was carried out. Peedrow not only met with Dr. Frazier almost every day but also with Moose Malone where he reported their progress to-ward the destruction of their mutual enemy.

Moose was supportive but cautious of what might happen if Peedrow was caught. Peedrow told Moose, "I ain't worried about being caught, and in some ways, I hope I am. I will be vindicated by an Alabama state jury who will understand that race traitors will not be tolerated in Alabama. Dr. Frazier has arranged for an anonymous letter to be sent to the wire services the night of the bombing detailing Pip Cooper's crimes against the South, the State of Alabama, Governor George Wallace, The Liberty Library, and the Christian faith. Dr. Frazier thinks that if I am caught, I could easily be elected to a statewide office when I turn twenty-one years old and could possibly be the youngest Governor of Alabama ever, once the current governor moves on to the White House."

As the fantasies of power and respect swirled in the head of Peedrow Walker, Dr. Bobby Ray Frazier was meeting with a convicted felon who had extensive knowledge of explosive devices and detonators. Bud Williams had been convicted of bank robbery in 1958 and had been out of prison for six months; however, he had found very few career opportunities for a bank robber on parole. When his old friend and fellow member of the Montgomery Ku Klux Klan, Dr. Bobby Ray Frazier, asked him to construct a bomb for one thousand dollars, he was ready and willing.

Bud was given two hundred dollars in advance to acquire the materials necessary to construct the detonation device and to pay for his time.

Bobby Ray told him, "Bud, I want this bomb hidden in a medium-sized table-top radio cabinet, and I want the detonation switch tied to the on/off knob." He told Bud that a young man would come by Bud's trailer and deliver the dynamite to be used in constructing the bomb on the afternoon of May 24th and that he was to deliver the finished radio bomb to the same young man at Furr's Café parking lot the next afternoon. He was told that he would receive the other eight hundred dollars after the explosive was detonated.

Bobby Ray explained to Peedrow how to get to Bud's trailer in the woods on the outskirts of Montgomery so he could deliver the dynamite and meet Bud. Peedrow was told not to discuss their plan with Bud and to leave as soon as he had made his delivery. After completing his explosives delivery, Peedrow was told to meet Bud at Furr's Café parking lot at 6 o'clock in the evening of May 25th and pick up the radio bomb and to then lie low until after midnight when it would be time to deliver the bomb to my bed-room's windowsill.

Dr. Frazier explained to Peedrow, "The radio bomb will explode ten minutes after you turn the on/off switch on. All you have to do is make sure the switch is turned on and placed on the outside of Pip's window ledge and then get the Hell out of the neighborhood before the bomb goes off." What Bobby Ray Frazier didn't tell Peedrow was that the bomb would be constructed to explode as soon as the switch was turned on. He didn't explain to Peedrow that he had no intention of leaving any witnesses to testify against him, and that he and Bud Williams were expendable.

The plan went like clockwork, the radio bomb was picked up as arranged, Peedrow showed up at my house at midnight and waited in his car out in front of my house until he was sure everyone was asleep. But Peedrow was missing two important bits of information: he didn't know about my need to generate alpha waves by setting my alarm clock every hour from the time I went to bed until I got up in the morning, and he didn't know that my next door neighbor, Mrs. Katz, was a New Yorker who couldn't imagine going to bed before 1 a.m.

Mrs. Katz had been watching Peedrow from her darkened kitchen window from the time he arrived and had watched him creep across the lawn with a radio in his arms. She left her house and confronted Peedrow as he placed the radio on my windowsill. My alarm had gone off only moments before she asked Peedrow what he was doing. I heard Peedrow say, "Pip used to be a friend of mine and I borrowed this radio, and I just want to return it to him without having to see him."

At this point in the conversation, I bolted from my bed and headed for the back door to sneak out quietly so I could confront Peedrow and find out what he was up to. As I rounded the side of the house, I saw Peedrow and Mrs. Katz standing at the other end of the house where my bedroom was located. I was too far away to hear what they were saying, but then I saw a flash of light and felt the intense heat waving over me as I was driven to the ground by the blast's impact. After that, everything went black.

I regained consciousness in my father's arms a few moments later amidst the screams of my mother, my siblings, and my next-door neighbor, Mr. Katz. Smoke and the smell of burning flesh surrounded me as I realized what had happened, and I joined the hysterical group with my own wails of pain at the loss of my wonderful friend and advisor, Mrs. Evelyn Katz.

The next sixty minutes was the longest hour of my life as I lived out Hell on earth, raw and violent, insane with grief and my own self-hatred. I had an absolute feeling of powerlessness and was horrified with the knowledge that I had killed one of the best people I had ever known by testing the limits of the sickest elements that American human culture could produce.

I was surrounded by firemen, policemen, FBI agents, paramedics, and even a very haggard looking U.S. Attorney, all prodding and pushing me for information that drew only shrieks and screams from me. Finally, I was given an injection that closed the door on the horror that would not leave me, the knowledge that I owned this nightmare and would for the rest of my life.

When I awoke the next day, I found out from Ira McDuffy that there were three deaths the night before in Montgomery: Peedrow Walker, Mrs. Katz, and a convicted bank robber known to make explosive devices, who had burned to death in a trailer fire. The U.S. Attorney explained that he was sure the three deaths were related and that he would assure the safety of my family while this horrendous crime was being solved and the guilty were brought to justice.

At this point, I stood up on my hospital bed and screamed that there was no God-damned justice in this insane fucking world I had been born into and that I knew there was nothing he or anyone else could do to change the fact that my friend was dead. This outburst got me another shot of quiet-the-boy-down medicine followed by similar injections for two more days.

After the authorities were sure I could be trusted not to throw a fit, I told my story of the night of the bombing. By this time, the police— with the unwanted aid of the FBI and the U.S. Treasury Department—

had tied Peedrow and Bud together with the bomb, by interviewing Peedrow's best friend, a very scared and cooperative Moose

Malone who implicated his uncle, Dr. Bobby Ray Frazier, in the deaths of Mrs. Katz, Bud, and Peedrow. Dr. Bobby Ray Frazier was arrested and was being held in the Montgomery City Jail without bond on a triple murder charge, but I knew he would never be convicted in a state court in Alabama. The U.S. Attorney said that it was ironic that there was no federal law that would apply to this crime, but that one was being debated before Congress at the very time this senseless act happened.

Moose Malone's testimony was disallowed as hearsay in Dr. Frazier's trial and the case collapsed for lack of evidence. However, the U.S. Attorney tried the evil Dr. Frazier on several federal liquor law and income tax evasion violations, and he was sentenced to twenty years in Federal prison where he served seventeen years of his punishment.

When Bobby Ray Frazier returned to Alabama in 1982, he found a state that was inalterably changed. All levels of government including the state legislature and the state law enforcement agencies were integrated. His hero, George Wallace, had recanted his racist views and admitted he was wrong, urging his followers to move beyond the bigotry of the past. The White Citizens' Councils were gone as was the National States' Rights Party, and the Ku Klux Klan was watched very carefully by the FBI and the

U.S. Justice Department. Dr. Bobby Ray Frazier was a broken man of sixty-five who had returned to Montgomery as a relic of a past who almost everyone in the state wanted to forget.

Dr. Bobby Ray Frazier, former National States' Rights Party vice presidential candidate and would-be superintendent of the Montgomery private white school system, lived out the rest of his life in poverty and bitterness. He was a man who reaped exactly what he had sown; he planted the seeds of hate and intolerance and was rewarded with twenty-nine years of misery as justice did, indeed, seek and obtain its due. Dr. Bobby Ray Frazier was finally dead, but it didn't make me happy.

My feeling as I sit here and remember those days and that evil man is that I wish he had not escaped the torment of this better world he had inadvertently helped create. I can taste the bile in my mouth as I remember those days of hate and rage. I know in my heart that the miserable, tortured man who departed this earth yesterday was the salve for an old wound that I acquired in those troubled times. I will miss his torment, because it was the only insulator between me and the fact that I was responsible for the death of the best person I have ever known, and as my life has turned out, the only woman that I have ever really loved. I know now that I had built my whole life around revenge and hate. I had let myself become what I despised, but I finally feel that justice has been served.

I know now that I must rebuild my life, to let go of the past thirty years of pain and torment, to find a positive reason for being here. There are so many normal human emotions that I have missed because of the need for revenge and justice and they have crowded out my emotional ability to love and be loved. Now, for the first time since the spring of 1964, I feel that I can be free at last.

Appendix I

Alabama Civil Rights Timeline August 1962–June 1964

Fall 1962 — Boycotts by African Americans of downtown Birmingham businesses result in a 40% drop in merchant revenue. The city responds by withholding U.S. Department of Agriculture surplus food destined for Birmingham's poor.

Fall 1962 — Southern Christian Leadership Conference (SCLC) plans for civil disobedience campaign in Alabama.

November 1962 — George Wallace is elected governor of Alabama on a segregationist platform that promises segregation in Alabama forever.

January 14, 1963 — George Wallace takes office and fires the director of the Highway Patrol, Floyd Mann (who single-handedly stopped the Freedom Rider beatings in Montgomery in 1961), and replaces him with Al Lingo, an ardent segregationist. Wallace re-names the agency the Alabama State Troopers.

April 12, 1963 — Dr. Martin Luther King Jr. is arrested and jailed in Birmingham. April 20, 1963 — Dr. King is released from the Birmingham Jail, even though Governor George Wallace passed a law increasing his bail by 1000%.

May 2, 1963 — The Children's Crusade for racial justice ignites a police riot where African American children are fire-hosed and attacked by police dogs and adult policemen with more than 1,000 arrested and detained in makeshift jails.

June 11, 1963 — Governor George Wallace physically blocks the registration of two African American students trying to register for classes at The University of Alabama until President John Kennedy nationalizes the Alabama National Guard and the governor is threatened with arrest by the National Guard's commanding general.

September 4, 1963 — White Alabama schools in Birmingham are integrated by five grade-school African American students and are confronted by a violent mob who are members of the National States' Rights Party.

September 15, 1963 — Four young African American girls are murdered and 20 others injured by a bomb planted by four Ku Klux Klansmen at the 16th Avenue Baptist Church in downtown Birmingham. Later that day, two African American children are murdered by segregationists.

November 22, 1963 — President Kennedy is assassinated, shaking the hopes of the Alabama civil rights community.

February 10, 1964 — Civil Rights bill passes the U.S. House of Representatives and the hopes of the civil rights community are invigorated.

June 9, 1964 — The U.S. Senate passes the Civil Rights Act and sends it to President Lyndon Johnson who is anxious to sign it. Most of the citizens of Alabama know that change is coming, but not before more violence and intimidation occurs.

Appendix II

"Letter from a Birmingham Jail" by Martin Luther King Jr. (April 16, 1963) is available to read for free at nlnrac.org (Natural Law, Natural Rights and American Constitutionalism): https://nlnrac.org/american/american-civil-rights-movements/ primary-source-documents/letter-from-a-birmingham-jail.html

Acknowledgements

Editors: Amber Derr, Steve Gamel, John Travis, and Mary Ann Travis.

Marketing and design: Deb York Salisbury, APR, Content Fresh®.

Cover design: Kai Gray.

Beta readers: Don Sawyer, G. Dan Lumpkin, Joe Formichella, Susanne Hudson, Skip Jones and Robert Reed.

About the Author

Phillip Norris was born in 1948 and grew up in Montgomery, Alabama in the 1950's and 1960's. His father was the state president of the Communications Workers of America (CWA) and active in the AFL-CIO Union movement. He was influenced by listening to his father talk politics with his friend Clifford Durr, a noted human rights lawyer, Rhodes Scholar, FCC commissioner, and the lawyer who got Rosa Parks out of jail in 1955.

Phillip graduated from the University of Alabama with an undergraduate degree in Communication and a Master's degree in Social Work. He then earned degrees in Education and Applied Behavioral Science at the University of Massachusetts at Amherst, and he was a post-doctoral fellow at Harvard University. He is the recipient of the Rush Silver Medal award from the American Psychiatric Association, a legislative citation from the Commonwealth of Massachusetts, and he wrote a syndicated series for the Los Angeles Times. He was the President of the South Alabama Institute and the Director of the University of South Alabama Baldwin County, a regional campus of the University of South Alabama, for 25 years.